Judy Sonksen
9 Aug '08
Union Book Sale

read 25 Oct '08 JS
Read Dec 08 MKS

SILENT WITNESS

SILENT WITNESS

CHARLES WILSON, 1939 –

Carroll & Graf Publishers, Inc.
New York

M

55152

This novel is a work of fiction. The characters, their names and other names, dialogue, incidents, and plot are the products of the author's imagination or are used fictitiously, and any resemblance to actual persons or events is purely coincidental.

First Carroll & Graf edition 1992

Carroll & Graf Publishers, Inc.
260 Fifth Avenue
New York, NY 10001

Library of Congress Cataloging-in-Publication Data

Wilson, Charles, 1939–
    Silent witness / by Charles Wilson. — 1st
Carroll & Graf ed.
        p.   cm.
    ISBN 0-88184-755-0 : $18.95
    I. Title.
  PS3573.I45684S58   1992
813'.54—dc20   91-29467
                                            CIP

Manufactured in the United States of America

To Kent Carroll, as much for the high respect I have for him as a person as for the guidance he has given me on my first two books. Also, for their technical advice used in this book and novels to come, John Edwards, former polygraph expert with the Mississippi Highway Patrol and an investigator for the Rankin County Sheriff's Department, and Dr. Steve Hayne, M.D. FCAP DCMEI, Medical Director Rankin County Morgue, Assistant Clinical Professor of Pathology University of Mississippi Medical School and Chief of Pathology Rankin Medical Center.

Also, to Tommy Furby, Shirley Blakeney, and Lynn Clark, and to those readers who have helped me with their opinions—Wanda Toney, Janice Champlin, Jeanne Kelly, and Mary Ann Norwood.

CHAPTER

1

Julie Richardson didn't like being alone in the house after dark. However, everything had its price. A smile crossed the blonde eighteen-year-old's face. Lifting the cordless telephone from its cradle on the table next to the rubber tree plant, she then opened the back door of the old Colonial home and stepped out into the night.

At the top of the back porch steps she paused to look up into the sky. Several large moisture-laden clouds were passing overhead, their dark forms dimming the bright glow of the full moon. But the sky was mostly clear behind the bank of clouds and the lightning didn't appear to be any closer than it had been earlier. The weather wasn't going to be a problem.

She had worried about that; she didn't want to have to come back to the house. *He could come back, too.* She had seen it in his eyes when he was threatening her.

She set her lips in a firm line and shook her head defiantly.

So why should she care if he did? She was no longer a child, too unsure of herself to call a halt to a game once it had begun. She had grown up a lot in the last few months—she was in control now. She would never suffer not being in control again. She glanced at the telephone in her hand. *There was one other, though.* She wasn't yet in control there. But it wouldn't be long and she would be free of that problem, too. Meanwhile she was smarter than he was. She slid the telephone's button to talk, listened to the dial tone for a moment, then moved the switch back to the receive mode. *Much smarter than he was.*

Her smile reappeared and she raised her face to look toward the rear of the yard, where the line of tall trees marked the subdivision's boundary with the heavily wooded Belle Colline State Park. Her smile broadening, she stepped off the porch and hurried across the neatly trimmed lawn toward the tall trees.

As she neared the park, a strong surge of wind swept across her back and into the trees. The long limbs of the oaks bent at the force, their leaves starting to whip wildly. Then a heavy cloud crossed the face of the moon, and the straining foliage faded into the darkness. A sense of anxiety settling over her, she stopped, glanced into the sky and waited.

The wind slowly calmed and a deep silence ensued.

She heard the twig snap behind her—*from the wrong direction.*

She whirled around.

The dog, a brindle boxer, his dark coat rendering him nearly invisible in the night, trotted toward her.

Julie sighed in relief and shook her head. "Peter," she said as she knelt to hug the animal's neck. "What do you mean scaring me like that?"

The boxer wagged his stubbed tail in metronome fashion and licked her cheek. Suddenly his ears picked up, and he pulled away from her to look into the park.

Rising to her feet, she stared in that direction, too. She saw only the blackness.

Another gust swept across her back, and the dog trotted forward to disappear into the dark.

She continued to stare.

The moonlight began to penetrate the thinner, trailing edge of the passing cloud, and the park's foliage gradually began to reappear. The latest surge of wind gone, the next series of gusts yet to arrive, the oak limbs straightened, their leaves becoming still. The deep quiet returned once more.

She glimpsed the shadowy movement within the park.

Coming from the right direction!

Her heart beginning to knock, a smile again spreading across her face, she moved forward into the trees to meet the figure.

Two hours passed before the first raindrops began to fall. They came down scattered and large at first, splattering clear spots in the dust accumulated on the rooftops of the homes in Belle Colline Heights.

They spread into the Belle Colline State Park, falling through the swaying Spanish moss and wind-tossed limbs of the hundred-year-old oaks.

They fell on the back of the brindle boxer scratching in the dirt at the bottom of a sinkhole in the park.

He raised his head. Above him a streak of lightning jumped between two clouds. The park quivered in pale-blue light, and there was the low rumble of thunder. The rain began to pelt his coat harder.

The animal glanced back at where he had been digging, then turned and made his way up the steep entrance and out of the hole, falling into a rythmic trot as he padded his way silently back toward the houses.

Almost to the boundary line between the park and the sub-division, he stopped abruptly. Ears coming erect, he lifted his muzzle and began sniffing the air. Tense and stiff-legged, he moved slowly in the direction of the scent, stopped when he saw the figure lying sprawled backward on the ground.

It was the girl who had hugged his neck, her arms now flung

out to her sides, her T-shirt gaping above her tight blue jeans, her open eyes staring blankly into the sky.

Edging forward, the boxer sniffed at the bloodstained T-shirt and the raindrops trickling pink across the narrow strip of exposed skin at the girl's waist. He nudged her cheek with his muzzle.

Suddenly a shrill ring filled the air. The dog started, sidling away from the cordless telephone which lay a few feet away.

There was a second loud ring.

And then a gust of wind blew toward the dog, and with the third shrill sound a faint echoing ring could be heard coming from within the old Colonial house a hundred feet away.

Inside the house, the shadowy figure standing in the hall outside Julie's bedroom had also tensed at the sudden ringing of the telephones. They rang a fourth time, then a fifth.

The figure hurried to the landing and down the creaking stairs, moved rapidly along the first-floor hallway to the back door, opened it, and disappeared out into the darkness.

CHAPTER

2

Leigh Ann stepped from her Lincoln and angled across the sunny, windswept parking lot toward the two-story building housing the offices of Ramsey Oil and Gas, Inc.

Mark Ramsey, his tall, athletic frame leaned against the side of a window in his second-floor office, watched her as she came toward the building.

She was walking fast, holding her hand at the back of her head in a losing attempt to keep the wind from blowing her hair. Several of the long dark strands whipped around in front of her face. She raised her other hand to help the first, and tilted her head back away from the sharp breeze. Her face was full in his view—her dark brows over big eyes, her high cheekbones molding into her perfectly shaped oval face, and all of it surrounded by the flowing dark hair.

He lowered his gaze to her figure, outlined as the wind plastered her light summer dress tight against her body. After two children and six years of marriage to Jack her figure didn't look any different than when Ramsey had first met her, her body still trim and well formed, with a small waist and long, eye-catching legs.

"Do I look all right?" she had asked him a long time ago as they stepped from a motel room. Remembering that, he smiled. Had she ever looked any other way but all right? He still couldn't understand why she hadn't found success when she had tried her luck at a modeling career. Somebody had to have been blind.

She hurried on beneath his gaze into the building.

He stood at the window for a moment longer, then turned and walked back to his desk, settled into the tall-backed leather executive chair behind it. He sat in quiet thought until his secretary knocked gently, then opened his office door and stuck her head inside.

"A Mrs. Leigh Ann Mueller is here to see you. She says you are expecting her."

He nodded. "Thank you, Shirley."

When Leigh Ann stepped through the doorway, he stood.

She smiled politely. "I appreciate your taking the time to see me," she said. "I know you're awful busy."

"No, not at all. In fact I was getting ready to hang it up for the day when you telephoned." He nodded toward the cushioned armchairs in front of his desk, and remained standing until she had seated herself.

"Would you like a cup of coffee?" he asked as he lowered himself into his own chair. "A Coke?"

"No, thank you."

"Anything?"

"No. No, thank you. I'm fine. I—" As she paused, her face tightened and she shook her head. "No, I'm not. I'm not fine at all. Like I told you on the telephone, I'm worried, really worried."

"Leigh Ann, there isn't any reason to be. What's happened has been traumatic, got you upset. Your next-door neighbor's daughter murdered, her body found almost at the edge of your backyard—that would upset anybody. But what it's done is put you on edge, made you start worrying about things there's no reason for you to be concerned about. The only reason the cops asked for Jack's fingerprints was so they could separate them from any others that might be on the girl's purse. He isn't concerned, is he?"

"Oh, *husbands*," she said, flipping her palms up helplessly. "To him I'm just a nervous wife, dreaming up things to worry about. But I just can't help it. It's not just his finding her purse. He saw our dog playing with it that morning, got it, and left it by the Richardsons' front door when he didn't get an answer— that's fine. But then his being the one to discover the sinkhole, especially after the officers had searched all through the trees and not noticed it—and then it turns out that's where she was raped, not where they found her body."

He shook his head. "You've lost me. The newspaper didn't say—"

"There wasn't anything about it in the paper. I found out when one of the policemen asked to use our phone. I had already started worrying about how Jack was beginning to look, so I went into the bedroom and listened in. They weren't sure how her body ended up at the edge of the woods. They were speculating about how that might have happened. But they were positive she'd been raped at the sinkhole. They were talking about her having sand on her that came out of the place. And they found a condom there that they think the killer used. It had . . . had semen in it. She didn't have any in her. One of the officers remarked that it was a pretty strange coincidence that Jack had just lucked up on a place they hadn't found when they were searching the woods. And that's when the other officer said maybe it would be a good idea if Jack took a lie detector test. It made me so mad I almost said something."

He had to hold his smile back. He could imagine the officers' reaction if she had suddenly screamed her displeasure into what they thought was their private conversation. And she was capable of doing just that—quick to lose her temper when she was displeased.

"Mark, Jack didn't just 'luck up on it.' Not in the way they were implying, anyway. He had been walking in the woods with Peter—that's our boxer. Just curious, looking around, not for anything in particular. Peter disappeared behind some bushes. When Jack called him, he wouldn't come. So Jack walked over to where he had vanished and saw the sinkhole. But you see how bad it makes him look to the police?"

"Leigh Ann, it doesn't."

"No? What about the hunting knife I told you about? He said he had one when they asked, and then it was missing from his hunting gear when he went to get it. It's been one coincidence after another, and I know they're adding up to make him look bad."

"Leigh Ann, listen to me for a minute. You hadn't told me about the cops finding the condom. That makes me even more certain they don't have the slightest doubt about Jack. If they did, then they would have asked him for a blood sample. I can promise you that the first thing the lab did was determine the killer's blood type from the semen."

She shook her head. "They might not have been able to. One of the officers on the phone was talking about the condom being partially melted from being next to the fire."

"Fire?"

"A campfire—down in the sinkhole. Evidently children had been there earlier, built it, and left it burning. The men on the phone were saying they were going to find out who the children were, if they were there after dark, when they left— maybe they saw somebody."

He shifted back in his chair and shrugged. "I don't know what else to tell you. That was idle speculation you heard on the phone. If I were you, I'd just try and forget about it."

"I can't . . . Mark, I know I've already been a terrible bother, but I want you to do me a favor. I want you to go and speak with the police. Find out if there's anything else that makes Jack look bad—something we might not know about."

"There isn't, Leigh Ann. Besides, they wouldn't tell me anything."

"Your brother would—if you'd ask him. If he tells you they're not concerned about Jack, then I'll be able to rest—get it out of my mind. Please do that for me. Please."

CHAPTER

3

The police station was located near the center of the town, in an area known by the local residents of the small bedroom community as The Square.

In the middle of the square, rising from a neatly trimmed plot of grass, was the Confederate Monument, a pillar of concrete five feet in diameter and thirty feet high. At the top of the structure, his forearms crossed and resting on the muzzle of a rifle standing in front of him, an-eight-foot-tall Civil War era granite soldier stared forlornly westward.

To the soldier's front and rear was the main highway running through the town—a two-lane blacktop dividing around and to each side of the monument.

To the soldier's left was a block-long line of two-story buildings—a mixture of freshly painted specialty shops and attorneys' offices. To his immediate right sat the hundred-year-old Davis County Courthouse, a two-story redbrick building graced with a large area of manicured grass and surrounded by an iron picket fence.

Next to the courthouse, but separated from it by a street bisecting the square on that side, was an old one-story redbrick building leased by the publisher of the local county newspaper. Close beside the newspaper office was a small white one-story building. It housed the mayor's office on one side and the police station on the other, the place Mark Ramsey now entered thirty minutes after having met with Leigh Ann at his drilling company offices.

"Afternoon, Mr. Ramsey," a matronly black lady said, looking up at him from her desk just inside the door and off to the right. To the left of the room a long line of filing cabinets were set against a wall. Toward the back, a dozen feet from the door, was a counter. It was slightly taller than waist-high and stretched wall to wall. No one was behind it.

"Afternoon, Lila. Is Ray here?"

"He's somewhere in the back. Go on in." She pointed to the swinging panel at the center of the counter.

At the rear of the room, Ramsey passed through a door into a narrow hall.

The three offices and the conference room were empty. Ramsey found his half brother and biggest fan, Chief Raymond Hopkins, in the small lounge near the back of the building.

He was sitting at a metal folding table next to the Coke machine. Heavy shoulders hunched forward, the top of his closely cropped, graying brown hair visible, he was eating a cheeseburger. A wadded-up sandwich wrapper and a pint carton of chocolate milk set on the tabletop in front of him. A wisp of smoke curled from the cigar butt perched on the edge of the table.

Ray looked up, smiled when he saw Ramsey, and boomed a greeting in his characteristic deep voice. "Hey, little brother. How in hell are you?" His stomach bulged when he stood and leaned across the table to shake hands, and Ramsey stared disapprovingly.

"Ray, you don't listen to a damn thing the doctor tells you, do you—diet or anything else?"

Dressed in the business suit he preferred over a uniform, Ray hid his bulge by pulling the front of his coat together and straightening to the limit of his nearly five-ten height.

Pointing toward the chair sitting on the other side of the table, he sat down in his own chair, then defended himself in a slightly growly voice.

"Fifty years old and with my diabetes actin' up like it is, how much time you think I got left? However long it is, I'm gonna enjoy myself while I can. Now what can I do for you? You didn't come down here to discuss my eating habits." His tone became normal again, a smile coming to his face. "By the way, been hearing you got a hell'uva well going down."

Ramsey smiled. Every well he drilled was a hell'uva well to his brother. In fact, everything he did, his brother became excited about. It was Ray who had been the first spectator out of the stands to reach him and hug him when he scored his first Youth League touchdown, and his last one in high school. Ray had always acted more like a proud father than a brother— and not just because of the over two decades difference in their ages.

Ray's father had deserted his wife when Ray was twelve. Ray's mother was left penniless, and Ray was forced to quit school to try and help feed them. When his mother remarried several years later, to a truck driver from Hattiesburg, and Ramsey was born, Ray didn't seem to take more than a normal brother's interest. But only two months later—the day after the new father had jackknifed his truck and died on an icy Oklahoma turnpike—Ray had sworn to their mother that his little brother would never have to face the same deprivation he had. He had immediately added a second job to his day and, ever since, had been Ramsey's father in every way but having sired him.

"We are drilling a good-looking prospect," Ramsey said as he slid a chair back from the table and settled into it. "But I've dry-holed many a one of those before."

His brother smiled broadly now. "Better not this one. Wives of a couple farmers you leased from are already talking about how they're gonna spend their share."

Ramsey smiled and leaned forward in his chair. "Ray, Leigh Ann asked me to come down and talk to you."

Ray's brow immediately wrinkled.

"Ray, it's a couple of coincidences—Jack's finding the girl's purse, her being killed at the edge of their backyard, his not being able to find his hunting knife—they've all added up in Leigh Ann's mind where she's worried what you all might be thinking."

Ray was silent a moment, then shook his head. "Mark, I can't believe she came to you wanting a favor." He shook his head again. "Looks like she could've found—"

"Come on, Ray. Don't start on that again."

"It just still sticks in my craw the way she treated you. Breaking off an engagement is one thing. But, hell, she was shackin' up with Jack while she was still wearing your ring."

"Ray, you don't know what she—never mind. That was six years ago."

"Yeah, and I still remember how you got down. Never saw you like that before. Don't want to again. Bothers me a little her running to you now when she needs somethin'. Not sure how you might start—"

"Ray, she's had two kids and I've been with a lot of women since then. In fact, I've got one now might be the best I've ever been around. I run into Leigh Ann in town a couple times a month. She's always nice and I'm always nice. Things pass. What do you want me to do, hold a grudge for six years?"

Ray shrugged. "I have."

Ramsey chuckled softly and shook his head. "Ray, I went off to school. She went off to be a model. We grew apart. What's the big deal? It happens."

"Big deal?" Ray exclaimed. "Damn right it was a big deal. She cost you a scholarship—cost me to have to work my ass off to help pay for your schooling the year you were here in

Jackson—not to mention I had five hundred in that ring, too. Big deal? Damn right it was a big deal."

Ramsey knew that to respond would only cause his brother to say something more, so he remained quiet.

After a moment a small smile appeared on Ray's face. "I get to going sometimes, don't I?" he said.

Ramsey returned the smile. "If I'd had to work as hard as you did back then because of an idiot brother like me, I'd get to going, too. Now, is there any problem?"

"With Jack? No, of course not."

"Do you have any suspects?"

"None yet." Ray's smile turned into a wry one. "Most calls we been getting say it's the devil worshipers' work."

"Devil worshipers?"

"Yeah—newest fad. Comes from all the play that kinda stuff's been getting on television lately, I guess. Nothin' happens anymore we don't get calls regarding that. Make things worse, we got a group of area kids running around drawing symbols on buildings and such, and now every time some farmer has a calf wander off, it's the devil worshipers again.

"Had a woman call last week, said her cat had been sacrificed. Says she was sure that's what happened to it. We go out there and it looks like it's gone through a meat grinder. While we're there this neighbor comes across the street and wants to bring charges against the woman for her cat attacking his coon dogs. Pair of fifty-pound hounds in his backyard scratched all to hell. That cat musta put up a hell'uva fight.

"Woman had probably already called ten neighbors and told 'em about her cat being sacrificed. Each of them might've called ten others. Word's probably all over the county by now." He shook his head in exasperation. "No tellin' what kind of speculation's going on about the Richardson girl's murder."

"Paper said she was stabbed."

"Yeah, bunch of times. Way more than was needed to kill her. We're dealing with some kind of nut or—" A smile crossed Ray's face and he leaned back in his chair. "Now listen to me running my mouth. Why in hell did I go telling you that? Everything I say here you're going back to Leigh Ann with."

"No. Only thing I'll tell her is she doesn't have anything to be concerned about. But you do have my curiosity up. You have anything you're holding back from the papers?"

Ray smiled, but didn't answer.

"Come on, Ray. I'm not going to tell Leigh Ann anything. I'm asking for myself—just morbid curiosity." He lifted his hand, holding it palm out toward his brother. "Swear."

"You were a cop for a year, Mark. You know stuff like that's not talked to everybody."

Ramsey held up his palm again. "Swear. Give you my word."

Ray glanced at the open door to the lounge and back to his younger brother. When he spoke he lowered his voice.

"Multiple stab wounds—more than enough. Forensics says it was a wide-bladed knife, like a Bowie knife. That's why my men were askin' everybody in the neighborhood what kind of hunting knives they owned." He lowered his voice further, nearly to a whisper. "She wasn't raped where she was found."

"Yeah, I heard."

Ramsey saw his brother's eyes narrow, but Ray didn't ask from whom he had heard, only continued with what he was saying.

"Appears like she got loose, almost made it back to her house before he caught her. You talking to Leigh Ann, I guess you know about the campfire. Had to have been some kids there—maybe that afternoon, or early in the night. We're gonna run 'em down and talk to 'em; see when they were there. Medical examiner put the time of death at between nine and one, so according to when the kids left, they might've seen or heard something. We found a rubber we think the guy used."

"Yeah, I know."

Ray's eyes narrowed. "Jesus! Sounds like you know everything I do. Got some damned big-mouthed law-enforcement officers in this county." He shook his head in exasperation, then nodded toward the front of the lounge. "Shut the door."

After Ramsey had closed the door and returned to his seat, his brother leaned forward over the table, rested his forearms on its top as he spoke.

"On your word that you won't be discussing any of this, I'd like to throw a couple facts at you. See if you might think of something that hasn't dawned on me yet."

"Fifteen years on the force in Jackson before you took this job, and I'm going to think of something you haven't?"

"Never can tell. Fresh perspective sometimes helps. I've seen so many cases they all run together. Sorta has me in a rut."

"Okay, go ahead." Ramsey shifted in his chair, trying to get more comfortable against the hard wood of the back and seat. He noticed that while he had gone to shut the door the cigar butt had disappeared from the edge of the table, and he smiled to himself.

"First," Ray started, "why did the guy use a rubber?"

"If he hadn't left it lying around, I'd have said to keep you from typing his blood from the semen."

"Yeah, and maybe that's what he did use it for. It was lying real close to the fire. Maybe he meant to pitch it in and didn't notice he missed." Ray leaned back in his seat as he continued speaking.

"Damn sure didn't need it for any other reason—she was already pregnant. Examiner says close to two months. Came as a hell'uva surprise to her parents." He paused a moment, stared blankly as he thought. "I been wondering why a guy would tote her all the way back to the sinkhole; not just stick it to her right in the house. I got to thinking maybe it wasn't a stranger busting in on her. Maybe it was someone she knew well enough to go back there voluntarily with him. Somethin' caused the guy to get upset afterward. If it was friendly at first, that could explain the rubber. With all the diseases nowadays, it could have been for that."

Ramsey nodded. "Did she have a steady boyfriend or was she dating around?"

"That was what shocked her parents so much about her being pregnant. I talked to her father—Dr. Richardson. He's a psychiatrist out at the insane asylum. According to him she had never dated the same boy more than two or three times; very seldom even went out. He gave me a few names and I talked to 'em—a class dance, double date at a movie, class officer's parties; things like that. I've got one of my men down at the high school talking to kids taking summer classes there, seeing if we can find out anybody else she might have dated. Her being pregnant certainly says she knew *somebody* more than casually."

"She was still in high school? Leigh Ann said she had already turned eighteen."

"Yeah, still there, and only gonna be a junior this fall. Father said she had flunked a couple semesters. Said it was from him having to uproot the family so much. In the last few years he's held jobs in New York, Memphis, Vicksburg, and here."

Ramsey glanced at his watch, shook his head and stood. "Sorry. Have to be going—unless you want another murder on your hands. Robert's going to be hot if I don't get out and look at the well today, and then I've got to get back and pick Janet up. I'm taking her out to the Lighthouse to eat. It's her birthday."

Ray smiled, came to his feet, and reached across the table to shake hands. Ramsey noticed his brother was making an effort to hold his stomach in.

"Mark, you be coming by more often now, you hear. I hardly ever get to see you any more what with you drilling wells all over South Mississippi. And I'm sorry about mouthing off about Leigh Ann—no call for it. I just—well, you know."

"Ray, when she came out to see me it passed through my mind how good-looking she was, same as I'd think looking at anybody that looks like her. And I remembered back to when we dated—of course. But that's all that happened. There was no little twinge in my stomach, no regret. Things pass."

"Good," Ray said. "You tell her for me that I said to quit worrying. Jack's the last person in the world I'd be thinking had anything to do with a killin'."

After leaving the police station, Ramsey used the cellular phone in his Cadillac to call the Mueller home. When Leigh Ann answered he explained to her that she and Jack had nothing to be concerned about.

"What if they do decide to ask him to take a lie detector test?" she asked. "Would he have to?"

Ramsey laughed softly and shook his head. "You said you would quit worrying if I talked to Ray."

There was a long silence on the line.

When Leigh Ann finally spoke again, there was a new timidity in her voice. "If he took a test, would they question him about other things? I mean something which might have happened years ago."

"What do you mean?"

There was another long moment of silence.

"Mark, if they ask him to, and they're asking him things about Julie—I mean, I've read about lie detector tests. I know they'll ask him everything about her. Will they ask him . . . will they ask him if he's ever been involved in something like this before?"

It was his turn to sit in silence.

"Mark, is there any way you can come over for a minute? There's something that I haven't told you that I need to. I don't want to do it over the telephone."

CHAPTER

4

Belle Colline Heights, the subdivision where Jack and Leigh Ann lived, was considered one of the more desirable residential areas in Davis County. Spread over two hundred acres of gently rolling hills, the subdivision was built on land that had been part of one of the largest plantations in Central Mississippi before being willed to the plantation's longtime manager by its last owner, childless, who also left three, two-acre home sites to families working for him, willing the remainder of the several thousand acres to the state.

The farm manager had lived on the two hundred acres until his death, whereupon his estranged wife, living in Biloxi, sold the parcel to a group of Jackson investors.

They had done a good job after deciding to develop a residential area, leaving the land in as near a natural state as possible—two small, cypress-dotted lakes at the subdivision's center, streets laid out without curb and gutter, and as many old trees left standing as were practical. But the area's prime attraction remained the plantation it came from, now a state park and giving the subdivision the unique privacy of being surrounded on three sides by a heavily wooded forest.

The Mueller home, a brick two-story of twenty-two to twenty-three hundred square feet, was one of the smaller houses in the development. It was especially overshadowed by the fact it sat next to the plantation's original columned mansion—the hundred and twenty-five-year-old house where the murdered girl had lived.

Leigh Ann was waiting outside her front door when Ramsey drove his Cadillac into the driveway and parked. She had changed out of the sundress she had worn during her visit to his office. She now wore a pair of low-cut blue slacks and a flowered cotton blouse, its unbuttoned ends knotted just below her breasts. Her bare midriff was highlighted by her tiny waist. Her full, dark hair was now wrapped in a tight bun at the back of her head.

The windy day, he thought. She hadn't been able to stand the strands of her hair whipping around in the wind, so she had gathered it into the protected bun. Had she changed out of the sundress because the slacks and blouse went better with the bun, or because of the blowing dust her dress had suffered when she had crossed the parking lot? He shook his head and smiled to himself. She was beautiful, and always looked like she had just stepped out of a fashion magazine—but at a price. She could drive you crazy with the time she spent primping. Everything had to be exactly right, from the smallest curl to perfectly applied makeup. He had never met a woman more finicky about her appearance.

"Thank you for coming," she said as she stepped up onto the porch.

Entering the living room, Ramsey was surprised that the furniture was not any nicer than it was, and that there wasn't all that much of it—a small couch near the center of the room and facing two easy chairs, a coffee table sitting in the middle of the arrangement; a compact china cabinet near a door leading into the master bedroom at the far end of the room, and, back against the wall to his left, a straight-back chair against the wall next to the entrance into the kitchen. Other than a small table and lamp next to one of the easy chairs, that's all there was—no built-ins, not even a television in sight. The home itself, well built and moderately expensive, had shown an exterior that gave the promise of much more inside.

Maybe he shouldn't have been surprised, Ramsey thought. It was no secret that three years prior, Jack, a real-estate broker, had been heavily involved financially in a failed rural residential development, losing most of what money his father, Dr. Jack Mueller, had left at his death the year before. The house was being built at about the same time the development was going sour—there probably hadn't been the money to furnish it as they would have liked—and Jack hadn't held any one job very long since then. It was doubtful they had much more money than what it took to get by each day.

Leigh Ann had stopped at the couch and indicated with a gesture of her head for him to sit down; she sat close beside him when he did.

For a long moment she was silent, her hands nervously fidgeting in her lap. Finally she asked, "If a person has been accused of doing something wrong in the past, would it show up on a lie detector test? Even if it's not what they're questioning that person about?"

"What are you trying to find out?"

"Would it?"

"I don't know. Depending what he's been accused of, I guess. They'd ask some broad questions. Yeah, I guess if a person had been accused of something and still was bothered by it, it could make him have a nervous reaction that would register. What is it you're getting at?"

She didn't answer immediately. When she did, she looked directly into his eyes.

"He can't take a lie detector test, then. I was hoping he could."

"I don't understand."

"When Jack was in New Orleans, at Tulane, he had some trouble. When he asked me to marry him, he told me about it the same day. He said he wanted me to know everything about him before I gave my answer . . ."

At her pause, not knowing what else to do, he nodded.

"Near the end of his junior year he was charged with rape."

She quickly placed a hand on his forearm and shook her head. "It's not like it sounds," she said. "He was dating this girl. She was a freshman, had finished high school early, and was only seventeen. Jack said he didn't want to go into all the sordid details. All he told me was the mother brought the charges against him when she caught him and the daughter together in bed one day. Talked the daughter into saying she had been forced—or scared her into it. There was a trial, at least the start of a trial. Then the girl admitted she hadn't been forced and the judge dismissed the charges."

He sat silent for a moment. "That's all there is to it?"

She nodded.

"You couldn't have told me this on the telephone?"

She dropped her gaze to her lap. "I'm sorry. I just wanted to know if it would show up. I shouldn't have bothered you." Her lip trembled.

He felt bad for the trace of irritation that had come through in his tone. He laid his hand on her shoulder, made certain his voice was soft when he spoke.

"I'm sorry. There was nothing wrong in your asking. I guess I got a little tense there, wondering what you were getting at. I'm sorry."

She smiled, raised her hand to lay it over his on her shoulder. "You're sweet," she said in a soft voice. "You know, I'd forgotten how really sweet you were." She lifted his hand from her shoulder, held it between the two of them, and looked at it for a moment before releasing it. He felt a little awkward.

As Ramsey drove away from Leigh Ann's, he used his cellular telephone to call his office. Shirley told him Piggott and Morrow's secretary had been rude, insisting he return their call. Snapper had forgotten to call in that morning's drilling report, again . . . *Less said about the rape charge the better* . . . Drilling a hundred feet high; should be in the Eutaw formation in five or six days if everything kept going well. Then two more days of drilling and they'd be in the Lower Tuscaloosa. Three hundred thousand dollars; a toss of the dice . . . *He was really surprised at the feeling that had come over him by the time Leigh Ann had released his hand—more than awkward.* He shook his head. That's all he needed now, start thinking about her again. Once was enough.

Glancing at his watch, he shook his head a second time. Robert was going to kill him. But if he took the time now to stop by the well, then Janet was going to kill him—might not come back to the house with him tonight. Not much of a decision to be made there, he thought. He reached for his radio mike, had to make several attempts at contact before he received a response.

"You got Unit Two. Whatcha need?"

"Robert?"

"Ain't none of him, Mr. Ramsey, this be's Snapper. Mr. Robert be's up on the derrick floor."

"Everything going all right?"

"Purrin'."

"Tell Robert I'm not coming back out to the well today. Tell him I had an important appointment I had to keep."

"Yessir, Mr. Ramsey. Tell Miss Janet I said happy birthday."

CHAPTER

5

The telephone rang just after ten that night. Ramsey silently cursed as he rolled away from Janet and fumbled in the dark for the receiver.

"Yeah?"

"Oh, God, Mark! The police came! They came and took him! *Please* go help him!"

He sat up straight in bed, nearly yanking the telephone off the bedside table when he did so. Janet raised up on her elbow.

"Leigh Ann, what are you saying?"

"My God, help me!"

"Leigh Ann, what happened?"

"They came after Jack!"

What in the hell . . . ? "You mean arrested him?" Sliding his legs off the bed, he sat on its side.

"Yes. Oh, God!"

"Leigh Ann, calm down."

"Please go help him. Please! They took him away!"

He shook his head, trying to think. "Did you call a lawyer?"

"Yes. Yes. Bennie Evans."

"I'm going to find out what's going on. Just wait by the phone. After I speak with Ray, I'll call you."

"No! Bring him home!"

"Okay. Okay."

After getting the dial tone back he quickly punched in a number, drummed his fingers nervously against the tabletop as he waited for someone to answer. Janet sat up in the bed, drew her legs up close against her chest and wrapped her arms around them, resting her chin on her knees as she waited.

"Police Department."

"Let me speak to the Chief."

"Do what?"

"Let me speak to Chief Hopkins."

"Mister, it's after ten o'clock—night. Look out your window. See, it's dark outside. Chief ain't required to work all day and night, too."

Hell, he was going crazy.

He punched in his brother's home number. It rang several times before Ray answered.

"Hello."

"You said there wasn't any problem."

The exasperated release of his brother's breath was audible through the receiver. "That was this morning."

"What changed?"

"Jack's charged with capital murder now. Not the kind of thing we ought to keep bullshittin' back and forth about. I think from now on maybe we need to start actin' proper like."

"Do they have him down at the jail?"

"Yeah. Sheriff just called me. I'm going down there in a minute. But I'm not gonna talk to you about it no more."

"Yeah, I understand."

"I'm sorry, Mark, but that's how it's gotta be."

"It's okay." He replaced the receiver.

Janet, her forehead wrinkled, continued to stare. He looked back at her. "I'm sorry, baby. I have to go down to the jail." He hurried toward his bedroom closet.

Janet reached to lift the covers and pull them up to her shoulders, leaned back against the headboard, and stared up at the ceiling.

Housed in an old three-story redbrick building, the Davis County, Mississippi, Sheriff's Department and Jail sat directly behind the courthouse and fronted a narrow, dead-end street lined on its opposite side with attorneys' offices.

When Ramsey arrived, he double-parked beside a line of Sheriff's Department cruisers and hurried toward the building's front door.

A television news team was already on the scene. Their white van, its antenna dish extended to the limit of its telescoping pole and pointed toward Jackson, was also double-parked. A reporter, bathed in camera lights as he broadcast live, was standing in front of the entrance. He never stopped speaking as Ramsey nodded, stepped around him, and moved inside the building.

Ray had already arrived. He was standing in the first-floor hall speaking with a woman reporter dressed in a tailored suit.

"Ray."

The reporter glared at the rudeness.

"I'll be with you in a minute," Ray said.

Ramsey leaned back against a wall until the reporter had finished and started down the hall, her thick-heeled shoes thumping against the concrete floor.

As Ramsey moved to his brother, Ray shook his head. "Not thinking any more about Leigh Ann than you would any other good-looking woman—right?"

"Ray, I'm not down here because of her. Jack was my best friend at one time. I know him better than anybody. I can't picture him being charged with something like this."

Ray stood silent for a moment. Finally he beckoned with his head toward an office door and walked in that direction.

Inside the room, he pointed Ramsey to a stiff-back chair, then walked around behind an old wooden desk at the rear of the room and seated himself. Leaning forward, elbows on the desktop, hands clasped together off the side of his face, he thought a moment before speaking.

"Well, first of all I didn't have nothin' to do with the arrest. I knew it was coming an hour ago. But I told the D.A. and sheriff I'd rather not be in on it—Jack spent too many nights at our house. They got him good." Ray paused for a moment, his brow wrinkling in further thought, then continued.

"Well, it's nothin' that's gonna be a secret after his lawyer gets through talking to the D.A., anyway. What's new is they lifted Jack's fingerprints from in the girl's bedroom. In addition to that, they've got his exact size footprints in a flowerbed outside one of the downstairs windows. If you were the D.A., wouldn't you be charging him?"

Ramsey shifted uneasily in the chair. "Tell me about the prints in the bedroom?"

"Well, when we got word a few hours ago that they matched his, the sheriff went out there to ask him if he'd ever been in the house. Jack indicated he and Leigh Ann had only been over there as dinner guests of the Parkers. That's the family who lived there until last summer. Said he hadn't been there since the Richardsons moved in. Then, as soon as the sheriff told him about finding his fingerprints upstairs—they were on the door facing—he immediately remembered having been upstairs. Said it was a month ago—he'd forgot about it. Said one weekend when the Richardsons were out of town he thought he saw somethin' move past a window in the house and he went over to check. Front door was locked, but the back door and the doors down into the cellar were standing open—according to him. He went down in the cellar first, and then went inside the house. Said he checked every room, including the girl's. Claims he left the fingerprints then. We know he couldn't have."

"What do you mean?"

His brother shook his head, pushed himself away from the

desktop, and leaned back in his chair. "Not gonna tell you that if you flat lay down on the floor and throw a tantrum. D.A. doesn't plan to bring it out in the preliminary hearing. You're just gonna have to wait on discovery motions to find out."

"What difference does it make, then or now? It's not going to change what you have."

Ray, his jaw firmly set, his lips tight, shook his head.

"For Christ sake, Ray, how can it hurt?"

"D.A. isn't gonna use it now, and told me to keep it to myself. You want to know, ask the D.A."

Ramsey knew he could talk his brother into almost anything. But there were rare times when Ray used a certain tone and, when he did, no one could persuade him to change his mind. He had just gone to that tone.

"Okay, Ray. Do you mind if I see Jack?"

"D.A. said no visitors. But you'll probably be able to see him soon enough. Bennie Evans is over talking to the judge right now. Not any secret they're friends. If I don't miss my guess, Bennie will have him out on bail by in the morning. Some people won't like that. But that'll be the judge's headache. Me, the sheriff, and the D.A., we've done our job."

Ramsey rose from his chair. "I appreciate you telling me what you have." He turned toward the door.

"Mark, one more thing. When they first brought Jack down here tonight he said he didn't need an attorney. The sheriff asked if he'd take a lie detector test. He agreed and—" Ray paused a moment and shook his head. "I got to be crazy telling you all this. You still got a job waiting for me in your company?"

"Always has been."

"Not liftin' anything?"

Ramsey smiled. "Desk job; air-conditioned office and a good-looking secretary."

"Well," Ray said. "They got Jack through the preliminaries, getting down his normal responses. Had just asked the first big question when Bennie busted in and said he didn't want his client on the polygraph. Guess Leigh Ann had called him.

Anyway, the testing stopped then. Jack had never answered—
but the pins had gone crazy right after the question was asked.
Question asked was as simple as you can get. Did you kill the
girl?"

"That's crazy, Ray. That could of just been a response indi-
cating he became nervous because it was the first critical question. The examiner would have to have had more than one
answer to be sure."

Ray nodded. "Normally I'd agree with you."

"What do you mean, normally."

"Champlin's the one who administered the test, Mark. You
know how careful he sets everything up. I got to go with his
opinion, one question or not. You ever heard of him being off
base?"

"He's got to be, Ray. God, think about it—you've known
Jack all his life."

"Thought I had."

"Come on, Ray, I can't believe you're thinking like this. I
don't believe for a minute—" He shook his head. "Hell, Ray,
if Jack was the killer, why would he agree to take the test in
the first place?"

"Maybe he was ready to take the consequences—guilt got to
him."

"Then why didn't he just admit it?"

"Mark, you were a cop long enough to know there's those
who want to get caught but don't have the guts to confess. Jack
wouldn't be the first one to let a polygraph do his confessing
for him."

CHAPTER

6

After leaving the Davis County Jail, Ramsey drove directly to Leigh Ann's, slowing when he passed the old Colonial next door.

It was a grand one—four fluted Corinthian columns gracing its front, and finished in its original lapped cypress siding. The developers had thought it would add to the subdivision, give the development a sense of character, and so they had renovated it and left it where it was, cutting out a large, well-landscaped lot around it.

And it had added to the subdivision's reputation. Not just northern tourists but visitors from other parts of Mississippi were constantly flocking to see the mansion, especially in the spring when its azaleas were in full bloom and the house was opened to the public for a week during the annual tour of old homes in the county. But, in a strange way, it had also taken away from the subdivision—none of the other houses in the development could compete with the grandeur it portrayed. Visually, it was a case of the Old South outshining the new.

But visually was all, for the people familiar with the house's history knew there was another side to the home, a darker side. Nothing to do with slavery—the original Jewish master used salaried whites to run a large herd of cattle and never was a slave owner. The home's curse was that in its hundred and twenty-five years of existence two separate families living there had suffered mysterious murders, with the culprits never apprehended. A lot of people said the house was cursed. It was all explained in the pamphlet printed by the Historical Confederate Society and distributed by the local Chamber of Commerce. He wondered how many years it would be before a paragraph about Julie was added to the pamphlet, and he wondered if her murder would be described as solved, with the killer listed as Jack—the only man Ramsey knew who had never gone hunting because he was too tender-hearted to shoot a living creature.

When Leigh Ann opened the door, she was wearing her nightgown. Completely proper, it was made of a white cotton material you couldn't see through; the scooped neck not excessive. Even then, after pointing him to a seat, she disappeared through the door at the side of the living room to reappear fully dressed a few minutes later.

She had regained her composure, but hadn't spoken since he had entered the home, only nodding at him as he had entered. She was still quiet as she crossed the room and sat down in a cushioned wingback chair across from the couch. He saw her hand tremble.

"Leigh Ann, you need to try and get some sleep."

"Was Jack okay?"

"Sure, fine."

"What did he say?"

"I'm sorry, Leigh Ann; they wouldn't let me see him. But I know he's fine."

A tear started from the corner of her eye and ran down the hollow between her cheek and nose. She reached with the back of her forefinger to wipe it away. Straightening herself in her chair, she took a deep breath and looked directly into Ramsey's eyes.

"He's not fine, Mark; hasn't been for a long time. I'm part of the reason. And now look what's happened."

He shook his head. "I'm sorry, I don't—"

"Jack didn't kill anybody."

"I know that."

"No, you don't," she said, shaking her head. "But I do. And yet I know they're going to try him and they're going to convict him, and they're going to kill him—and I'm the reason it's going to happen. It's going to be my fault."

She shook her head again when he started to speak. "No, let me finish. You know why I'm positive Jack didn't rape Julie? He didn't rape her because he didn't have to. He'd already had sex with her."

Ramsey knew his face had betrayed his surprise when she nodded her head.

"Yeah . . . already. I should have seen it coming when that whore moved in next door—" She shook her head once more, bit her lower lip.

"I shouldn't be speaking about a dead girl like that, but that's what she was. When Jack was out in the yard she didn't just sunbathe, she put on an exhibition. I almost went to her parents and told them." She shook her head again, a faraway stare glazing her eyes for a moment. Then she turned them back to Ramsey.

"But I didn't say anything to them. I wish I had, but I didn't. It happened late last summer, about two months after they moved in. I was down in Ocean Springs for the weekend and it turned out her parents were out of town, too." She looked down at the hands clasped in her lap, took a deep breath, then raised her face to his once more.

"The old story," she said. "I came home early and I caught them. I became the typical woman scorned. What else could I have been? I ranted and raved about a divorce; called him everything I could think of; told him he'd rot in hell." She shook her head and frowned.

"Well he did rot in hell. Right here in this house. If you ever need anyone to put a curse on a person for you, you're looking at the devil's best. I made him crawl, made him feel ashamed, guilty; all the things I wanted to make him feel. And then it got worse. He came down on himself like you wouldn't believe. Soon he was telling me how he was like an animal, couldn't control his urges, was no good. He became deeply depressed. I even began to worry about his committing suicide. I mean really worry . . . You know his grandfather killed himself."

Ramsey nodded. Jack had been the one who had told him. The old man had been president of the first nationally chartered bank in the county, and had been unable to face the humiliation when he had been discovered embezzling funds.

Leigh Ann shook her head once more. A bitter smile crossed her face. "I should have found help for him then, somehow gotten him to a doctor. But I didn't do anything.

"Then he got it in his mind that losing our first child must have been his punishment for what he did with the girl at Tulane. Jesus! Punishment for what? A mother catching a couple of young lovers in bed together? It . . ." She stared at him for a moment. "You didn't know about my miscarriage, did you?"

He shook his head.

"It happened the first year we were married, the year before the twins were born. I was three months pregnant. Most people don't know. It was just a miscarriage. A sad time in our lives, but just a miscarriage, not punishment. Jack didn't think it was, either, then. But right after I caught him with Julie, he started talking about the miscarriage being some sort of delayed punishment that had happened because of what went on at Tulane. It makes no sense, but he did." She took a deep breath before continuing. Her voice was becoming labored, on the verge of breaking.

"Then he started worrying that something was going to happen to the twins because of what he had done with Julie. He's

developed a guilt complex you wouldn't believe. First remark
he made when they discovered Julie's body was that she was
dead because of what they did, and that he'll be punished for
it, too. He's just waiting for it to happen. If he goes to trial,
he's going to sound so guilty he might as well admit to having
murdered her. He's insane with guilt.''

Ramsey sat silent a moment, finally decided to tell her what
Ray had said.

"Leigh Ann, Jack consented to a polygraph before Bennie
got there. He hadn't answered any questions, but they were
just asking him if he had killed the girl when Bennie walked in
and they said the machine registered—" He shook his head.
"I'm afraid the response he showed—"

"No!" she exclaimed, her eyes widening, a look of panic
sweeping her face. "No! Oh, God, what am I going to do?"

"They can't use it against him, Leigh Ann. They won't even
be allowed to mention it in the courtroom."

She began shaking her head back and forth. "But he didn't
do anything and now they're going to be sure he did, there's
not going to be any doubt in their minds. They—it's his guilt
complex. That's what it is. They might not use it in court, but
they're going to—" She suddenly moved her hands to clasp
the sides of her face, her eyes widening again.

"Oh, my God, Mark, they're going to know about the girl at
Tulane, too. I'd forgotten about that."

"What do you mean, know about her?"

She looked him directly in the eyes. "Will you go talk to
her?"

"Go talk to her?"

"Yes. Yes, you have to. Then come back and tell them Jack
didn't do anything wrong. They'll believe you. They wouldn't
me. And with his family dead, he doesn't have anybody else.
You have to. If they think he's raped a girl, they're going to be
even surer he killed Julie."

"Leigh Ann, they're not going to know anything about—"

"Yes, they are. She lives in Biloxi now. Last year one of
Jack's friends attending a convention down there met this girl

named Honey. Hearing him talk about where he lived, she asked about Jack and said she knew him from Tulane. The girl there had been named Honey; Honey Rutherford. From the description his friend gave him, Jack knew it was the same girl. Mark, the girl told this man that Jack had ruined her life—said he raped her."

"You told me she admitted he didn't—to the judge."

"She did. But then it turned out she was pregnant, had an abortion. Then when he quit dating her she went crazy, blamed him for her having the abortion. I saw some of the letters she wrote him; she was threatening to get even with him. If she hears about the trouble he's in—what if she calls up and says Jack raped her?"

"It won't come up, Leigh Ann. Even if someone finds out about her, she won't be brought in to testify. It's unrelated to this case."

She shook her head. "No. That's not right. You're talking legal. I'm talking real life. If she does call, then the police are going to be even more positive Jack's guilty of Julie's rape, too. Even worse—if she does call, word will get out in a town this size. Some clerk at the sheriff's office, the district attorney's secretary, will tell somebody. The man who was at the convention might already be telling people. What if it gets to someone who's going to be on the jury? Please. Please go talk to her. Get her to tell you the truth and then come back and tell everybody. Please. I told you in your office that this awful chain of events was adding up. Jack finding the sinkhole, his knife lost, and now this. Mark, please. He can't stand anymore. At least talk to the girl so that he won't be hurt by that, too."

He sat quietly for a moment. He did have two leases that he hadn't yet tied down on the next block he was going to drill. One of the owners lived in Ocean Springs, just a few miles from Biloxi. There was no hurry to get the lease signed; he had planned on getting it after the current well he was drilling was down—combine the trip with a couple of days of relaxation on the Coast. But then neither was there any reason to put off getting the lease.

"Please," Leigh Ann said. She shook her head again. "I know you were hurt by us. I'm sorry. But please don't get back at us this way. You're the only one who can help us that the police will believe."

"Leigh Ann, I wouldn't do something like—"

"Mark, I'm sorry I hurt you. But it wasn't any of his doing. It was me."

"Leigh Ann, I wouldn't—Never mind, I'll go—'course I will. I'll run down there tomorrow."

On his way back to his house, Ramsey used his cellular phone to call the drill-site trailer.

"Yeah."

"Robert, it's me."

"Mark, where in hell were you all day? If I'm going to be the only one that sets this well, you might as well give it to me."

"They've arrested Jack for the girl's murder."

"What?"

"They say they've got his fingerprints in the house. It doesn't look good for him."

"Christ Almighty. That's hard for me to believe."

"I knew you'd want to know. I'll see you in the morning. Then I'm going to run down to Biloxi."

"What in the world for?"

"I don't want to talk about it over the phone. I'll tell you in the morning."

"Don't want to tell me over—Something about Jack?"

"Something I told Leigh Ann I'd do for her."

There was silence for a moment. "Comes to you in her hour of need. You never know do you? Feel funny about it?"

"Jesus, Robert. You sound just like Ray. I know I didn't act that bad back then."

"Yeah—well, appreciate you letting me know about Jack."

CHAPTER

7

Janet was waiting in the game room when Ramsey arrived at his home. She was completely dressed and sitting in the big overstuffed easy chair in front of the television. She stood and faced him when he walked into the room.

"Do you mind if I borrow your car to go home in?" she asked.

"Go home?"

"Go home."

"Hey, Janet, I'm sorry, but I had to go to the jail."

"I know you *had* to. That's why I want to go home."

"You've lost me."

"No, I never had you. Thought I did, but Leigh Ann still does."

"Come on, Janet; Jack's an old friend."

"Can I borrow your car? I'll have it back to you first thing in the morning."

"If you really have to go, I'll drive you."

"I don't want you to drive me."

"Come on, Janet. I—"

"I thought you were over her, but you're not. How can you . . . Never mind, it's none of my business. Can I use your car or not?"

He stared at her a moment, then nodded. "The keys are in the ignition. I'll send somebody after it tomorrow."

"You won't have to. It'll be at the office by the time you get there." She walked past him toward the door leading into the living room.

He stared after her until he heard the front door shut, then he turned and moved to the easy chair, sat down and leaned back in it.

I thought you were over her, but you're not. First Ray had hinted at it, not too subtly. Robert had, too, and now Janet had just plain said it.

The two and a half years he and Leigh Ann had dated had certainly left an impression on everyone. If an earthquake had struck the county it wouldn't be much better recalled. *An earthquake*, he thought—quick, powerful, memorable, and then, when it was over, the destruction it left behind . . . That was as good a description as any of what he had gone through with Leigh Ann. He smiled. He could smile now.

It had all started a month before he was to report to Ole Miss for his sophomore year, something he hadn't been really looking forward to. On a football scholarship, the only way he could afford to attend the university, he had spent his freshman year as a scout team tackling dummy, and saw little prospect of much more than similar duty in his future.

Even if his athletic experience had been more favorable, he still wasn't sure he would have wanted to return to the school —at least not under the circumstances he faced at the time. A mostly fraternity-sorority school, that part of the Ole Miss life was completely out of the question for him—neither his mother nor Ray had the money for him to enjoy such a luxury.

He had worked a part-time job during the summer, but had spent most of what he had made during that time on dates and partying and was almost down to the embarrassment of not being able to afford to go out with anybody. Quitting school and going to work would solve a lot of problems—at least the problems he was most concerned about at that age.

Then he had met Leigh Ann at a club at the reservoir. She had been with three of her friends, all of them upcoming high school seniors. She had ended up letting him drive her home. They had gone out the next night, and the next, and the next; would have gone out every night except for her mother not being happy about Leigh Ann being so serious about one boy.

But Leigh Ann didn't care what her mother thought; he was what she wanted and he was what she was going to have, she told him. They would be married as soon as she was old enough not to need permission. Until then she wanted to be around him every night, not just when he could come home from school. But that was up to him. *She* couldn't drop out of high school, but *he* could drop out of Ole Miss. There were colleges in Jackson he could attend.

After making the decision not to go back, the worst thing he had to face was his mother's disappointment. She had her heart set on him being the first member of their family to get a college education.

He had explained to her about the amount of time he had to put in on the football field, and how by working the same number of hours while attending the local community college he would not only be more rested and better able to concentrate on his books, but would probably be able to save up enough money to pay for his last two years at a four-year college. Besides, there would no longer be any chance of his being seriously injured in football. That had persuaded her he was doing the right thing. She had always worried about his being hurt.

His brother wasn't so easily convinced. Ramsey smiled as he remembered what had happened after he told Ray he was quitting school. That very night Robert had called from Oklahoma State where he was studying geology. Jack, who was attending Tulane in New Oleans, just "happened" to call the next morning. Both of them had ended up giving him a pep talk. Ray had put them up to it. Who better to give you a pep talk but your two best friends—Ray would have looked at it like that.

Two best friends—one for all and all for one. The Three Musketeers. Silly now, but that's what they had called themselves in high school; the quarterback, fullback, and tailback of the best backfield in the state—or so they liked to claim at the time.

One thing that wasn't silly was their friendship, ever since they had started grade school at the same time. And now there were two. Was that how the *Three Musketeers* went? Ramsey wondered. He had forgotten the exact story. But not *their* story—he and Robert left, still best of friends, and now prospecting for oil together, Jack having taken a different route. Ramsey shook his head. He really hadn't given Jack any choice, had he? But that was now. Back then they were all still friends. "Don't let us down," Jack had said when he called from Tulane. "I'm always telling everybody you were the worst football player of the three of us—we just didn't care anything about playing college ball."

But he had held steadfast to his decision, and Ray said no more—until the second week of Ramsey's first job, when he was fired for skipping work two days in a row to take Leigh Ann water skiing at the reservoir.

Ray asked Ramsey what was happening to him—said that he was getting out of control. Ramsey knew he was, too, and was serious about it, sitting Leigh Ann down and explaining to her that if they were to have a life together that he had to have a way that he could make an adequate living for her, and that meant having a college degree.

Everything settled down for the rest of his sophomore year. Then Leigh Ann graduated and simultaneously got her big break. She had entered a modeling contest the year before and had won it, receiving among her prizes a photography session at a well-known agency in New Orleans. They still had her portfolio on file and called the day after she graduated, asking her if she would like to try a three-month stint as one of their models.

She accepted the offer and, to her mother's chagrin, asked him to go with her. He couldn't. He had also just received a break. With his year at the community college over it was then time for him to go on to a senior college. Yet, despite what he had promised his mother he would do, he hadn't saved any money. Then a small college in California had called. It was one of the schools that had earlier recruited him, but having only a mediocre reputation in football, it had had no chance at enticing him. During the second call he had to suppress a shout of joy.

Leigh Ann didn't like it, and cried more than once as she tried to persuade him to go on to New Orleans. Tulane was there—a highly respected school. But it was also a private school and there was no way he could afford it. No, he told her, he had nearly screwed up his chance of an education once. He wouldn't again. And, thank God, he did go on at that time. His mother died of a heart attack only a week after he had signed the grant. Had she died at anytime prior to that, he was sure he would still feel guilty about disappointing her for dropping out of school.

In school in California he did well academically, but never did start for the football team—though he played quite a bit as a junior, lettering, and was projected to be a starting wide receiver his senior year. Then, prior to the opening game of that year, he suffered a shoulder separation that prevented his even practicing again.

But football wasn't the main thing on his mind then, anyway. It was in third place, behind his second-place desire to get a degree, and his primary goal of marrying Leigh Ann—his purpose for attending college in California in the first place.

Meanwhile, Leigh Ann seemed to be headed in the direction she wanted, too. With his work in the off-season he had saved enough money that he had flown to New Orleans half a dozen times, and had her out to California once. She always seemed proud of what she was doing and expected to "break out" any day.

Then one day Ray had told him during a telephone conversation that he had heard she wasn't doing well. That in fact, except for her mother supporting her, she couldn't have afforded to remain in New Orleans. That bothered him, but he didn't say anything, realizing it could hurt her pride.

It was during the Christmas break his senior year that he had given her an engagement ring—a pretty damn expensive one costing him most of his savings plus a five-hundred-dollar loan from Ray.

He flew to New Orleans once in the spring, then cut two days of classes prior to spring break to have his time at home coincide with hers.

Ray had met him at the airport and handed him a letter from Leigh Ann.

Inside the envelope was a ring wrapped in tissue paper and a simple message. Leigh Ann had fallen out of love with him and in love with Jack—one of his two best friends.

He hadn't gone back to school. Angry at being made a fool of, sick of study, and ready to go to work somewhere, he told his brother that he would finish up his degree through night courses. But he really didn't know what he would end up doing, except for one thing—he was certain that he was going to beat Jack half to death the first time he ran up on him. The earthquake had reached its climax.

Ramsey shook his head and rose from his chair, walked to the bar at the side of the game room and opened the small refrigerator there. He lifted out a Coors, popped the tab back, and turned and leaned back against the counter.

Of course there had never been a fight, though for all that was left of the friendship there might as well have been, and that bothered Ramsey; had for a long time, but especially did now. How could he fault Jack for doing the same thing he had done—fall in love with Leigh Ann?

How could he fault Leigh Ann, either? She had begged him

to go to New Orleans with him and he hadn't. He had known her modeling career was a failure and had said nothing to comfort her. He knew her mother was always pressing her to marry somebody *worth* marrying, and Jack was a good person, as well as the son of a rich doctor—small-town Mississippi rich, anyway.

All the signs were there for her to bounce in Jack's direction and he—Jesus, he hadn't played all this over in his mind in years. And it was suddenly starting to bother him. Tonight, going down to the jail like he did, then agreeing to go to Biloxi to try and talk to some woman named Honey Rutherford— was he really doing it out of concern for Jack or because of Leigh Ann? And if he was doing it out of concern for her, what kind of concern?

He took a sip of beer and placed the can on the counter. *Come on, Mark, baby,* he told himself; *be sure why you're doing this. We don't need to start any backsliding here. One earthquake was enough for anyone.*

CHAPTER

8

In the entire Belle Colline State Park, only three small plots remained in private ownership, the two-acre homesites the old plantation owner had willed to the men working for him at the time he died. All three of the sites were located off the old logging road which ran along the crest of the hill above the subdivision where Leigh Ann lived. Two of them, now used as fishing cabins, were located on a small river several miles down the road. The third one was located directly above the subdivision, and contained the old house trailer Ramsey now approached in his Cadillac.

He had earlier been out at the well to check on the drilling progress, was ready to go to Biloxi to try and talk to Honey. But before he did, he had to speak with Leigh Ann—question her about what his brother had just told him.

On the way to her house, a mile before the subdivision entrance, out of curiosity he had taken a turn onto the logging road which ran above the subdivision. The road was one direction from which the killer could have entered the subdivision. His coming down through the woods from the road would have allowed him to come out directly at the site of the murder without any chance of anyone in the subdivision having seen him enter the area.

Ramsey had come upon the old, rust-streaked yellow trailer, its location less than a quarter mile from being directly above where the old Colonial house set.

A vehicle could have parked on the road in sight of the trailer. Someone living there might have noticed.

Leaving his car at the edge of the road, he walked across the dusty red clay of the plot, stepped up onto the railroad ties which served as the trailer's front porch.

Seconds after his knock, the door opened as far as a safety chain would allow.

"I'm Mark Ramsey." He could see only darkness through the three-inch crack.

"Whadda ya want?"

"I'd like to ask you a question—about any cars you might have seen up here a few nights ago."

For a long moment the crack remained unchanged, then the door shut to reopen wide. He was surprised the deep, gruff voice had come from a child no older than eleven, and maybe five two in height. He was skinny, had shoulder-length blond hair, and was dressed in a pair of blue jeans; no shirt and no shoes.

"Your parents in?"

The boy shook his head. "Nope."

"When will they be?"

"Ain't got no mom. Paw will be gettin' in when he takes a mind to. You a cop?"

The boy's stare was cold, his lips tight. Ramsey imagined police officers had visited the trailer in the past. "No, son, I'm not a cop." He heard the rumbling of a vehicle on the road and turned toward the sound.

Leaving a cloud of yellow dust behind it, an empty pulpwood truck was bouncing along the road, coming in their direction.

"That's Paw."

Ramsey met the boy's father as the truck's wrinkled metal door swung open with a screech and a man about five eight stepped out onto the rusty running board.

"I'm Mark Ramsey."

The man stared down on him with narrowed eyes. "Whadda ya be needin', brother?"

"You heard about the murder last Wednesday night?"

"Yep."

The man raised a hand to scratch at the side of his head. His shoulder-length brown hair moved along with him, as if every hair on that side were matted together. He didn't wear a shirt, only blue overalls over bare skin. The outfit's straps ran back over dirt-streaked shoulders rippling with wiry muscles.

The man dropped from the running board to the ground, spit a brownish stream of tobacco juice with the wind, and, wiping his mouth with the back of a forearm, raised his face to Ramsey's. "What of it?"

"I was wondering if you or your son . . ." Ramsey began, glancing back over his shoulder toward where the boy had been standing.

The youngster had come from the trailer and now stood close behind him, hands stuffed in his pockets, a cold stare on his face.

Ramsey looked at the boy for a moment, and turned back to his father. "I was wondering if your son or you might have noticed anybody that night; maybe a car or a truck parked off to the side of the road?"

The man shook his head as he twisted an arm back over his shoulder to scratch at another spot. "Didn't. Cops already asked that. Told 'em, didn't. Whadda you be wantin' to know for?"

"I'm a friend of the family. There was some kids supposed to be camping out that night."

"Wouldn't know 'bout that. Told the cops that, too."

"Do you mind if I talk to the boy?"

"Yeah, I do," the man replied. His eyes had once again narrowed and now exhibited the same cold stare as the boy's. "That all you be wantin'? I come in for a saw blade, not to be a visitin'."

Ramsey wasn't about to be intimidated by a man he was nearly half a head taller than, and who he outweighed by thirty to thirty-five pounds, especially when there was no justification for the man's behavior. He stared into the pulpwood cutter's eyes for a moment, then turned toward the boy.

"Son. You know any children who ever camp up here?"

The boy glanced toward his father.

Ramsey looked to see the man spit another brown stream, then nod at his son.

"Ain't never heard tell of none," the boy said. "Rangers don't allow no campin' out in the park."

"Some kids have been. Three or four of them did last Wednesday night."

"Beats hell outta me. I don't see why they would. Skeeters and bitin' flies, they're bad down there this time of year. Lots of puddled water for 'em to be breedin' in." The boy turned and started toward the trailer.

Ramsey stared after him for a moment. *"Son!"*

The boy stopped and turned back to face Ramsey.

"Son, where's down there?"

The boy frowned. "What do you mean?"

"Where is down there? You said the mosquitoes and flies were bad down there. Where specifically were you talking about?"

The boy glanced at his father before settling his eyes back on Ramsey. "Just there," the boy said, nodding toward the woods on the side of the road opposite the trailer. "Ever'where round here."

"Then you weren't talking about near the subdivision? That's the way you glanced when you were speaking. That's where the boys were that night."

"Paw," the boy said, looking with slitted eyes toward his father. "He's confusin' me. I'm gonna start frettin'."

Ramsey heard the spit and the splat of the tobacco juice next to his feet, then felt the strong fingers of the pulpwood cutter's hand on his shoulder, and turned to face the man.

"My boy says he don't know, he don't know. Told you in the first place I didn't want you to be a talkin' to him. Don't do it no more. I'm tellin' you straight out now."

He *was* the pulpwood cutter's son, and Ramsey was an uninvited visitor on their property. He nodded. "If your boy does happen to remember, I wish you would call the police station and let someone know."

"I'll be doin' just that iffen somethin' comes around to him." The man walked past Ramsey toward his trailer.

After stepping up onto the railroad tie porch, the pulpwood cutter stopped and turned back to face Ramsey. Reaching into the side of his jaw with a crooked forefinger, he removed his wad of tobacco and placed it in an overall pocket before speaking.

"I'd appreciate your not botherin' my son no more. He gets nervous, real easy. The doc says it's not good for him. Good afternoon to ya."

After driving back to the spot he calculated should be directly above the Richardsons' home, Ramsey guided his car to the side of the road and parked it. Stepping from the automobile he worked his way through the roadside brush into the forest.

Inside the tree line the thick canopy of leaves and limbs overhead had shaded out most of the undergrowth and moving was easy.

He walked forty to fifty yards before deciding not to go any farther. It would only be luck if he managed to find his way through the trees to the subdivision. If he moved completely out of sight of the road, he wasn't even sure he could keep his directions straight.

Turning back toward the road, he saw the face. It was staring at him from around the trunk of a large sycamore.

The face disappeared behind the tree. An instant later the pulpwood cutter's son emerged and started moving back up the hill, glancing back over his shoulder as he walked.

Ramsey ran after him. When the boy noticed, he began to run.

Ramsey caught him before he reached the gravel road, grabbed him by the shoulders, and turned him around.

"Hands off'n me, Mother!"

Ramsey released the boy. "Son, if you don't know who was camping down here last Wednesday night, you do know the boys who have a club here, don't you?"

"My paw warned you. He told you not to be askin' me no more."

Ramsey took a deep breath, forced himself to keep his voice level. "All I want to know, son, is a name of just one of the boys in the club. If you don't tell me, I'm going to have the police come back out here again and take you down to the station to talk. You wouldn't like that, would you?"

A sneer contorted the child's face. "My paw will kill 'em sure as hell," he said. Then he lunged backward, turned, and sprinted up the slope toward the logging road.

Ramsey stood staring after him for a moment. Making a mental note to have Ray send some officers to question the boy and his father, he turned and retraced his steps to his car.

CHAPTER

9

Leigh Ann answered the door wearing a simple white linen skirt and a sleeveless red blouse. She was wearing her hair the way he liked it most, loose and flowing free over her shoulders. Smiling, she invited Ramsey inside and walked ahead of him to the living room.

He sat on the couch as she arranged herself in the easy chair across from him, pulling her legs up beside her.

"I hoped you'd stop by to see me before you left for Biloxi," she said. "They let Jack out on bail."

"Ray told me. Is he here?"

"No. The judge gave him permission to go down to a fishing cabin we have on the Pascagoula River. He wanted to be alone for a few days. I think it's a good idea. He doesn't have a phone or TV, even a radio there. He needs some quiet . . . Have you eaten? I'd fixed something for myself and the twins before I went to pick them up from Vacation Bible School.

They decided they had to go over and visit Margaret Wheeler's children. It's hard to turn little Jack down when he wants something. He gets so upset, becomes so insistent. As usual, I let him have his way."

The boy with her black hair and her eyes. Evidently her personality, too. The other twin—they were fraternal twins and nobody would think they were that closely related without knowing them—was a girl, a cute little blonde who looked a lot like Jack.

"I'm not really hungry. I'll stop on the way to Biloxi."

"It'll just go to waste. Please."

He hadn't eaten breakfast, having gone to the well site just after dawn to check on the drilling progress. Leaving there he had driven straight to the old logging road, then to Leigh Ann's. Besides, staying to eat would allow him time to find the right opportunity for asking Leigh Ann about what Ray had told him.

He nodded. "Okay."

She smiled self-consciously. "I'm a little embarrassed. What little Jack wanted was chicken, mashed potatoes, and fried green tomatoes. That's all I have. Fried green tomatoes are his favorite. We have to have them every day all summer. If we run out, he throws a fit. His father has half a dozen plants along the fence and we hardly ever have one ripen."

"Sounds fine. Mother used to fix them all the time."

"Good, I got hot enough picking them in this weather; still sticky." Reaching under the edge of her skirt, she fluffed it several times. "Even with me keeping the air conditioner as low as it is, it takes forever to cool off when you've been outside on a day like this."

Her movement had left part of a tucked leg exposed. Only the lower part of a thigh and the knee and the calf, it was less than a bathing suit would show. But the tanned shapeliness, lying against the background of the bunched white skirt, was a sight he had to force his eyes above.

She grinned, swung her feet to the floor, and stood, walked toward the kitchen.

"Come on," she said back over her shoulder.

In a minute she had fixed two plates and brought them to the table. They sat down across from each other.

The food was unusually good. For some reason that surprised him. When he finished, he leaned back in his chair and shut his eyes. "Perfect. Couldn't have been any better."

She smiled politely. "You're awfully nice."

"Really. It really was."

"Thank you."

He dropped his gaze for a moment, then raised his eyes back to hers. "I went by to see Ray just before I came over here, Leigh Ann."

She nodded.

"He said you told him that the night the girl was murdered that you and Jack had been over to Dennery's to eat. Ray said that a man parking cars there knew you and Jack. He told one of Ray's officers you two had a fight when you left."

Her eyes narrowed, and she shook her head. "We argued over something. Not what I would call a—"

"He said more than an argument."

She looked into his eyes for a moment, but said nothing, finally dropping her gaze to the center of the breakfast table.

"He said Jack shook you and you slapped him."

She slowly raised her face. "That's just going to make Jack look worse, isn't it. It was my fault. He drank too much and was insistent on driving. I pushed him. He shook me—more pushed me away. I hurt my back on the sideview mirror and slapped him before I thought. If the attendant saw everything, then he also saw I apologized, and that we hugged. It was my fault."

"He didn't see that. He said after you two got in the car he thinks Jack hit you."

"No! He didn't! That's not right. How could the man see inside the car? We were parked at the side of the building. It was dark. You don't believe something like that, do you?"

He didn't answer.

Leigh Ann, her lips pressed into a firm, thin line, sat quiet for a moment, staring at him, finally rose and lifted the plates from the table and carried them toward the sink.

He glanced after her, then stood and walked to the break-fast-room window to stare through the panes toward the state park.

The doorbell rang.

Leigh Ann, her hands under the running faucet as she rinsed the plates, looked at him.

He nodded. "I'll answer it."

The doorbell rang a second time, and quickly a third.

He hurried his steps.

Reaching the door, he pulled it open to see the pulpwood cutter. He also saw the shotgun the man held in his right hand, the barrel swinging up.

Ramsey slammed the door shut, turned the deadbolt, and leaned back against the wall.

"Who was it?" Leigh Ann asked, walking from the living room toward the door.

"Get back, Leigh Ann! He has a gun!"

"What?"

"Get back! Now!"

He flinched at the slam of the gun stock against the outside of the door.

"Get in your bedroom! Lock the door! Call the police!"

She disappeared into the living room.

There was a long silence.

He edged from the side of the door toward a window, sliding his back along the wall as he moved.

Slowly, carefully, he leaned away from the wall to look through the window. He saw the man's twisted face staring back at his. He jerked his head away from the opening.

The shotgun stock struck the window and glass went flying. Pushing himself off the wall, he dashed for the living room and on through it to the closed bedroom door.

"Leigh Ann!"

He heard the latch turn. She swung open the door. Her face was white.

He stepped inside, shutting and locking the door behind him. "Did you call the police?"

She nodded.

"Is there a gun in the house?"

She shook her head back and forth repeatedly.

He used the back of his hand to nudge her out of the way of the door. He stepped to the side and leaned back against the wall. Then he noticed on the far side of the room the large expanse of glass in the big French doors leading out onto the back porch.

"Leigh Ann, go in the bathroom. Lock the door behind you. Now! Stay away from any window."

As she shut the bathroom door behind her, Ramsey heard the faint sound of a siren.

Continuing to lean against the wall next to the door leading back into the living room, he watched for any movement on the porch outside the French doors, and waited.

The siren grew louder.

He took a deep breath. He moved his hand to the doorknob. Bracing his left foot at the bottom of the door so he could stop it if someone suddenly pushed from the other side, he turned the latch. There was an audible click as the door unlocked.

He waited a moment, then slowly turned the knob, eased the door open a little, and looked through the crack.

Opening the door further, he cautiously stuck his head outside and glanced around the living room.

The sound of the siren was piercing, then the shrill noise suddenly ceased.

He crossed the living room in short, careful steps, his head swiveling back and forth, his eyes jumping between the opening to the kitchen and the one to the foyer.

The shape he glimpsed through a front window was that of a uniformed policeman.

Hurrying to the front door, he opened it and stepped out onto the porch. A black police officer, three stripes on the sleeve of his uniform, started to raise his revolver, then relaxed his forearm.

"Who was it?" the sergeant asked.

"I don't know his name. He lives on the logging road. In a trailer."

"Luttle!" came the exclamation from Ramsey's right. He turned to see a second, younger white officer standing there, a revolver also in his hand.

"It figures," the sergeant said.

"What did you do to piss him off?" the young officer asked.

"You don't have to do much of anything to get Luttle's pants in a wad," the sergeant said before Ramsey could answer. "That's the meanest little son of a bitch I know. Should'a been charged with attempted murder last fall. Got mad at his brother-in-law. You know the guy, Mr. Ramsey. He owns Floyd's Carpets. Luttle wrapped him up in a roll of vinyl floor covering and left him standing upside down in his storeroom. Wife didn't find him until the next day—wonder it didn't kill him."

The white officer walked up beside Ramsey and nodded toward the front door of the house. "You better go on back in the house and lock the door—in case he's still out in the woods. We'll have the station call back here after we've caught him."

Ramsey glanced to his left, toward his car, then strode toward it.

He opened the passenger door, unlatched the glove compartment, and pulled out the .38 Smith & Wesson revolver he kept there. Carrying the weapon in his hand, he moved back to the policemen who were stepping into their patrol cruiser.

The white officer nodded. "We'll have him in a jiffy, sir. You just stay inside until you hear from us." The officer looked at the revolver in Ramsey's hand. "He does come back, go ahead and use that thing. If somebody would just blow the nut away, it'd save us a passel of work."

The sergeant could be heard using the patrol car's radio, explaining the situation and asking for a backup to be sent to the trailer on the logging road.

After the police drove away, Ramsey stepped back into the

house, shut the door behind him, and locked it. He walked toward the master bedroom. Inside it, he knocked on the bathroom door.

"Leigh Ann."

The door slowly opened. Her face was still pale.

"It's okay now, Leigh Ann. The crazy bastard's left. They've gone after him."

She looked at the weapon in his hand.

"In case the nut comes back," he said.

She shook her head back and forth. "I was afraid he was going to kill you. I was so scared for you." She stepped forward and laid the side of her face against his chest, wrapping her arms around him. She started crying.

Leaning, he reached his hand out to the side and set the revolver on the top of the chest of drawers against the wall. Then he put his arms around her and held her tight, patting her on the back.

"It's okay now, Leigh Ann. It's okay."

He felt her shake her head against his chest. "I was afraid he was going to kill you," she said once more.

She lifted her head from his chest, raised her face to his, her big eyes moist, staring directly into his. Her brow wrinkled slightly with her thought and she shook her head again. For a long moment she continued to stare, then suddenly raised on her tiptoes and pressed her lips hard against his. It was like a jolt of electricity. He hesitated a second, and then he was kissing her back, hard.

She moaned into his mouth as her arms encircled his neck and she pulled his lips tighter against hers, their tongues working, she catching his between her teeth. He shuddered involuntarily as she moved her body against his, and he moved back against her.

The doorbell rang.

He pushed her back.

She stared at him, a quizzical expression on her face.

She heard the second ring, her eyes widening as she turned her head toward the open bedroom doorway.

He lifted the revolver from the chest of drawers, then stepped from the bedroom, pulling the door shut behind him.

Ray rang the doorbell another time, glancing irritably at his watch. He started to push the button a fourth time when the door opened.

Ramsey, his cheeks still flushed, nodded at his older brother.

"I'm sorry I couldn't get here sooner," Ray said. He looked at the revolver in Ramsey's hand. "You forgotten how to use one of those things?"

"It was in the glove compartment."

Ray looked past Ramsey. "Afternoon, Miss Leigh Ann."

"Afternoon, Ray."

Ramsey felt Leigh Ann's palm at the small of his back, and her gentle squeeze.

He glanced at her, saw her mussed hair and the top buttons of her blouse undone—he didn't remember doing that. He looked back to his brother.

Ray, his face now clouded, still looked past him toward Leigh Ann, held the stare for a moment longer before turning back to Ramsey and speaking.

"Well, I just wanted to check on you. I need to be getting on back to the station. Those kids painted symbols all over the sidewalk in front of the First Baptist Church last night. Then somebody hung the preacher's phone number up on grocery store bulletin boards all over town with a message saying, 'Yards mowed, any size, five dollars, call after eleven P.M.'— preacher's hot." He turned and walked toward his white Ford LTD.

Ramsey glanced back at Leigh Ann, and started out the door.

"Mark!"

He stopped.

"Could I talk to you for just a second?" she asked.

He stepped back inside the door.

She stood still a moment before speaking.

"I'm sorry about in the bedroom. I—"

"You don't—"

She held her hand up, palm out, and pressed her fingers against his lips. "Mark, please, let me. Please . . ." She dropped her hand, lowered her eyes a moment before raising them once more back to his.

"Mark, I don't want you to think I'm trying to make an excuse for what happened in the bedroom. There isn't any excuse for that, and I'm sorry it happened. I . . . I just . . ." She shook her head. "Mark, my marriage was falling apart even before Jack's depression. I had decided to divorce him, had been thinking about it for a long time, but hadn't because of the twins.

"That's what the fight the attendant saw was over. I had told Jack I was going to get a divorce, and he got mad. And *I am*— I *am* going to divorce him.

"I'm not going to leave him now, not with what he has facing him—I couldn't live with myself if I did that. But when it's all over—I mean when the real killer is found—I'm going to go ahead and file." She looked directly into his eyes for a long moment, twice started to say something. Finally she simply said, "I wanted you to know that."

CHAPTER

10

Less than three hours after leaving Leigh Ann's house and following 49, the highway running alongside open pasture land, past thick pine forests, and through small, tranquil towns on its nearly straight shot to the coast, Ramsey turned off onto the four-lane scenic drive paralleling the white sand beaches of Gulfport and Biloxi. After driving into the nearest service station he walked to the bank of pay telephones at the building's side and began going through the directory.

Honey Rutherford's address as well as her number was listed. She lived on a dead-end street in an out-of-the-way neighborhood tucked behind Back Bay. It took him some time to locate the address.

A young, slim brunette in dark slacks and a white blouse answered the doorbell. She was attractive, her thick hair reminding him of Leigh Ann's. She smelled like honeysuckle.

"Miss Rutherford?"

"She's not here. May I help you?"

"Thank you, but I don't believe so. Do you know when she might return?"

"Who's inquiring?"

"Mark Ramsey."

"You wouldn't be with the police, would you?"

A curious question asked so matter-of-factly it sounded routine. "No, ma'am."

"Ma'am—? Do I look like a ma'am? I'm Katey."

He smiled. "Force of habit. Sorry."

She laughed. "You're sweet . . . You're not one of her regulars, are you? I know most of them. A reference from somebody?"

A regular? Know most of them? Asking about the police? Honey was a prostitute. "No, ma'am—Katey. I just want to ask her a couple of questions."

The woman's eyes narrowed. "You're starting to sound like a cop."

"I'm not. Really. When do you expect her?"

"Not until late this afternoon."

"Are you busy?"

Her smile came back again. "I was starting out the door for an appointment when you drove up. But I should be free in a little over an hour."

"Then I'd like to spend some time with you until I can see her."

"Both of us?" Her eyes swept him, her smile widening as she did so. "I believe you can handle it. You from out of town?"

He nodded.

"Have a motel room? We don't use the house."

"The Broadwater."

"Let me have your key. I'll meet you over there in about an hour and a half."

"I haven't checked in yet. When you get there you can call my room."

A one-sided smile lifted a corner of her mouth. "Don't want

to just leave your key with anybody, huh? Don't blame you with the things that happen nowadays. Fine. I'll call you when I arrive. One more little thing. I can tell by looking at you, you can, but I don't want to take a chance on wasting both our times. You can afford a hundred, can't you?"

He had forgotten to stop by the bank and cash a check; had a little less than a hundred dollars in his billfold.

She must have recognized his expression, asking, "Do you have a credit card?"

"Yes."

"It'll do fine. Credit cards, personal checks after we get to know you. About anything except I.O.U.'s." She glanced at her watch. "I have to run now. See you in an hour and a half, baby."

The highest structure sitting on a man-made promontory into the Mississippi Sound, the sixty-five-foot lighthouse of the Broadwater Beach Hotel and Yacht Marina, was visible to Ramsey long before he turned off Highway 90 into the resort complex.

The hotel was one of his favorite relaxing spots. He often stayed long weekends in one of the cottages behind the main building, occasionally chartering a boat for a day of deep-sea fishing, often doing nothing but resting, seldom going anywhere but to the Hook Line & Sinker to eat.

After checking in, he stood by his car a moment and looked across the highway to the marina. He could hear the clanking sound coming from the wind whipping lines against the metal masts of the sailboats; several dozen large motor yachts sat under the arched concrete canopies that gave the marina its distinctive look. The Gulf breeze was cool, removing the August heat from the air. A wry smile came to his face at his thought. *Heat.* That was the image of a Mississippi summer.

Heat, sweltering heat, people standing around fanning themselves. How crazy, he thought. Like many other of the images the state had, it was simply untrue. If somebody wanted to see what oppressive heat was like, they should go to

Florida in the summer. Mississippi summers were much cooler. Then in the winter you couldn't ask for any better weather— south of Highway 80, anyway; that half of the state more often than not seeing people in their shirtsleeves on Christmas Day.

Ramsey looked at the line of charter fishing boats sitting on the marina's west side. He wondered how many people knew there was big game deep-sea fishing off the Mississippi coast. For that matter how many people even knew the state had a coast?

As he stepped inside his car he caught himself smiling at his next thought. Though he often became irritated when he thought of the state's unflattering images, overall he was probably glad they existed. It was like the silver lining in a cloud. The images kept the state from being overrun with newcomers, let the relaxed life remain. That was just fine with him.

After entering his room he called Robert and checked on the drilling progress, then whiled away the time watching television.

Katey was punctual—ninety minutes on the dot. Stepping into the room, she repeated her earlier concern. "You're not a cop, are you?"

"No, I told you I wasn't."

"And it was you who invited me here, right?"

He smiled a little. What if she was an undercover cop setting him up? He would hate to have to explain that to Ray.

"If you say so, that's what I did."

"Good." She held out her hand. "Now the hundred."

"You said a credit card would do."

"Oh, yeah." She opened her oversize purse.

Another little smile came to Ramsey's face when she produced a credit card machine. She laid it on the room table and held out her hand again.

He handed her his American Express card and she turned to the table to begin filling out a credit slip.

Prostitutes, Inc.? he wondered. "How's the bill going to read?"

"Tours Unlimited," she answered, and glanced around her shoulder and smiled.

He smiled, too.

"Now," she said, holding the slip and an ink pen out to him. "Sign on the dotted line and we've got a deal."

She moved toward the bathroom, beginning to unbutton her blouse as she walked.

"Wait a minute," he said. He signed his name and handed her the slip. "I only want to talk."

She frowned. "You serious?"

He nodded.

"Ordinarily that'd tickle me to death. But I'd sorta counted on maybe enjoying this."

He smiled, walked to the bed, and sat on its side. She walked to the bed, then slowly knelt, rested her forearms on his knees, and lowered her hands to clasp his upper legs, pressed her thumbs into the inside of his thighs. He could smell the honeysuckle again.

She smiled up at him. "You sure all you want to do is talk?" She moved her thumbs again.

"Sure." He had been more sure of other things.

She shrugged, her sly smile now leaving her face. "Okay. I'm paid to please."

She rose to her feet and walked to the easy chair by the wall, plopped into it. "Okay, so what do we talk about? Why I'm in the business? What I enjoy doing? Some old war stories? You name it."

"Your roommate, Honey."

Her eyes narrowed. "You sure you haven't been with her before?"

He shook his head.

A wry grin came to the woman's face. "She just turns you on, huh? You want to talk about her—sorta secret-like?" She winked at him.

"I've never met her. I need to speak with her. Yet I didn't know if she would talk to me cold. I thought if I made friends with you first, you could vouch for me."

She cocked her head. "Go ahead, baby. Explain a little better."

"I'm not a cop. In fact, I'm working on the opposite side. I have a friend who's charged with murder. The girl who was murdered was also raped."

He noticed her glance from the corner of her eyes toward the door. "You're not getting around to something weird, are you?" she asked.

He smiled a little, shook his head. "No. I really need some information. That's all."

"Go ahead." She glanced toward the door once more.

"A friend of mine's charged with murder based on some circumstances I don't believe will hold water. Nevertheless, he's going to have to stand trial. To make a long story short, I'm working with the defense to make sure we don't get any surprises during the trial. This guy used to date Honey when they were both in college together at Tulane. There was some kind of incident there and he ended up being charged with raping her. The charge came from her mother. I need the details. If our district attorney finds out about it, and the incident turns out to be more than we think it is, obviously that's going to create a problem."

Katey was nodding her head. "Mueller . . . Something, Mueller."

He nodded. "Jack Mueller."

"Mister, if he's your friend, you're not going to be a friend of Honey's."

He didn't like this. "What do you know about it?"

"Only that she was a virgin when she met him, wasn't when he left, and she didn't have any say in the matter."

"Are you saying he did rape her?"

"Flat out did!"

"Honey told you he did?"

"Tells me every time she gets drunk, every time she gets depressed over this business. He's always to blame. I don't buy the psychiatric bit. She's in this business because she makes a good living at it. His raping her didn't cause crap. But he did rape her. And she doesn't look at it like I do. She's not just pissed off over the rape, she's pissed because he ruined her life."

"Would you mind giving me the details?"

"All I know for sure is he raped her."

"When will she be back at the house?"

"Told you she's not going to be wanting to talk to you."

"Could you persuade her to?"

"Why would I want to get involved? Even if I owed you a favor I wouldn't try. I have to live with her."

"You have another credit-card slip?"

She shook her head. "Money won't get it, buddy. There's some things I don't sell. One of them is talking my best friend into doing something she doesn't want to do."

He held out his hand. "Give me a slip."

"I told you—"

"Just give me a slip."

She stood. "I think you've had your hundred's worth." Her tone was suddenly cold and her face had the first stern look he had seen on it.

"Katey, I'll give you a hundred more dollars. Two hundred all together. Just for introducing me. If you do it in a way where she'll at least listen to what I have to say."

She studied him a moment. "You already spent the first hundred, baby. That's no longer on the negotiating table."

"You haven't had to do anything to earn it."

"You're the one who wanted to talk—time's money."

"Two hundred fifty dollars for you and another two fifty for her—if she tells me everything I want to know."

She looked into his eyes. "In addition to the first hundred?"

He nodded.

"You serious?"

He nodded again.

She reached to the table for her purse. "It'll have to be in advance—mine anyway." She fumbled around in the purse for a moment, produced another slip, and handed it to him. "If Honey doesn't give you what you want, there'll be no refunds from me. If I convince her to sit down and talk to you, I've done my part."

"Agreed!"

"You won't even have to leave the Broadwater. She's out on a yacht that berthed here last night. The guy's old lady is flying in from Texas at seven. He'll drop Honey off before then for sure. We can wait over at the marina lounge. It's right at the entrance into the Sound. The yacht will have to come in through there when it returns. We can catch her then."

CHAPTER

11

It was a little after five when Katey looked out a window of the marina lounge and said, "There they are. You wait here and I'll bring her back."

Ramsey watched as the gleaming white fifty-three-foot Hatteras backed into its transient berth. Stenciled on its stern was: *Granddaddy's Toy.*

After the captain and a mate had tethered the craft bow and stern and secured the spring line, a man and a woman emerged onto the deck from the Hatteras's salon.

The woman was a long-legged blonde, dressed in white slacks and a pink blouse. The most noticeable thing about her to Ramsey was how young she looked. She could pass for a teenager—she had to be at least twenty-five by now. The man, much older and looking it, dressed in white shirt and shorts and wearing a blue captain's hat, spoke to her as they walked down the gangway to the concrete pier.

Katey met the couple when they stepped onto the sidewalk. After a brief conversation, the man hugged Honey, then moved toward a black Mercedes parked at the front of the berth. The two women started down the line of yachts toward the marina exit.

They stopped a couple hundred feet farther, engaged in conversation as the man in the Mercedes drove past, waving at them as he went by. They turned and started walking back toward the restaurant.

"This is Honey," Katey said as the two walked up to Ramsey's table.

He stood and nodded. She was even prettier than he had first thought, and didn't look the least bit cheap; instead was rather classy. She looked like she belonged on a yacht, though as somebody's daughter rather than what she was.

"That's my real name, Honey, not a stage name or anything."

He smiled politely. Both women seated themselves and then he sat.

"Katey tells me you want to know about Jack."

"If you don't mind."

"I do. But for two fifty I can put up with it. That is the amount, right?"

"After you give me the details."

"Before."

He saw Katey reaching to open her purse and he laid his hand on her forearm. "Just the slip. You can write my credit card number on it."

She glanced around at the several old couples sitting at tables in the lounge. "You certainly are a shy one," she said. "Okay, I'll write the number in."

She handed him a slip and he quickly signed it and gave it back to her. Slipping it inside her purse, she came to her feet. "Honey, baby, I'm not real interested in listening to your life story again. I'm going to look at the boats. Holler at me when you get through."

Ramsey stood. "Thank you."

Katey smiled. "Thank *you*. If you ever come this way again, remember me." After giving Honey a parting pat on the shoulder, the brunette turned and walked across the lounge.

Ramsey reseated himself.

"What exactly do you want to know?" Honey asked.

"Just what happened."

She glanced at her watch. "We're going to have to make it quick. I've an appointment at nine and would like to eat and get off my feet for a while. So I'll cut straight to the dirty details. You tell me if I leave anything out you want to know." She looked over her shoulder, then back to Ramsey. "Could you order me a bourbon over ice—you know, that's actually all a mint julep is, bourbon over crushed ice sprinkled with sugar, then a little mint."

He ordered the drink and then leaned back in his seat to listen.

"I'd been dating Jack about six months. Thought we were in love. I was seventeen; didn't know any better. I had made up my mind I was never going to give it away until I was married. But that didn't count playing around. We got each other off in every way short of him popping me. I've made money in this business off some of the things we dreamed up.

"One night he came to my apartment earlier than he was supposed to—or I was late, who remembers. I had to step out of the shower to answer the door—only had a towel around me. He came into the bedroom and sat on the bed talking while I dried my hair. I had this urge. I just dropped the towel and kept brushing. He had never really seen me like that. Usually it was clothes half on, half hanging off, hands going everywhere.

"He came over and I told him to get back to the bed and just watch. He didn't want to; got to playing around. Next thing I knew he was pushing me toward the bed. I didn't mind that. But I wanted to get a little something on because—you know, without *anything* on it's hard to guard all the avenues. He wouldn't let me. Maybe if I'd stopped it there . . . I didn't, though. It got wilder and wilder. Then he was trying to enter me and I told him no, tried to force him away. He got insistent. I told him I meant it. He knew I did. He still didn't stop. I started fighting. Then he hit me—"

"What do you mean, hit you?"

"He hit me."

"I mean did he hit you hard?"

"Jesus Christ, you macho bastard! He hit me to make me quit resisting. What in the hell difference does it make whether he hit me at eighty-two percent or ninety-seven percent of his strength. He raped me and he did what it took to do it. If I'd kept resisting, he'd have hurt me bad, real bad. He went crazy."

The waitress paused to stare as she set the bourbon on the table. Honey glared at her and the woman quickly moved away.

Ramsey noticed Honey's eyes were beginning to mist. "I'm sorry it happened," he said. "I really mean that. I have one more question. Your mother and you brought charges against Jack. What happened to them?"

"The judge dismissed the charges."

"Why?"

"I backed down. I told the judge Jack didn't force me; that it was voluntary. Said I was just mad at him so I claimed he raped me."

"Why?"

"Because I found out I was pregnant. I didn't want my baby's father to be a rapist."

"Baby's father? But you had an abortion."

She nodded.

"I don't understand, Honey."

"I thought he would marry me, but I was afraid he wouldn't if he was pressured."

"He told you that; said you had to have the abortion before he would marry you?"

"He never said it like that. He was just talking one day and said a marriage couldn't ever work for him if he was forced into it; said he wouldn't let it work—his pride wouldn't let him.

I was wrong. I shouldn't have had the abortion. I—" She shook her head. "I really don't feel like talking about it anymore. Is that enough?"

She rose before he answered, looked like she was about to cry. He nodded. "Thank you."

After she had left, he slid her untouched bourbon in front of him and tasted it, then pushed the glass back across the table and stood.

At the pay telephone outside the lounge he punched in Leigh Ann's number. She answered after the first ring.

"I just met with the girl."

"And . . ."

"It wasn't just the mother, Leigh Ann."

"What do you mean?"

"I believe Jack raped her. I'm sorry, but the girl said he did and she sounded convincing."

"No! There's something wrong! He told me—Oh, God, Mark. What do we do now?"

"I don't know. I have to think a while. I'd like to speak with Jack."

"If you do that, he'll know I told you about Honey."

"Can you tell me how to get to the fishing cabin?"

She didn't protest further; gave him the directions.

He told her he would call her in the morning.

CHAPTER

12

The lower end of the Pascagoula River is a fisherman's paradise, the river's deep channel cutting through thousands of acres of marshland and swamp on its way to the Mississippi Sound and the Gulf of Mexico.

Dozens of fishing cabins, from structures not much more than a lean-to up to retreats designed for millionaires and featuring large yachts pulled up to private piers, line the west bank, while the east bank, mostly owned by large timber companies, has only a scattering of cabins. It was on this east side, four miles north of the Interstate 10 bridge, where Dr. Jack Mueller, Jack's deceased father, erected his favorite retreat—a structure of weathered cypress resting on thick piers of indestructible drill stem pipe. It could be reached only by boat.

Ramsey, arriving in the area a little after seven-thirty, rented a twelve-foot aluminum fishing boat complete with a twenty horsepower Evinrude motor from the little marina on the west bank.

Following the natural chute from the marina, he paralleled the river until he was able to guide the boat into the main channel where he turned east and crossed to the far bank.

Securing the craft to a cypress knee, he walked to the cabin and up its steep stairs to the entrance.

Jack opened the door only moments after the knock. He looked terrible. A couple of inches taller than Ramsey's six feet, he had always been heavier, too. Now, swallowed in a rumpled terry-cloth robe, he didn't look as if he weighed a hundred and sixty pounds. His blond hair was longer than Ramsey could ever remember seeing it, and in disarray. And this change had all taken place in—what, Ramsey thought? Five, six months since he had last seen Jack?

A puzzled expression came to Jack's face. "What . . . what are you doing out here, Mark?" The creases on his forehead deepened. "Not the twins. Nothing's happened to the twins, has it?"

"Nothing to do with them."

The acrid odor coming from inside the cabin was strong. Ramsey didn't know what it was, but had immediately noticed Jack's dilated pupils—something else unexpected from the man he had thought he knew so well.

Jack's expression was still puzzled. "What then?"

"I want to talk to you about Honey Rutherford."

Jack's face went blank. His shoulders slumping, he shook his head. "You already know, don't you?"

"She gave me her version of what happened at Tulane."

"I knew somebody would find out. It's true. I did it, raped her. Did it surprise you when you found out?"

Stunned that Jack so easily admitted the rape, Ramsey only nodded, said nothing.

"Good. I'm glad you thought enough of me for it to surprise you." He turned and walked inside.

Ramsey followed him into the big living area. Its only illumination was supplied by a pair of kerosene lanterns—one on a desk sitting near the back wall, the other on a table next to a white wicker easy chair.

Jack pointed to the chair as he seated himself on an old fabric couch a few feet away. "What all did she say?"

"Told me about what took place, why she asked the judge to dismiss the charges; about the abortion."

Jack nodded slowly. "You know I've killed two children now."

At the calm matter-of-fact statement, Ramsey felt a coldness sweep his body. "What do you mean, Jack?"

"You can't help me, Mark. Nobody can."

"Will you explain to me what you meant?"

He noticed the eye tic.

"Mark, I didn't know about the baby. She never told me. She said afterward she had kept it from me because she didn't want to force me into marrying her, didn't want to start a life together on that basis. If she had told me, I would have married her. I swear. Being responsible for the death of the baby —you don't know what it did to me. I know now that's why my second child was taken."

"Leigh Ann's miscarriage?"

Jack nodded.

"Is that the second child you killed?"

Jack nodded again.

"You feel the miscarriage came about because of the abortion?"

"It did." He nodded his head. "I first thought about it when it happened—now I know for sure."

Ramsey sat a moment staring at the pained expression on Jack's face. Leigh Ann was right. He needed help badly.

"Two children," Jack mumbled as he dropped his gaze to the floor. "And now Julie."

"What do you mean, Julie?"

"You're not going to believe this. I seduced her—a kid. It wasn't over a year ago. She had started working for me, just part-time some days after school—filing, answering the phone, things like that. One day I got to watching her and I had to have her—right then. It was easy. She didn't know any better."

Leigh Ann had talked about catching them in the house. "In your office?"

Jack nodded. "Yeah, eight years after Honey, and I'm still a worthless son of a bitch. I can't control myself. I've tried. I want you to know I've really tried. I don't know what it is, but I'm just different—not like you and Robert." He leaned back against the couch, his gaze moving to the ceiling, and he shook his head.

Ramsey noticed the capsules lying on the table next to the couch. They were clear, filled with colored crystals. He didn't know what they were. Jack had hit Leigh Ann, maybe not for the first time. He had raped Honey. Possibly intentionally tricked her into having an abortion and then left her. What else was he capable of, been capable of? *Done?*

Jack started to say something, his mouth opening but closing again without his speaking. He was still staring at the ceiling.

"What, Jack?"

Jack slowly lowered his gaze back to Ramsey's. "I have to pay for all I've done. I've known that for some time. Being convicted of her murder is as good a way as any." His eyes stared questioningly. "It doesn't make any difference how, does it? Just so long as I pay—so long as I can quit hurting."

"Hurting?" Ramsey shook his head. "Hurting . . . Hell, Jack, Honey's hurting—you raped her. Leigh Ann's hurting—worried sick about you. And now knowing you lied to her about Honey—bound to be wondering what else you've lied about.

"But you talk about hurting, you haven't seen anything yet. Wait until the twins have to go to school with the other kids knowing their father has been convicted of rape and murder? You got a yen to be punished—that might not be a bad idea considering all I've heard today. But, yeah, it makes a differ-ence how. If you didn't kill her, and yet allow yourself to be convicted because of some guilt obsession you've worked up, then you're sentencing your family to face hell right here on earth."

Jack sat silently for several seconds, his eyes downcast. Slowly he began to nod his head. He raised his eyes to Ramsey.

"You're right, Mark. I would be, wouldn't I? If I was convicted I would be destroying the twins, too; adding them to the list. I never thought of it like that. I guess I was thinking of myself. I get so down. Thank you, Mark."

CHAPTER

13

The light from a television flickered against the wall of the otherwise darkened game room in a sprawling redwood house twenty miles southeast of Jackson.

Ramsey, a Coors Light in his hand—the third one since returning home from Jack's cabin—was slouched low in his brown overstuffed recliner. He was watching the end of a film he had transferred to video tape a few years before. The end was all that mattered to him—in more ways than one.

It was fourth down and goal to go from the three-yard line. The small high school scoreboard had a zero under each team's score. The clock showed four seconds left in the game. They had just used their last time out. The scene switched back to the field and there was Jack taking the snap.

He dropped back a hitch step, then started down the line. Robert, making sure to stay in the proper position to throw a block with his head to the outside of his target, headed toward the outside linebacker. Ramsey watched his younger self, five yards deeper than Jack and sprinting in the same direction.

The defensive end made a mistake, came too far across the line of scrimmage. Jack faked the pitch, cut inside the frozen defender.

The linebacker had no choice but to take the quarterback. He did, and Jack pitched.

Ramsey planted his foot and made his cut toward the end zone at the same time he gathered the ball into his hands.

Robert, the linebacker gone, slammed his shoulder into the cornerback, doubling the defender backward.

The safety had the last chance. Ramsey cut back against the grain, left the red-jerseyed figure sprawling on the ground.

Ramsey's teammates buried him under a pile of their bodies.

The next scene was of the three friends standing close together at the middle of the field. Their arms over one another's shoulders, they were posing with the State Championship Trophy sitting on the ground in front of them. Flashbulbs were shooting bursts of light over the scene.

Ramsey watched the ten-year-old film with a half-smile on his face. He had often wondered what the team's linemen had thought of all the publicity the three backs had received. He suspected he knew by the fact that after the team voted by secret ballot, an interior lineman emerged as the year's Most Valuable Player.

There she was.

He pushed the reverse button, and watched the skinny little cheerleader walk backward from where she had disappeared behind the three heroes. He froze the frame.

His smile broadened. She really was skinny then, though the noticeable swell at the top of her frilled uniform signaled what she was to become. But the face; it was already there, like no other he'd ever seen. And he had not even noticed her—a sophomore cheerleader for the opponents that humid November night. He wondered if things would have turned out differently if he had met her then—What if?

What if a lot of things—good and bad. What if he had stayed at Ole Miss and not come home? Would he have gone ahead and gotten his degree? If he had, would he be sitting at a desk somewhere hoping for another promotion up the ladder? He would hate to have to work indoors so much of the time. Thank God he did leave Ole Miss.

What if, after Ray got him a job with Jackson P.D. when he didn't go back to school in California, he had liked it rather than have become disgusted with the constant exposure to the city's seamy side of life? Would he be a detective now, looking forward to an appreciation certificate and a bare-bones retirement check in another thirty years or so? Thank God, again.

What if, after leaving the force, he had taken the higher paying salesman job he was offered rather than opting to work in the outdoors, taking a job as a landman for an oil and gas leasing company?

What if, after being able to obtain a personal lease in a big Shell Oil Company play, he had sold it for the good profit he was offered rather than taking a chance and holding on to it as the well was drilled—the well that ended up being the discovery well for one of the largest oil fields ever found in the state. His first month's check had been over twenty-five thousand dollars. And from there he had gone on to hire Robert, a geologist fresh out of school, and started the small drilling company that had been so successful the last four years.

The what if's—or lack of them—had obviously gone his way. He had been fortunate, blessed. Except for that one *what if*. What if he had gone to New Orleans to live with her? He glanced back at the figure on the screen. It was beginning to bother him. He raised the remote control and switched off the television, then turned on the lamp and walked toward his kitchen.

Inside it, he opened the refrigerator, stared at a molded slab of bacon, a carton of milk that was soured the last time he had drank out of it, and two Coors. Not much like what one would expect to find in a top-of-the-line dual refrigerator-freezer combination, was it?

He lifted a beer out, popped its tab and took a drink, then leaned back against the counter, stared at the specially built commercial oven. He had used it what, four, five times since it had been installed? That had been three years ago, right after he had the house built.

He had everything he had always dreamed about—even the Cadillac. That's what his mother said his father had always dreamed of owning. Ramsey had felt good the day he bought his first one—he did it for his dad.

The fancy house, the fancy furnishings and built-ins, the Cadillac—the boy who couldn't afford a new bicycle when he was young was now a man driving a fancy Sedan de Ville. He had everything he had ever dreamed of, except for one thing— a woman he could enjoy it with, someone who could make a home out of his house.

He had told Ray that Janet was the best he had ever met. That was a lie—Leigh Ann was. Damn the earthquake and damn the consequences. He glanced at his watch. She would probably still be up—be glad to get up if she wasn't.

On the east bank of the Pascagoula River, the flickering light of a kerosene lantern could be seen through the windows of a cabin on that side of the river.

Inside the cabin, Jack Mueller stood on a white wicker chair in the center of the big living room.

He had tied a half-inch nylon rope around one of the exposed cypress beams running across the ceiling. At the lower end of the rope, he had fashioned a crude hangman's noose and looped it around his neck.

Now, finding it difficult to maintain his balance as he did so, he stretched out his arms and slipped the looped end of a second, smaller rope over his hands. Pulling back with his arms, he tightened the loop snugly around his wrists. The other end of that rope was strung across the room and tied to the front doorknob.

He had calculated carefully. His chair was not directly under the cypress beam, but a foot out in front of it. The rope from the doorknob now had only a few inches of slack in it. When he kicked the chair from under himself, his body would swing back under the beam, stretching the rope to the door tight and yanking his locked wrists out in front of him. That way, if the initial jolt didn't break his neck, and he began to lose his nerve as he strangled, he wouldn't be able to loosen his hands and reach for the noose around his neck.

With a last apology to those he had wronged, he kicked the chair back.

CHAPTER

14

Ray was meeting in his office with a pair of highway patrol investigators so Ramsey had to wait outside in the hall for several minutes.

The door finally opened and the plainclothes investigators emerged. He nodded and stepped around them to the doorway. "Have a minute, Ray?"

"Hey, little brother. Come on in." Ray pointed at one of the straight-back chairs facing the desk. "You're looking better than yesterday. Jack's suicide hit you harder than I would have thought. Hit me harder than I would have thought, too."

"Is the investigation going to shut down now?"

Ray nodded. "Pretty much. Won't be official. The note Jack left about being responsible for the girl's death was too vague to really be a confession. But the district attorney's satisfied he did it."

"Hell, I told the D.A. Jack felt guilty over making it with the girl. That's all the note meant."

"D.A.'s considering the evidence, too. He says Jack did it. I got to admit it's hard for me to dispute him."

Ramsey shook his head. "I keep thinking back to when I was at the cabin and told Jack if he wanted to punish himself, that was great, just not be taking his family down with him. I believe he might have killed himself because of what I said."

"Don't be starting any such talk, Mark. Doesn't matter what you said to him. Couldn't have made any difference one way or the other. A guy in the state of mind to do what he done is gonna do what he's gonna do."

"I believe he was planning on letting himself be convicted— had made up his mind that would be his punishment. If I hadn't told him a conviction would destroy the twins, maybe he'd have come back to stand trial."

"Yeah, and then hang himself one day during a recess in the trial. Mark, his granddad killed himself. Stuff like that can run in families—like alcoholism."

"His dad didn't kill himself."

"Mark, let's talk about somethin' else."

"You know, all I really had on my mind was Leigh Ann. I'd let her get back in my head. I was telling myself I was wanting to help an old friend who was in trouble, and really all I'm thinking about was her. There he was thinking about killing himself, and all I was thinking about was putting the make on his wife."

"Thinking's no sin, little brother; only saying it out loud is."

"What?"

"That's the only thing I remember my real daddy telling me. Said the devil can't hear you thinking, only if you say it out loud. So the good Lord knows you don't really mean it, unless you say it out loud. I've always hoped Daddy was right on that. Now let's get to discussing somethin' a little lighter. You want to go get a sandwich? Fay didn't fix me much of a breakfast this morning."

"Ray, I've thought about it and I've thought about it, and I still can't see Jack killing the girl. I'm going to try to see if I can come up with an idea of who did. It's probably stupid, and I probably won't know any more afterward than I do now. But I have to try; at least make myself believe I tried. I have to. It's something to do with the friendship we had and me breaking it off like I did, then acting like I was trying to help him when all I really had on my mind was—" He shook his head. "I have to do something for Jack, now—I have to if I'm ever going to be able to stand myself. I want to know if you'll help me?"

"Like how?"

"I need to know everything you do about the case, all the evidence, observations, anything regarding the murder."

"I think you'd be better off making up with Janet and running down to the Coast for a couple days—get your mind on something else."

"You going to help me or not, Ray?"

Ray shrugged. "Okay. Nobody's gonna object to you knowing anything now. I'll get you one of the evidence folders."

"There's a couple of things I'm not going to be able to tell by the folders. I need to speak with Dr. Richardson. I can't do that without your help. There might be somebody else I'll need your help with later; after I've had time to think."

"Why do you want to talk to him?"

"Hell, I'm not really sure myself. I want to go through the evidence folder, go look at the spot they found her, go to the sinkhole. Maybe later, somehow, see if I can find out the name of the kids who were there—if they saw anything. I don't have a specific thing I'm looking for, just want to get a general feel. I've got to start somewhere. Maybe something will click. It just doesn't make sense that Jack would have done it. What reason would he have had to have a knife with him? She had submitted to him freely a few months before, and for all we know maybe again since then. Even if she turned him down and he became enraged, it doesn't make sense that he took the time to go back to his house and get a knife and come back. Not unless there's something I'm missing; missing bad. And he was willing to take a lie detector test. He wasn't stupid. He wouldn't have agreed to take it if he had killed her."

"Maybe," Ray said. "And maybe not. Maybe he wanted to be punished for it, but didn't have the balls to just up and confess—I already told you there's been those who let the polygraph confess for them. You said yourself you thought he was thinking about letting himself be convicted."

Ramsey shook his head. "He felt guilty, wanted to be punished—he was almost crazy."

"Yeah, crazy enough to kill himself. You can't get any crazier than that—including crazy enough to kill somebody besides yourself. But I said I'd help you, and I will." A wry smile spread across his face. "I've got two undercover investigators. One hangs out around the pool halls trying to spot dealers. The other one's on loan to the State Narcotics Bureau right now. When he gets back, one or the other of them's gonna have to take a hike; mayor says a town our size can't afford two. For the moment, though, I've got authorization for two and only one working." He reached down and opened a drawer in his desk, pulling out a badge and sliding it across the desktop.

"I'll have the ID drawn up that goes with it. It'll open some doors you wouldn't otherwise get through." He chuckled. "The idea of using undercover investigators is having someone nobody would suspect. I've damn sure done that now."

Ramsey leaned forward and gathered the metal shield into his palm, stared at it a moment, then tilted sideways to slip it into his trouser pocket. "Thank you. All I needed was a little help in speaking with a couple of people. You sure doing it this way's not going to cause you any problems?"

"That's up to what you do. Mayor and board of aldermen aren't gonna be any trouble. I can't see any cop getting upset over it. First of all, what harm will you be doing? Second, most of the law-enforcement people around here like you. I'm sure your company barbecues for the department already cut down on your speeding tickets. D.A. grew up with you, though. He knows about you and Leigh Ann. If he gets wind of what you're doing, he's gonna figure quick you just didn't have a sudden yearning to become Mr. Good Citizen. Won't make any difference, though, unless you do somethin' stupid. You do, and I'm not only fired, I won't be able to get another job in law enforcement, even washing patrol cruisers."

"Ray, you said Jack couldn't have left the fingerprints the time he said he was in the house."

His brother nodded. "Well, first place, I don't believe they'd been there that long and the maid not have dusted them away. But even if you want to give Jack the benefit of the doubt on that, they still wouldn't have been there. As a birthday present to his daughter, Dr. Richardson said he personally painted her room. Didn't have any white paint for the facings. He specifically remembers scrubbing 'em to brighten 'em up until he could get back to 'em later. That was two weeks before she was killed—days after Jack claimed he was in the house. Those prints were put there after the girl's birthday. D.A. thinks about a week ago Wednesday night."

"When do I see the evidence folder?"

"I'll have Lila make you up a copy."

"Pictures of how the body was placed?"

"Everything's in the report."

"Lab ever get a blood type from the semen?"

Ray shook his head. "Wasn't able to. The rubber was too charred."

"Was there anything missing from her purse or from in the house?"

"It wasn't a burglar who suddenly decided he'd also knock off a little, if that's what you're getting at. Nothin' gone from inside the house. And she was wearing a watch had enough diamonds on the band to strike you blind."

"What else do I need to know?"

"There was a cordless telephone found close to her body."

"A telephone? Were there any fingerprints on it?"

"Only hers. You already know she was pregnant. There weren't any underclothes found with her body. Take your pick why. One, whoever killed her took them with him; or, two, she didn't fancy wearing 'em. Probably are other reasons hadn't popped into my mind, yet. And there were the holes in the T-shirt. When she was found the shirt was covering her breasts, bunched up under them. But arranged that way the holes in the shirt don't match the wounds. The shirt had to be higher when she was stabbed—bunched above her breasts."

"The shirt was rearranged after she was dead?"

"Maybe. Or could of been she did it herself—in her agony."

"Leigh Ann said the girl's father and mother spent the night in Vicksburg?"

"They had some antique furniture stored from when they lived there. Visited some old friends until about nine, then stayed in a motel. Met about eight the next morning with some hands they'd hired to help 'em load the stuff, then drove in about eleven."

"You any closer to knowing who built the campfire?"

Ray shook his head again. "Had to be some kids living outside of the area. We questioned everyone who lived in the subdivision, plus those living on the logging road. Questioned parents and youngsters. None of 'em went camping. No one stayed over at a friend's house where they might've slipped out together. No bunking parties. From the footprints around the fire, there were at least three or four of 'em there. Whoever they were, they had to be gone before it happened anyway. We were hoping for a long shot; thinking maybe they saw a car or a truck or somethin' pull up on the road. Road's only about a hundred yards from the sinkhole."

"I don't guess there were any prints on the packet the condom was in or you would know Jack didn't do it."

"I'm not sure that's what we'd be knowing. But, no, not a point of comparison. One other thing. The hunting knife that was used—medical examiner says one time when it was jabbed into a bone, left an impression that leads him to believe the very tip of the blade's broken off, maybe about the last half inch." He leaned back in his chair. "Now you know all I do—everything anybody does except for the guy that did it."

Ramsey stood. "Appreciate it. When can I meet with Dr.

Richardson? Psychiatrists deal with some pretty rough people at times. One thing I'd like to know is if he can remember anybody he might have particularly peeved; maybe bad enough they might have decided to get even."

"That's one of the first things we asked about. He said he couldn't think of any."

"Like to ask for myself. See if I can jog his memory."

"Okay, but I'm gonna go along with you. He gave a couple of my officers a rough time when they questioned him. Then called the mayor and said they were insulting. Won't hurt for you to have a witness along in case he decides to call the mayor again."

"Fine. What about now? Let's go out to the hospital and speak with him during lunch. I don't have to wait until I've studied the folder."

"Let me call first, *ask* him, show a little politeness up front."

Ramsey pointed toward the telephone on his brother's desk.

Ray shook his head in exasperation. "You're the most impetuous bastard I've ever met. Do you have to do everything as soon as you think of it?"

"Haven't I always?"

Shaking his head once again, Ray reached for the receiver, hesitated, and drew his hand back. He glanced at his watch. "I forgot; I'm going to be out of pocket for a little while. Mayor wants me to run over to the Chamber of Commerce luncheon with him. They're worried about the image the county's getting with those devil symbols being painted on everything. Mayor wants me to give a talk on what we're doing to catch those kids. I gotta make up somethin' before I go over there.

"Don't know how long the luncheon's gonna last. When I get through, I'll call Dr. Richardson and then call you and let you know the time. Where you gonna be?"

"I guess the park. It's as good a place as any to start—where it happened."

"Call me when you finish," Ray said, then reached down into the still-open drawer in his desk. "Here." He lifted a holstered snub-nosed .38 revolver and held it out butt first toward his brother.

Ramsey smiled. "Remember, I have one. Don't believe I want to be that official anyway."

"One you got has a long barrel," Ray said. "Too cumbersome. Can carry this one on you. It goes with the badge and asking questions of people that you might oughta shouldn't be. Never can tell, you might come up and prove everybody wrong. Find out Jack wasn't the killer; stumble on the man who is. If you do, and you happen to be alone with the guy when you realize it, just you and him, this might come in handy."

CHAPTER

15

Ramsey drove slowly as he approached Leigh Ann's home, looking first out one side of his automobile then the other.

The street was a cul-de-sac. Richardson's Colonial was located on the left near the end, then Leigh Ann's two-story brick setting to the side of the actual turnaround.

Directly at the head of the cul-de-sac was a wooden, one-story ranch-style. On the other side of the turnaround, across from Leigh Ann's and on a lot which sloped down toward a small man-made lake, was another one-story, a big brick contemporary design of around three thousand square feet.

A man with rape and murder on his mind would be unlikely to drive or walk down a dead-end street where the residents, familiar with most of the vehicles belonging to the families living there, would be likely to remember a strange car or truck. And if something went wrong with his plans, the killer would have only one way out, and that way under the full illumination of bright street lights.

Directly behind the rear of the house sitting at the end of the cul-de-sac was the backyard of the house at the end of a similar cul-de-sac coming from the other direction. Anybody entering that way would have the same problem with being seen.

That accounted for the north and south approaches the killer could have made. Both were unlikely.

To the east, across the street from the Richardsons' home and down the slope behind the homes on that side, was the lake. Anyone entering from that direction would not only face the problem of still another cul-de-sac, but also have to pass through several backyards while circling the ten to twelve acres of the lake.

He guided his car into Leigh Ann's empty drive and sat a minute looking in the westward direction he now faced.

It was the only reasonable direction from which the killer could have counted on entering the area unseen—through the heavy foliage of the park.

He opened the car door and stepped outside. Leaning back against the automobile, he let his eyes wander idly, searching for anything.

After a moment he pushed himself away from the car and walked to the front door of Leigh Ann's home.

No one answered the doorbell. She hadn't answered the telephone earlier. More than likely at the funeral home— Jack's funeral was the next day—or maybe she was at her mother's house. His mind intent on how the killer might have entered the subdivision, he hadn't even glanced at the driveway of her mother's home when he drove by it. She lived in a one-story ranch-style house about a half mile back toward the subdivision's entrance, in fact had been one of the first to buy a lot in the subdivision, bought two—hers and the one Jack and Leigh Ann had built on after receiving it as a wedding present.

Her mother had always spoiled Leigh Ann rotten, from

making sure Leigh Ann as a teenager outdressed most any other girl in town, right up to her buying the lot right next to the Colonial for her daughter. No telling what the old woman had paid for the site; it was considered one of the best in the subdivision because of its proximity to the old mansion. Yet the final result had been for the old Colonial to diminish Leigh Ann's home, make it appear small and plain.

Ramsey wondered if the woman was now comforting Leigh Ann in her pain, or cussing Jack's memory for causing the pain. He imagined the latter. One thing he was certain of—her only sincere compassionate thoughts would be those she had for Leigh Ann. Outside of the affection the old woman showed for her daughter she was one of the coldest people he had ever met.

Stepping away from the doorway, he walked around to the side of the house, then followed the property line between it and the Colonial, moving up the gentle slope of the yards to where they ended at the big oaks of the national park.

The yellow police ribbon was at the very edge of the yard. It was looped in a triangle shape, a post oak trunk and a small cedar its base, a large oak trunk its apex. It had been under the shadows of the oak's thick limbs where the body was found.

Ducking under the ribbon, he noticed the footprints left in the soft ground—too many and too clumsily placed for police officers. The yellow warning barrier had no more deterred the morbidly curious than it had him.

There was nothing to be seen there. Except to visualize how her body had lain, and try to relate her position to anything in particular besides the spot where she died.

T-shirt bunched up under her breasts, blue jeans removed and cast to the side, legs splayed wide—whoever had killed her had gone to a lot of trouble to leave the impression she was raped where she was found. Too much trouble. It was an exaggerated impression; almost as if the body had been ritually arranged.

He had thumbed through the copy of the police report, only glancing at the pictures of the body. He didn't know if the officers writing the report had come to the same conclusion he had just reached or not. Surely they had. It was obvious. The folder was locked in his trunk. He would study it in detail that night.

Before entering the trees he looked back toward the rear of the homes—the view the killer would have had as he stepped from the woods.

In Leigh Ann's yard, a mower still sat where Jack had left it the morning the girl's body was found. To the mower's left the grass was neatly trimmed; to its right, taller and uneven with a few weeds showing.

The old Colonial didn't seem as large when viewed from the rear. The front's more massive appearance was probably due to its thick columns and wide, overhanging roof. Several over-size windows, a broad and deep back porch, and an inclined set of doors leading into the cellar beneath the house were the features that caught his eye. He turned and entered the park.

Even following the map he had taken from the report, he walked past the heavy foliage surrounding the sinkhole once, and almost a second time, before spotting the flash of yellow ribbon behind a bush.

Following the short, winding path through the bushes to the hole, he stopped at its front edge and looked down into it.

Sunk into the gentle slope of the hill, the depression was five or six feet deep at its back, its flat bottom only three feet deep at its front and downhill side. The entire area of the hole wasn't more than fifteen feet long by ten-to-twelve feet wide.

The charred remains of a campfire were near the back and up against the bank to the left. A small area of white sand, a dog's prints noticeable across it, was leeched out from under the bank a couple of feet from the burnt wood.

The dog had been on the right side of the hole, too. The animal had scratched a shallow hole next to a narrow, eroded gulley which split the bank and meandered down the hill. He stepped down into the sinkhole.

The children's footprints were obvious; impressions imprinted with the webbed design of tennis shoes. The police had made plaster impressions of the one set of hard-soled prints.

Being careful not to tread on any of the impressions, he picked his way through them to the remains of the campfire.

He smiled. It didn't take much work to ascertain who had built the fire. Candy bar and gum wrappers dotted the ground.

A scrap of paper protruded from the small mound of dirt the dog had pulled up with his scratching. It wasn't a wrapper. He bent and plucked it from the loose dirt.

He smiled again.

It was a torn lower corner of a comic book page—a yellowed, partially faded peasant woman recoiled at the edge of the page as a red-faced creature, devillike horns protruding from its forehead, raised an axe over its head. The ink had run together on the back of the page and nothing was distinguishable.

As he let the fragment spiral to the ground, he noticed a short piece of lumber barely visible through the loose dirt at the bottom of the scratched hole.

Kneeling, he lifted the blocky five-inch section of two-by-four and shook the dirt from it.

It had several small designs cut into one of its sides. The carvings were crisp, carefully done. Other than a crescent-shaped etching, which could represent a half moon, and an obvious star, he didn't have the slightest idea what the symbols were. But his mind was immediately drawn to Ray's talk of kids playing at being devil worshipers.

Reaching into his back pocket, he pulled forth his handkerchief, folded it around the section of wood, then bent and used his cupped fingers to dig in the ground at the bottom of the small hole. But there was only moist dirt, becoming solidly packed a couple of inches deeper.

He stopped his digging, remained motionless a moment, then moved his hand to sift through the mound of dirt the dog had left.

There was another fragment of paper, not as soiled as the first. He examined it.

He had been wrong. The fragments were not part of a page from a comic book.

He stared at the drawing of the woman, the details of her total nakedness sketched vividly, exaggeratedly. She was embracing the red-faced, devillike creature he had seen on the other piece of paper.

He turned the fragment over to see the two now engaged in wild intercourse, again in extreme detail. In red ink at the top of the page someone had printed the words, PALO MAYOMBE.

He looked to where the first piece had floated to the ground and leaned to lift it into his hand. He slipped both fragments into his pocket, then began sifting through the loose dirt once again. He found nothing else.

Suddenly experiencing the sensation of someone watching him, he raised his face to look into the bushes and vines surrounding the depression. He glanced over his shoulder. A smile coming to his face, he shook his head and chuckled at himself.

Rising to his feet, he moved back to the center of the sinkhole.

He lowered his eyes to study the ground a last time, making sure he hadn't overlooked anything in the shadows cast by the moss-draped oak branches overhanging the hole.

Satisfied there was nothing else, he turned and walked up the steep slope out of the sinkhole.

He heard the sound. It was behind him, and he quickly turned to face it.

The noise was coming from the tangle of vines on the far side of the hole. He saw the leaves shake, and he moved back a step.

A brindle boxer poked his muzzle through the thick cover.

Ramsey felt his muscles relax. "You wouldn't be Peter by any chance, would you?"

The boxer tilted his head to the side, its ears pointed forward in curiosity.

"Peter!"

The stubby tail wagged, and the boxer trotted around the lip of the hole.

"Bet you know who camps out here, don't you?" Ramsey said, leaning to pat the dog on top of its flat head.

The animal allowed his head to be patted a moment longer, then moved away and trotted back toward the subdivision.

A hundred yards farther up the hill, Ramsey topped the crest and looked in both directions down the gravel logging road.

The pulpwood cutter's trailer sat about a quarter of a mile up the road and off to the left. He started back toward the subdivision.

At the yellow ribbon near the edge of the park, he paused to look a last time at what the killer would have viewed from the spot. Peter came trotting slowly from deeper in the trees to stop next to him.

And then Ramsey saw his brother's white LTD stopping in front of the Richardsons' house. He walked toward it, Peter trotting along after him.

CHAPTER

16

Moving from the tree line toward the Richardsons' driveway and Ray's car, Ramsey noticed the Chrysler New Yorker traversing the end of the cul-de-sac. Through the windows he could see the heads turning slowly, the faces staring alternately at the Mueller home and the old Colonial. The street had two tourist attractions now.

Nearing the white LTD, Ramsey saw the cigar butt fly out the driver's window. He smiled and shook his head. Opening the door and sliding into the passenger seat, he handed Ray the handkerchief-wrapped section of two-by-four. "You're going to like this."

Ray unwrapped the handkerchief. His eyes widened when he saw the carving. "Out of the campfire in the sinkhole?"

"In the hole, but nothing anybody missed. It came out of a hole a dog just scratched out. The loose dirt was still pretty damp, dog might have dug it up as late as this morning."

Ray rewrapped the wood and stuffed it into an inside pocket of his coat. "That's why no kids are admitting they were camping that night. It's that damn bunch of smart alecks. I just caught hell over 'em for the last hour. Didn't even get to finish my plate. I'm gonna find out who their little asses are. When I do . . ."

"One more thing," Ramsey said, handing his brother the first fragment of paper. "It's from the hole, too, out of the same spot. I thought it was from a comic book—" He handed Ray the second fragment. "—until I found this. You know anyone who could tell us what it's from?"

His brother's eyes narrowed as he looked at the second fragment and its explicit scene. "F.B.I. might be able to. Obviously some kind of girlie magazine."

"Turn it over."

Ray did. His eyes slitted again. "Porno magazine."

"Yeah. See what's printed at the top of the page—Spanish?"

Ray shook his head. "Don't know. I'll get it to the F.B.I. this afternoon." He placed the fragments in his pocket. "Kids nowadays got a little different reading matter than we used to have, huh?"

"You think there's any chance they're not kids?"

Ray shook his head. "Camping out—campfire and all—they're gonna be kids. You heard of Dr. Jones in Jackson?"

Ramsey shook his head.

"Any law-enforcement people in this area need to know somethin' about cult stuff, he's who they call. It might not be a bad idea to run this piece of wood over there and let him have a look at it. I know what he's gonna say, it's people messing around with Satan stuff; that's obvious enough. But could be somethin' in particular he might be able to tell us that could be of some kind of help. I'm not gonna be able to run over there until in the morning. You could take it on over now, if you want."

"What about the meeting with Dr. Richardson?"

"That's what I was coming out to tell you. He says he can't meet with us until after he gets off work. Says he'll meet us here at five-thirty. You got plenty of time to run over and see Dr. Jones. I can call and tell him you're coming. You can take my car so you can look a little more official."

Arriving at the small Jackson college where Dr. Roosevelt Jones taught two courses in theology and was also Dean of Admissions, Ramsey was unable to find a parking place. He finally took advantage of driving Ray's automobile, leaving the marked LTD in the NO PARKING ZONE nearest the center of the campus.

He found the doctor's office on the second floor of the two-story brick building housing the college's administrative offices.

The small outer office was empty. When Ramsey stuck his head through the doorway into the inner office, the large black man sitting at the desk looked up. He was wearing an old torn sweatshirt, and had a ragged straw hat pulled down tight on his head.

"May I help you?"

"I'm looking for Dr. Jones."

"Yes, I'm Dr. Jones." The man glanced down at his sweatshirt and a smile came to his face. "I've been cleaning a storage closet," he explained. "Slipped this on to keep from soiling my shirt." He glanced up at the brim of the old hat, chuckled, and reached to remove it. "There were cobwebs in the closet." His pleasant smile grew broader. "I certainly hope you're not a member of the Board of Trustees."

"I'm Mark Ramsey. Chief Hopkins called about my coming."

"I was praying that's who you were. Glad to meet you."

The man stood to lean across his desk and shake hands. He was even bigger than Ramsey had first thought—at least six three or six four, and considerably over two hundred fifty pounds.

"So the chief has someone playing at devil worship over in Davis County."

Ramsey handed over the section of two-by-four. "Yes, sir, it looks that way. We were wondering if these symbols might tell you something we wouldn't know."

"Please have a seat," the doctor said, his eyes already studying the carvings as he sat back in his own seat.

Among the pictures hanging on the wall behind the desk, Ramsey noticed one of a man posing on his knee in a New Orleans Saints uniform, the number 62 on his jersey. Seeing that, the doctor's quiet voice seemed even softer when after a moment he raised his face and spoke again.

"Well, there are satanic symbols here. But that's not all. This . . ." The doctor held up the piece of wood and pointed to the largest carving.

Ramsey leaned forward.

"This is a specific, little-known black magic symbol most commonly related to Voodoo. So here you have a group using parts of Satanism and parts of Voodoo—obviously not well versed in any singular belief. The Voodoo symbol, by the way, quite properly used, if I correctly understand where this section of wood was found. At a meeting place, wasn't it?"

"It was found where we know some kids were camping one night."

Dr. Jones nodded. "Camping, or perhaps having a meeting. In its proper use, this symbol would be buried or otherwise concealed at the entrance to a place where gatherings of a cult are held. It is a symbol meant to guard and protect an important place. This mixture of two different practices—Voodoo and Satanism in this case—is not all that unusual. Particularly in this country, where your typical cult members are new to their beliefs and not bound by longstanding tradition. Groups here quite often pick bits and pieces of whatever pleases them out of the various practices."

"Doctor, do the words 'Palo Mayombe' mean anything in particular? They were written on a fragment of a book page I found in the same place as the wood."

"Yes, it is still another one of the religions."

"Religions?"

"Yes. Palo Mayombe, Satanism, Santeria, Black Magic,

Voodoo—all religions. Even though I use the term devil worship myself, it is really a simplistic catchall term largely foisted on us by the news media—and not entirely correct. While some of the religions do worship the devil, in many of the others he is not even referred to. More often the central figure in most of these religions comes from a god out of ancient African beliefs; occasionally from old Caribbean and Latin American beliefs.

"Like your different denominations of Protestant Christianity—Methodists, Baptists, and so on—there are widely varying practices among these religions, too. Most of them are relatively benign. Voodoo has been practiced quite harmlessly in Louisiana for over a hundred years, but those cults that adhere to Palo Mayombe, at least those whose members are known to practice the most ancient African form of the religion, can be dangerous. There have been instances of human sacrifices committed by cult members involved with various twisted tenets of this particular practice.

"But I don't mean to alarm you with my comments. It's very unlikely you have anything more here than what Chief Hopkins indicated he believes, children play-acting—at least somebody of some age play-acting. I base my opinion to a large degree on the Chief telling me you have had no verified cases of animal mutilation. If this were a group involved in the type of cult activity that you would need to be concerned about—whether children or adults—you would almost definitely at least be finding mutilations." He glanced at his watch, then pushed back from his desk and stood.

"I know I haven't been all that enlightening, Mr. Ramsey, but I've told you about all I can from this." He handed the section of two-by-four back across his desk. "And now if you'll excuse me, I have a lecture session awaiting me."

After pulling the sweatshirt over his head, the doctor reached to lift his coat from a wall peg and slipped it on, then walked around to the front of his desk.

The two men shook hands.

"I appreciate your time, Doctor. One last thing. The page

fragment the words 'Palo Mayombe' were written on is evidently part of a page out of a porno magazine. Would that indicate anything special to you?"

"No, it doesn't. A wide variety of normal sexual activities is quite common in . . ." At his pause a little smile came to Dr. Jones's face, and he chuckled softly. He shook his head and looked back at Ramsey.

"Mind you now, when I say normal sexual activities I don't mean to be stating that pornography is normal. This is a church-sponsored school; wouldn't want it known I made a statement like that.

"I meant normal only in comparison with some of the more dangerous cult sexual practices—the kind that *would* raise a warning flag. For example, necrophilia, the abuse of the dead —quite frequently sexual abuse.

"I name this particular practice because it is probably the dangerous practice found most often in this country. In its most widely reported and simplest form, it is evidenced by incidents of grave robbing where the corpse is removed from its interment and then ritually desecrated during perverted black magic ceremonies. The danger comes in the tendency of an occasional group to graduate from corpses to live victims.

"If Davis County were experiencing incidents on the order of necrophilia, I would be concerned. But just pornography, that doesn't concern me at all. No, your page fragment indicates nothing, at least nothing out of the ordinary."

CHAPTER

17

"I've always wanted to see the inside of that house," Ray said as the two brothers sat in the LTD in front of the Richardsons' home waiting for the doctor to arrive for their five-thirty appointment. "Been wanting to ever since I was in the fifth grade and Mrs. Swilley told us about all the things that had gone on in there. Give my eye teeth to see if I could find a secret passageway in there—idea always intrigued me."

"That's a new one on me."

"It was back in the late eighteen hundreds. Some guy was running from the law and was seen going in the back door of the house. When the sheriff and his men got there, they couldn't find hide nor hair of him. But the plantation hands swore he was in there and that he hadn't come out. Scared the old lady living there so bad that she had some of the hands stay in the house with her.

"One morning three days later, the guy was seen running

across the yard from the back of the house. Evidently he'd been inside the whole time. Never did catch him. Turned out the guy was the son of the chief carpenter who had built the house and since died. Everybody immediately said there must have been a hidden passageway built in the house. But the original owner had passed away, too, and none of the few men still around who had worked on the house knew anything about it."

Ramsey glanced down the street and then back to his brother. "What background do you have on Richardson?"

"He moved into the neighborhood last summer. Not much on friendliness; hasn't made an attempt to get to know any of his neighbors. Originally came from some state job in New York to Memphis to work in the V.A. complex there. Spent about a year at that, best as I can remember. Then spent six months in Vicksburg in private practice. Supposed to have had a falling out with his partners there. That's when he came here. Think he does a little private practice, but his business card lists him as—Wait a minute, I've got one here."

Reaching inside the Ford's glove compartment, Ray fumbled through some papers before producing a small white card.

"Reginald X. Richardson. What in the hell would 'X' stand for? Assistant Chief Psychiatrist, John H. Douglas State Hospital."

He pitched the card back into the glove compartment, and shut its door. "From the interviews we got, most of the people around here won't be disappointed if the doc's current employment doesn't last any longer than his earlier jobs. He's generally an ass.

"His wife seems nice enough, though. A couple of people on the street brought some cakes over to 'em right after they arrived. They said she went out of her way to make 'em welcome, even promised one couple she was gonna visit their church, though she hasn't yet."

The doctor's silver Lincoln Town Car drove past, the round-faced, bespectacled man behind the steering wheel staring across his shoulder as he slowed for the turn into his driveway. The shiny automobile moved on into the garage.

As Ramsey and his brother walked up the drive, the garage door started down. They changed directions and crossed the lawn to the front door.

They stood waiting a while, then Ray rang the doorbell. Another minute passed before the door finally opened.

"Come in, gentlemen."

The doctor, dressed in a rumpled gray suit that seemed at least a size too big for him, was a surprisingly slight man, not over five five. His daughter had been a tall, big-boned girl. He wore gold-rimmed glasses and, despite not appearing overweight, had a round face and double chin. Though he didn't appear to be any older than his middle forties, when he turned he flashed a noticeable bald spot in the middle of his straight brown hair.

Stepping inside the home, Ramsey and Ray were greeted by a long, wide hall. Pieces of exquisite antique furniture placed against the walls gave promise of an authentically decorated interior. They weren't to find out, though, for the doctor ushered them into a formal sitting room to the immediate left of the entrance.

He followed them inside, moving to sit in a high-backed Victorian chair while they stood.

"Now, what is it you gentlemen desire?"

"I'm Mark Ramsey."

The doctor nodded. "I know who you are. I saw your picture in the local county paper. Some kind of charity barbecue you were attending. The best I can remember, you are employed in the oil business. It is my recollection that the story referred to you as being a redneck."

Ray grinned.

Ramsey didn't. Redneck to Ray was a common expression that everybody used—a harmless expression. But spoken by this northern doctor it was meant as a slur, a dismissive term showing his contempt for southerners—the last racial epithet that could be used in polite company and gotten away with. "I think the story you're referring to said I had worked as a roughneck in the oil fields."

"And you're representing the police department now?"

Ray answered. "Undercover investigator; has always been a big help to the department."

"I see," the doctor mused. Then he glanced at his watch. "Well?"

"You've already answered a lot of questions," Ramsey said. "I apologize if I ask you any of the same ones, but there's a couple of things I wanted to ask personally."

"I would have thought that after the suicide the authorities would have all the answers they needed. But I am ready once again to respond to whatever it is you wish to ask."

Surprisingly, Ramsey caught himself feeling sorry for the doctor. He knew the man had been asked the same questions several times. Part done intentionally, to make sure his answers remained the same. Some done just out of idle curiosity or because one officer was not aware of what the others had previously asked. Ramsey could imagine the stress the man was under. It had been only a few days since his daughter was buried.

"I am sorry, Doctor. I'll try to be brief."

The man nodded, rolling his eyes openly. Ramsey's compassion ebbed at the gesture.

"First, Dr. Richardson, would you give me an idea of your feelings toward Mr. Mueller? I mean prior to your daughter's death—and his."

"That's simple. I had diagnosed him as a pedophile within days of moving here. Every time my daughter was outside, especially when she was in her bathing suit around the pool, I would observe him staring at her. The only mistake I made was in assuming it was a harmless, controlled tendency on his part. Did disturb me enough, though, to where I repeatedly cautioned Julie to be careful of her body language."

"So you think he was the murderer?"

"Certainly! There is not a doubt in my mind."

"I see. I understand you have already been asked my next

question, but I wish you would answer it again. In your practice, especially since you moved to this area, here and in Vicksburg, are there any patients you might have treated who would have reason to dislike you?"

"You're correct. I have been asked that, not once but twice before. All psychiatrists have patients who dislike them. Especially at first. Obviously much of the initial phase in any treatment is forcing the subject to remember things he often doesn't wish to recall; trying to get at the root of whatever the patient's personality disorder might be. But, assuming you mean dislike me so intensely as to kill my daughter, that's ludicrous."

"Dr. Richardson, back to your first statement, about your diagnosis of Mr. Mueller. Your daughter was not a tiny built person, was she?"

"What are you referring to?"

"How tall was she?"

"Five eight or nine. I had no occasion to ever measure her."

"And, one hundred thirty, one hundred forty pounds? Heavier?"

"If you're trying to make a point, which I suspect you are, state it more clearly."

"Isn't a pedophile—?"

"That's what I thought you were leading up to," the doctor said before Ramsey could finish. "Of course those with pedophiliac tendencies are attracted to smaller, fine-featured, childlike individuals. That in itself is the definition of their problem. But they are also attracted to the chronologically young, whatever the particular individual's body type. Age alone, so long as the pedophile is aware of it, is quite sufficient attraction to trigger their compulsion. In retrospect, it obviously was sufficient for Mr. Mueller, and I *resent* your defense of him."

"I wasn't defending him. I was simply asking a question. I assumed you would answer professionally."

Ramsey noticed his brother shaking his head at him.

Richardson evidently also noted Ray's gesture, a small smile coming to the doctor's face. "Oh, it is quite all right, Chief Hopkins. I do not take umbrage at Mr. Ramsey's words. He is correct. My statement was poorly phrased. The emotions of a father overpowering the professionalism of his station, I am afraid. I am sure you understand, but I apologize in any case."

He turned back to Ramsey. "According to how much makeup my daughter might wear and her style of dress, she could very easily appear to a stranger as much older than her chronological age; even in her middle twenties. But Mr. Mueller was well aware she was only a child, and it is my professional opinion he viewed her in such a light."

"Thank you, Dr. Richardson. There's just one more—"

"Mr. Ramsey, excuse me for interrupting, but going back to when you asked me if there were any patients who might be angry at me. I have just recalled one who might be." The doctor dropped his gaze to the floor, brought his hand to the side of his face, and tapped his cheek with the tips of his fingers as he thought further. A smile briefly crossed his lips, and he nodded and raised his face to Ramsey's.

"He was a patient I treated in my private practice while I was in Memphis—John Gregory. 'Red' is the nickname he is best known by. He is a male Caucasian, actually resides in Southaven, Mississippi, but listed in the Memphis metropolitan area telephone directory. If you desire to contact him— and I assume such will be your intention—and you find that his number is no longer listed, you might inquire at most any of the strip bars in the city. To my knowledge his only civilian employment since his early teens has been as a bouncer at such establishments.

"His specific problems are, of course, protected by the ethical standards I subscribe to as a psychiatrist. But I will tell you my chastising the man could well have planted a seed of hate in his mind. Yet, that is not the only reason I bring his name to your attention.

"The gentleman was originally sent to me as part of a plea bargain his defense attorneys struck with an assistant attorney general in Memphis. Not as a prisoner or anything of that nature—as I said he was one of my private-practice patients and I treated him at my office on Poplar. Among his problems, which I have no ethical reason not to discuss as it is listed on his police record, was his tendency to follow women home and harass them.

"The particular incident which led to his being assigned to me was one where he followed a woman from Memphis to St. Louis. He made advances to her when she stopped to eat at a truckstop, but went away when she rejected him; then resumed following her. She sought assistance from a state trooper who detained the man for questioning. It was discovered he had on his past record more than one incident of harassing women." He glanced at Ray and then back to Ramsey.

"Please excuse me for expatiating to such a degree," the doctor said, "but I felt I needed to give you a brief overview of the enormity of this man's compulsion so that you might better understand my mentioning him.

"My daughter visited my office once when he was undergoing treatment. This was a little less than two years ago, and her arrival coincided with the session's end. He became notably agitated when she entered the office. She knew better than to come into the office with a patient present. But you know teenagers.

"When she departed, I was by happenstance standing at the window watching her on her way to her automobile. As her automobile departed I observed the man emerge from behind a hedgerow near the building. He hurried to the curb and looked in the direction she had driven. He ran to his automobile and left, driving in the same direction.

"It concerned me so much that I immediately called the police and then went to my car and drove toward my home. Evidently he lost her, for I came across him parked off to the side of the road. Still worried, I flagged down the first law-enforcement vehicle I saw, but by the time we got back to where he had been parked, he was gone. I had his case transferred to another psychiatrist and never saw him again. But . . ." The doctor raised his forefinger to make a point. "I later received a telephone call from his new psychiatrist, the doctor informing me that Mr. Gregory was irritated with me for having refused to continue treating him.

"One last thing. The man has the potential for violence. If I were you I would tell him you are a law-enforcement officer the moment you confront him. Make sure you intimidate him from the very beginning." He stood. "Now if you gentlemen would allow me, I have another engagement I need to prepare for."

"There's just one more thing, Dr. Richardson. I would like to look at your daughter's bedroom."

The doctor shrugged, then stood and walked toward the door without comment.

The sounds emanating from a bedroom in the expensive, French Provincial house four streets over from Dr. Richardson's were much lower now. The woman had stopped screaming long before the men were through raping her. Only an occasional whimper or guttural, choked groan had continued to escape her swollen lips, but she had continued to move all the time they took turns with her.

Sometimes she had struggled violently. Sometimes in only a half-hearted, nearly submissive manner, once or twice almost appearing to experience some kind of vile pleasure. But always moving, never lying completely still.

The last man to rise from her now reached down to grab her by her limp wrist. One of his companions grabbed her other. They began to drag her toward the sturdy oak table with the large leather restraining straps and the knives already arranged on it.

Johnny looked at the old man who had been standing silently by watching the attack. He knew what the old geezer had on his mind. To the others the table and its knives were only for further sport, to be abandoned when the woman's screams no longer entertained them. To the old man who would not move forward until after the rest had left, the table was the altar at which he would perform.

But really not much of anything was going to happen right now—nothing interesting anyway. The scene would fade off into another one before the man had done much. Johnny glanced at his friend. The older boy, intent on the action before him and barely breathing, was certainly finding it interesting. But then he hadn't seen it before.

"Fast forward it," Johnny said.

The boy glanced back over his shoulder, then quickly returned his attention to the TV screen.

"Fast forward it," Johnny repeated. "Nothing happens here. Get past the next few minutes and there's a good part, though —real good. It looks like the old man might have really offed her when he does it."

"For real?" the older boy asked as he looked back over his shoulder again."

Johnny nodded. "Looks like it." Except for near the end of the scene when the camera caught the supposedly dead girl smiling. That always made him mad.

The older boy rose and stepped to the VCR, pushing the fast-forward button. The screen swarmed with jerky pornographic moves.

"Okay," Johnny said.

The boy depressed the play button, then walked around to a side of the bed. Sitting on it, he swung his legs up on the covers and crossed his ankles.

Jimmy pointed down at the boy's shoes. "Off my bed with those, man. I sleep here."

The boy leaned forward, slipped off his white loafers and dropped them to the floor beside the bed.

CHAPTER

18

The second floor of the old Colonial was as elegant as the first. The hall was so wide that even with a large rolltop desk against one wall, Ray and Ramsey were able to walk side by side down the corridor toward Julie's bedroom. Dr. Richardson followed along behind them.

There were four bedrooms on the floor, plus two large bathrooms and a spacious walk-in linen closet bigger than an average home's bedrooms.

Julie's room was on the right in the middle of the hall directly across from the linen closet.

Entering the room, Ramsey saw an antique dressing table topped with a large mirror, then the canopied bed. Beyond the bed, a sitting area contained a large three-seat couch, an easy chair, and an oversize study table complete with chair and lamp.

Faint traces of blue fingerprint powder were still noticeable in the room—on the door-facing and knob, and on the handle of a miniature souvenir baseball bat lying on the dresser top.

Other than a towel on the bed, and a hair dryer and brush lying on the dressing-table chair, nothing seemed out of place. The hair blower was plugged in, its cord running to the wall socket at the side of the dressing table.

"Might I ask when we will be once again allowed access to this room?" Dr. Richardson asked.

"Excuse me?" Ray said.

"Your sergeant stated quite plainly," the doctor said, "that we should touch nothing in this room or the bathroom until further word from your department. We had thought that would be forthcoming after Mr. Mueller's suicide."

"I am very sorry, Dr. Richardson. There is no need for that now."

The doctor snorted. "It would have been thoughtful of your department to have already conveyed the message. It would have saved my wife much grief if the maid could have at least moved the towel from the bed and removed Julie's clothes from the bathroom."

Ray shook his head. "I am very sorry; an oversight on our part. I apologize."

Ramsey stared at the towel. "It was lying on the bed that morning?"

The doctor shook his head. "Yes, it was. Nothing has been touched, either here or in the bathroom."

"Where is the bathroom?"

"She used the one at the head of the stairs."

Walking from the bedroom, Ramsey moved back down the hall and across it into the large, ornate bathroom. Lying in a pile in the middle of the tiled floor were shorts, a sweatshirt, white socks, a pair of tennis shoes, and panties and bra.

He turned, stepped past Dr. Richardson, and returned through the hall to the teenager's bedroom.

"To answer what is obvious before you ask," the doctor said as he followed Ramsey back into the room, "and already known by your department. She had taken a bath. The water was still in the tub. It has seeped out since. The clothes lying in the bathroom are the ones she was wearing when we left. The clothes she was wearing when I . . . found her were, again, obviously, the ones she changed into after bathing.

"As I told the officers who first questioned me, when she took the bath and changed is pure speculation. It might have been when she returned from playing tennis. That's where she spent the early part of the afternoon, at a lesson with Dr. Thompson's daughters. It could have been late at night when she was preparing for bed and Mr. Mueller broke in on her and forced her into the clothes she was found in. It could have been at anytime and for any reason."

Ramsey nodded. He stepped to the only window in the room, an enormous one with thick panes. He looked across at the Mueller home, stared at the two windows directly in his line of sight. He thought a moment then asked, "Were these curtains open? Just like they are now?"

"Again, Mr. Ramsey, nothing has been touched. This room is the first place I came into in my search for her. Those are expensive, quality curtains, and when they are drawn the room is quite dark. When I entered the room it was bright. I noticed the open curtains immediately."

Ramsey glanced from the corner of his eyes to the towel on the bed, then back through the glass to the Mueller windows.

"Thank you very much, Dr. Richardson. You've been very cooperative and I appreciate it."

When Ray and Ramsey emerged from the house, two neighbors at homes directly across the street were standing at the hedges between their yards, looking toward the doctor's home. Down the block, a man worked with his hands at a lawn mower, while his face remained turned toward Ramsey and Ray.

"Okay little brother, what are you gonna do now—go to Memphis?"

"Yeah. This 'Red' character had reason to be mad at the doctor, was attracted to the daughter, and traveled three hundred miles following one woman. Sounds like he's worth speaking with." He looked at his watch. "There's a couple more flights out today. If I don't have any trouble finding him, I can find out all I need to know tonight and come back early in the morning."

Ray smiled. "Don't guess it would do any good for me to tell you I can get the Memphis P.D. to check him out for you—save a trip."

"Naw, I'd rather do it myself—be able to look him in the eye when I question him."

Ray's smile broadened. "I didn't think it would do any good for me to mention it. You have to know right now, don't you. God, you're impetuous . . . What about your well?"

"After the drilling starts, the wells are mostly Robert's babies anyway. About all I do when I go out on a site is stand around and twiddle my thumbs. He likes it better when I'm not bothering him." He glanced back at the Colonial.

"Jack was thirty, Ray, a little over a year older than me. Maybe the way some people look at it, that's too old to be making eyes at an eighteen-year-old—especially in the mind of a father who noticed it. But it's a hell of a long way from evidence of pedophilia."

"What does it matter?"

"Doesn't. Doesn't matter that she didn't date much, either. Just thinking out loud."

Ramsey looked across his shoulder to Leigh Ann's home. Her Lincoln was now in her drive, parked off to the side where he would be able to back out his car. "I need to look at something over there before I go to the airport."

Ray nodded. "If you need me for anything, I'll probably be at the house. I'm gonna go home and lie down for a while. Starting to feel a little puny."

As his brother walked toward the white LTD, Ramsey turned to look up at Julie's window, then back to the two upstairs windows in Leigh Ann's house. The distance between the two homes was not much more than the length of a couple of large backyard swimming pools.

He walked around to Leigh Ann's front door and knocked.

After a few seconds of waiting, he glanced toward her car and then knocked again. Another minute passed. He tried the door. It was unlocked. He opened it and stuck his head inside.

"Leigh Ann!"

There was no answer. He looked self-consciously back across his shoulder, then stepped inside the house and walked toward the staircase.

Upstairs, there were two doors off the hall to the side of the house that faced the Richardsons'. The one at the head of the stairs led to a bathroom. The window in it was over a tub, and was of frosted glass. He walked down the hall toward the second door.

It led into a room arranged into a study. On the far side of the room were a chair and a large office desk. The window next to the desk was hung with a set of white plastic blinds. He walked to them, reached out, and used his forefinger to pull down a slat.

He peered through the opening directly into Julie's oversize window. He could have easily hit it with a football—and watched her catch it.

He withdrew his finger from between the slats, stood in thought for a moment, and then turned and left the room.

Walking down the stairs, he saw Leigh Ann standing off to the side of the stairway looking up at him.

"Mark?"

"I was wondering where you were, Leigh Ann."

"I was outside in the back, at the edge of the park. Peter hasn't come in to eat today—probably after a stray female. I thought maybe if he was close enough he'd hear me calling him."

Ramsey circled off the bottom of the staircase and stopped in front of her. "Leigh Ann, was Jack with you all night?"

Her eyes narrowed questioningly. She glanced up the stairs, and then back to him. "What do you mean?"

"I didn't pay any attention to your statements in the police report. Knowing you all had a fight—argument—I was wondering if maybe you'd slept in a different room."

"You're thinking Jack might have—"

"I'm not thinking anything. Just the more I know the better. Maybe something will fit together."

"We were together all night. Neither one of us left the house after we came back from Dennery's . . . You wouldn't be asking that unless you were starting to think Jack might have killed her. He didn't."

"I told you I'm not starting to think anything. But I'm not trying to prevent any thought from entering my mind, either. I'm trying to think of everything, learn all I can—absorb as much as I can." He shook his head at her continued worried expression.

"Leigh Ann, I'm trying to get two and two to equal something other than four. I don't know any other way to put it. I learned when I was on the force that sometimes all the initial evidence in a case can seem to point in a certain direction. But later, almost the very opposite is proved—just have to be patient. The key to not coming to a wrong conclusion is being able to take everything in and catalogue it, but still keep it separate in your mind. Sometimes the next little thing you find out, the next thing that happens, makes everything suddenly fit together in a way you would have never dreamed possible in the beginning."

CHAPTER

19

Ramsey's back pressed into the seat as the Northwest Airlines jet, engines whining, released its brakes and lunged forward down the runway of the Jackson International Airport.

In a few moments he felt the liftoff, watched the ground dropping away. He saw the traffic moving along the four lanes of Highway 80, then Interstate 20 passed under the wing. Moments later the big airliner banked to the right, circling to settle on its northward course to Memphis.

He was on his way to question John Gregory, but his mind kept coming back to something else. Still staring at the ground, he pictured Julie's window in his mind once more. He recalled the towel on the dead teenager's bed, and thought about her having to pass the window on her way to the bed from the bathroom.

He remembered the brush and hair blower lying on the

cushion of the dressing-table chair, the blower plugged into the wall socket.

Maybe after stripping the towel from around her, the teenager had moved to sit in front of the large mirror, drying her hair.

From the window of the study she would have been in clear view. Ramsey had seen her pictures in the folder. She was built solidly, too solidly; would have had a problem retaining her figure as she grew older. But at that moment, young and still firm, anyone watching her overdeveloped body would have found it sensual. She had once been willing to take Jack in her arms, those months before when Leigh Ann had gone to Biloxi. Had she remained in the same frame of mind? And if she hadn't, what would have been his reaction if he had been watching her and decided he wanted her again? The same as it was the time at Tulane when Honey had dropped her towel and stood brushing her hair?

If I'd kept resisting, he'd have hurt me bad, real bad, she had said.

In only a few minutes the double ribbon on the ground that had paralleled the short flight was once again growing into Interstate 55. Then they were passing over homes, each one growing larger as they neared the ground.

While still in the terminal, he telephoned the Memphis number listed for John Gregory and listened to several rings before replacing the receiver. After copying the address on the back of a card from his billfold, he walked to the nearest rent-a-car office.

Gregory wasn't at home, but another man was; one who didn't know much of anything.

Yes, it was Red's home, the man admitted and, yes, he was a friend. But, no, he didn't know where Red worked—if he did —or when he would be in, if ever.

Armed with a list of the city's strip establishments torn from the Yellow Pages, Ramsey entered the first club near dusk.

There had only been a few cars parked outside, and there were even fewer people inside—a couple of salesmen types and an aging member of a motorcycle gang, his gray hair in a ponytail.

A topless dancer, skinny and blonde, was gyrating on the stage in the middle of the club to a scratchy record blaring from the jukebox. The sullen man who had collected the four-dollar admission fee and a fat, bearded man behind the bar, were the only other employees visible.

He walked to the bartender.

No, the man said, he had never heard of Red, didn't know who worked there on the night shift; didn't know anything.

Ramsey took a seat and ordered a Coors from the blonde who had been dancing and, clad only in an unbuttoned robe, was now doubling as a cocktail waitress.

When she returned to the table he paid for his drink with three one's, then held out a twenty-dollar bill in the other hand. A broad smile came to her face, but faded when he pulled the bill back.

"There's a man named John Gregory. He goes by the name of Red, supposed to work as a bouncer in a strip club."

She shook her head. "There's a lot of these joints in town."

"I understand he's worked at most of them."

"Could have."

He reached in his pocket, added another twenty to the first.

"I really don't know," she said, her tone becoming more sincere. "The night shift comes in about an hour. Maybe one of them knows him. Between the bunch of 'em, they've worked just about every club in town."

He nodded, handed her one twenty, put the second back in his pocket, then leaned back to drink his beer.

She stared at him for a long moment, then walked away.

A short buxom black woman had stepped onto the stage. Dressed only in cowboy boots, a bandanna, and a large Stetson, she was bumping to a country western tune.

When she finished, he called her over, gave her the second twenty, and received the same response.

The night shift was a step up in class. He caught himself paying more attention to the numbers the girls performed, but received no more helpful information than from the afternoon crew. Pulling the Yellow Page from his pocket, he studied it a moment, then rose and walked from the club to his car.

He had no better luck at his second stop than at the first. He walked through the doorway of a third club a little after nine.

Here he had a dancer try to gain possession of a second twenty in a different way. Despite his protestations, she climbed on the small round table in front of him and began to strip, her high heels clicking in time to the fifties favorite blaring from the jukebox. He moved his Coors off the tabletop into his lap, held it there until she had finished, and hopped to the floor.

It was a young long-haired bartender working his way through Memphis State who finally gave Ramsey the information he desired. Red worked as a bouncer at a place on the corner of Airways and Winchester, a location not over a mile from the Memphis International Airport; a club Ramsey had passed without noticing when he drove his rental car from the airport property.

At that club he asked the man taking up tickets if John Gregory worked there.

"He has. Haven't seen him tonight."

The bartender hadn't seen him, either.

Moving on to a table against a wall, Ramsey took a seat and looked around. The club was like all the others—maybe a little bigger at approximately a hundred feet by fifty feet. A stage surrounded by tightly grouped tables was at the building's center, with other tables spreading out in a more open fashion the farther they were from the stage. The lighting was virtually nonexistent except for the spotlight on the stage, and there was no way Ramsey would be able to pick out a man with red hair.

When a waitress stepped in front of his table he tried again. "I'm looking for a John 'Red' Gregory."

"Sorry, honey."

"I was told he worked here."

"What would you like to drink?"

He pulled his billfold from his pocket, lifted out two twenties. "If he's here and you point him out or tell me when he's going to be here, these are yours."

She looked at the bills. "It'd irritate him if he knew I told you."

"He won't know."

"Don't look anywhere but at me right now," she said, "but he's in the far back corner sitting with two of the girls." She took the money from his hand.

"Why all the big mystery about whether he's here or not?"

"Red's got a hell of a temper, and he doesn't like to be bothered. Don't look over that way for a while after I've left." She turned and moved back toward the bar.

Ramsey sipped from his beer for several minutes, finally stood and made his way through the tables in the direction the waitress had indicated.

As he neared the corner he could make out the red hair of the man sitting with the two strippers.

"John Gregory?"

The man came to his feet, turned to face Ramsey. "Yeah," he said in a sullen tone. He was big, at least six three, and broadly built; his biceps stretched the sleeves of his T-shirt. His blue jeans looked like they were about to burst at the thighs.

Dr. Richardson and, just a few minutes before, the waitress, had spoken of the man's temper. The doctor had advised Ramsey to show his badge immediately. He reached in his pocket and pulled forth the identification case, opened it where the man could see.

The redhead stuck out a hand to grasp the case, pulled it close to his face, and studied the shield for a minute. A sarcastic smile coming to his face, he looked back to Ramsey. "Damn Mississippi cop—that badge don't give you no more authority in this town than I've got; less."

"I just wanted to identify myself."

The redhead held out the case, purposely dropped it as Ramsey reached for it. Ramsey glanced at the case. The two strippers hurried away from the table, looking back over their shoulders.

Ramsey remained motionless a moment, then slowly knelt. Without taking his eyes off the big man looming over him, he retrieved the case and came back to his feet.

Gregory put out a big forefinger and thumped Ramsey on the chest. "You better be going now."

"I just wanted to ask you a couple questions."

The big redhead thumped his forefinger harder against Ramsey's chest, and then a third time, finishing with a brisk push.

Ramsey stepped back. He had no authority in Tennessee; the big redhead was right about that. A fight in the club could end up putting them both in jail, to remain there until at least in the morning—and nothing gained. He turned and started back across the club, heard the chuckle behind him. At tables along his way several people who had witnessed the confrontation stared at Ramsey. One big man wearing an Arkansas Razorback cap glanced back at the redhead, then to Ramsey, and shook his head in disgust.

Outside the club Ramsey leaned back against his car. He could call Ray and get him to contact the Memphis Police, get some cops to come out to the club. But if the redhead was seasoned in dealing with the police, which there was no doubt he was, he could ask to speak to a lawyer and even the Memphis cops would be afraid to press it any further. Gregory would do that, or just refuse to say anything.

As he weighed his various possibilities, the waitress who had told him where Gregory was seated stepped from the club. Seeing him, she made her way across the gravel parking lot to stop in front of him. "Didn't get very far, did you, mister?"

He shook his head.

She glanced back over her shoulder. "It could have been worse," she said. "You're lucky he didn't lay you out right there."

"For talking to him?"

"They said you were a cop. He's got it in for cops. His dad

was killed by one several years ago—he hates them. I've seen him get up and walk outside just because a couple came in to check around. He won't have anything to do with one no kind of way. I believe if someone was out to kill him he'd rather move out of town than ask the cops for help."

"That bad, huh?"

She nodded. "Yeah. In fact if he knew I was the one who pointed you out, he would've said something to me—or worse. I've seen him slap a woman across a table. I wouldn't be standing out here talking to you if I thought there was any chance he'd come outside, but when he goes out it's always the back door—check on his love from time to time." She smiled and shook her head. "He's really nuts."

"What do you mean?"

"Nuts—crazy."

"No, I mean, 'check on his love?' "

"His car. A '56 Chevy he's got all slicked up and looking like it's fresh off the showroom floor. He spends more money on it each year than my old man does on me. He parks it out back when he comes to work. Steps outside two or three times during the night to check on it, or maybe to keep it from being too lonely. I've seen the son of a bitch speak to it. Low, sweet voice; really, like a lover or something."

"When does he get off?"

She glanced at her watch. "About an hour—he came in early today." She looked directly into his eyes. "You're not thinking about trying to talk to him again, are you? I wouldn't advise it. Especially outside where there's not any witnesses."

"No, I was wondering if I had time to go downtown and get some officers to come back out here with me—some that do have authority."

"He's working the same hours tomorrow."

Ramsey nodded. "Thank you."

"Well," she said, "if that means your day's over . . ." She smiled. "Mine is, too. I'm going to go get a bite to eat. Interested?"

He gave her a friendly smile. "Wish I could, but I've got to report back in."

After she had driven off, he climbed into his car and drove to the nearest all-night grocery, went inside to the hardware department, then drove back to the club, parked at its front, and walked around to the back.

For a few moments he stared at the car protected by a dust cover, then walked around to the front of an old pickup sitting next to it. In less than ten minutes the back door of the club opened and a woman walked out, made her way toward the pickup.

When she started to open the door she saw Ramsey. Her eyes widened and she took a step backward.

He stepped around the front of the pickup, his hands working with his belt buckle. "Too many beers," he said.

The woman, her brow wrinkling, moved farther back out of his way as he moved past. He realized he should have come up with something better—there were obviously bathrooms in the club.

The woman, continuing to stare cautiously at him, stepped back to her pickup after he had gone past. As he moved on toward the side of the building she climbed inside the truck and locked the door.

After she had driven past, he walked to the back of the club again. There were no other vehicles there, but a garbage dumpster sat about thirty feet away from the left side of the car. He walked around behind it.

When Gregory stepped out of the club he was alone. He walked to the right side of his Chevy first and gently folded back the cover, then stepped to the car's rear and folded the light material forward. Moving around to the left side of the car, he lifted the material toward him.

Ramsey, moving silently out from behind the dumpster and toward the car, tried to be as quiet as he could, but the gravel moved under his feet just before he reached Gregory's back.

The redhead glanced over his shoulder.

Ramsey swung his forearm hard into the redhead's back.

With a loud grunt the man slammed hard against the side of the Chevy.

Ramsey pressed the barrel of his revolver into the redhead's thick neck.

"What in the hell's going on!" Gregory yelled, looking sideways down at the pistol.

"Shut up! Put your hands behind you."

"This ain't damn Mississippi. You can't do this."

Ramsey pressed the barrel harder into the man's skin. "Put your hands behind you. Now!"

Glancing again at the pistol, Gregory slowly did as he was told.

Ramsey looped the reinforced packing tape he had bought at the store around the crossed wrists. Quickly sliding his revolver into his waistband, he made several more turns of the loop.

The redhead glanced back over his shoulder, tried to see down to his crossed hands. "What the hell is that?"

Ramsey used the edge of the plastic dispenser to cut the tape, then raised his hands to the sides of the redhead's face and quickly pulled a section of tape across the man's mouth.

Gregory twisted his head, tried to blow the tape from his lips; said something unintelligible.

Ramsey ran another strip across the man's mouth, looped two turns of the tape across the mouth and around the head, then pulled him back away from the car, opened its door and forced the redhead inside.

His cheeks red now, still trying to speak but only succeeding in bringing forth loud, unintelligible sounds, Gregory began jerking his arms, trying to break the tape binding his wrists.

Ramsey grabbed a handful of red hair and forced the struggling man forward against the wheel. The horn sounded.

The unintelligible mumbles grew louder. Ramsey circled a section of the tape around Gregory's head and the steering wheel, locking the man's head sideways against it.

Ramsey looped the tape once more, cut it, then reached to

pinch Gregory's nostrils shut. The angry eyes suddenly widened.

"When you settle down, I'll let go."

Gregory immediately stopped struggling.

"Good. Start again and I'm going to hold your nose until you pass out—might accidentally hold it too long. You understand?"

The redhead gave a half nod.

Ramsey smiled, turned his back to the car and placed his hands on the fender, suddenly sprung to sit backward down hard on the hood.

Gregory moaned loudly, began to struggle again.

Ramsey leaned around to the open driver's window, and shook his head, pointed his finger at the man's nose.

Gregory quit moving, fell silent once again. Sweat was breaking out all over his face. He was trying to look sideways out of his eyes at the hood where Ramsey sat.

"You don't like me sitting on your car? How about me standing on it—dancing? Yeah, what about dancing on it?"

The redhead's neck bulged so violently Ramsey wondered if the tape might snap. He leaned back to the driver's window.

"Now, Mr. Gregory. What I want to do is ask you some questions. I'm going to expect you to answer me honestly. You do, and I'll cut you loose and be gone in no time. You don't . . ." Ramsey straightened, slipped his revolver out of his waistband and turned the weapon in his hands, then smashed the butt hard into the windshield, cracking it. The red head's eyes dramatically widened.

Ramsey hit the windshield again, and then a third time, a several-inch section of the glass frosting and falling back into the car, leaving a round hole in the windshield.

Gregory's face was beet red. The noises he was making now were more moans than mumbling.

Ramsey leaned close to the hole. "Only thing, Mr. Gregory, if you lie to me I'm not going to keep working on the window —something easy to replace. I'm going to work on the hood, and the door panels, and the trunk—a different mark on a different panel everytime. That's what's going to happen when I think you're not being honest with me. Understand?"

He hoped he didn't have to go that far. The waitress said if someone was out to kill Gregory the man would more likely leave town than go to the police. But he didn't want to make him so violently mad he might act out of character. He didn't think he'd have to go much further.

He slid off the car and moved around to the window. "I'm going to cut your head loose from the steering wheel now and take the tape off your mouth. I want you to keep your voice civil, low. You raise it one time and I'm going to retape it, and then work on the car for a few minutes before giving you your next chance."

He reached inside the window and used the edge of the tape dispenser to saw the tape loose. Then he unwound what was around Gregory's head.

As soon as the redhead was loose from the wheel, he glanced through the windshield to his hood, groaned audibly, then slowly turned his face back toward Ramsey's.

"Now, Mr. Gregory, my questions are simple. First, where were you a week ago Wednesday night?"

The redhead, his eyes slitted nearly shut with his fury, didn't answer.

Ramsey reached into his pocket and lifted out his keys, arranged one between his forefinger and thumb. Lowering his hand to the side of the car, he dug the end of the key into the metal.

"No! I was in Mississippi."

The redhead could have said anything else and Ramsey wouldn't have been sure whether or not he was lying. But had the big man in any way been involved in Julie's murder, the last place in the world he would have admitted to having been at that time was in Mississippi.

"Doing what?"

Even as angry as he was, a sheepish look briefly crossed the redhead's face. "I got stuck on a paddle-wheeler."

"Stuck on what?"

"A kid owes me some money, been owing it. I found out he was on a big society cruise a paddle wheeler was making from Memphis down to Vicksburg. I went on it to get my money. I knew his old man and mother were along. With all their friends around, I knew they weren't wanting me to be saying anything about why their kid owed me the money. I knew they'd pay up for him. The kid saw me and tried to get down to his room—did get to it. I went inside after him. He got to whining and begging, asking me to give him more time; swore he'd steal the money from his old man as soon as they got back, but to not tell them about him owing me. The next thing I knew the damn boat was moving. There wasn't any way for me to get back to land. I had to wait until it got to Vicksburg."

Ramsey knew he was once more hearing the truth. Nobody could dream up an excuse like that that fast. He reached inside the window and patted the red cheeks. "You've been a good boy."

The eyes instantly slitted again.

Ramsey smiled. "I'm going to leave now. I'm sure you can find somebody in the club who'll cut your hands loose." He glanced at the hood of the car and back to the slitted eyes. "Not much damage done to speak of. If you want to keep it like that, then don't come looking for me. If you do, I'll send someone back here to dismantle this thing, and you'll never know who it was."

CHAPTER

20

In Davis County, Mississippi, Benjamin Jerome McAlister sat up in his bed with a start. He looked around wildly. Realizing he was in his own room, he relaxed his taut muscles and exhaled audibly.

"Jesus!" he said. "Only a dream." He glanced at his watch. "Three damn A.M." He shook his head, then swung his feet to the floor and reached with an unsteady hand for the half-empty pint of Old Crow sitting on his bedside table. He took a long swig.

Setting the bottle back on the table, he then fumbled for the pack of cigarettes and lighter lying there. He lit a cigarette, took a deep drag, and exhaled the smoke slowly. Still shaky, he stood and walked to the only window in the small bedroom. Propping his hands on each side of the window frame, he leaned to look outside.

It was a bright night, the sky clear, a light wind causing the branches of the nearest big oak to sway gently.

Beyond the oak, the granite tombstones, light gray in the moonlight, rose endlessly from the ground for as far as he could see.

He saw a movement near the marker of the closest grave, maybe a hundred feet away. His eyes narrowed. He saw it again.

A rabbit, up on its hindquarters, nibbling at the flowered wreath. B.J. wondered what filler was woven in with the flowers. Certainly not artificial, whatever it was.

A sudden blur in the air above the grave, coming down at the rabbit, and suddenly the white fur disappeared.

There the white was again, a few feet from the grave, jerking frantically, now gone again.

Again a flash of white, something black across it, the black fading into the background. No more movement.

B.J. continued to stare.

Nothing.

Forehead wrinkled with his curiosity, he turned from the window and walked to his bed, began slipping on his trousers.

Moments later, dressed only in the trousers and lace-up shoes without socks, he stepped from the small cottage the management of Davis Memorial Gardens provided their caretaker.

Walking slowly through the warm night, he made his way toward the grave where he had seen the movement.

He stopped cautiously a few feet from the headstone.

Nothing. No trace of the rabbit—as if the animal never had been there.

B.J. recalled the blurred flash in the air above the grave. An owl.

Well, he hoped it carried the rabbit's carcass well clear of the property, or ate it all. In a couple of days the stink of a rotted carcass would be enough to cause visions in any group laying a loved one to rest.

It had happened once before. Those assembled for that service had cast glances at one another when the odor washed over them just as the pallbearers carried the casket by. The bereaved widow had began to scream uncontrollably. He had caught hell for that.

But it hadn't been his fault. The wind had been out of the west for two days, just beginning to shift to coming from the east when the hearse had parked near the grave.

It had been an opposum's carcass that time. The excess fat of such an animal carried a much worse stench than a rotted rabbit would produce. But a rabbit carcass would be enough. Any stench was too much.

He would search the grounds carefully the next day.

Turning to leave, he momentarily glimpsed a dim light a few hundred feet away, or thought he did.

It had come from down within the grove, an area of several dozen pecan trees that until a few years before had been an active commercial venture. Since the cemetery had accepted it from the old lady in exchange for perpetual care, the only harvesting that had taken place had been that done by the many resident squirrels. That was probably where the owl lived, too—close to a ready supply of furry food.

B.J. continued to stare toward the grove for another few seconds, then began walking that way.

Just inside the first row of trees he glimpsed the dim light again. He had not been mistaken. But what in the hell from?

A hundred feet farther and he saw there was more than one light, several, in fact, all dim, flickering—*candles*. He reached into the rear pocket of his trousers and pulled forth a handkerchief to wipe his brow.

Moving cautiously now, he crept quietly to the cover of a thick pecan trunk.

He peered out around the tree. His blood chilled at what he saw.

Several candles sat on the ground around a grave. The grave had been reopened, the casket partially pulled from the ground and tilted up. The lid was open. The flickering light from the candles danced on the pale, plasticlike features of the

young woman who had been buried there only two days before. She stared with blank eyes someone had propped open.

Kneeling in front of the coffin, hands clasped in prayer as he
stared at the dead woman, was a figure dressed in a dark
hooded robe.

Two figures! Both in robes. The hoods extended forward
past their unseen faces.

One of them rose to his feet, the other remaining on his
knees. B.J. noticed the white shoes. The only distinguishable
characteristic about either of the two was that the one who was
still kneeling wore white shoes.

The figure that had risen to its feet now moved around the
mound of loose earth to stand beside the open coffin.

A knife blade flashed in the candlelight, and the standing
figure leaned forward to grasp the lace bodice of the dead girl.

Behind the caretaker a sudden fluttering. He whirled
around, gasped in shock at the blur, and tripped backward
over a pecan root, sprawling to the ground.

The owl flapped its wings frantically, stopped its dive in mid-
flight, and rose back into the air.

The caretaker quickly looked back toward the grave.

Both figures were disappearing into the trees to the far side
of the candles; the last glimpse he got was of the white shoes
fading into the dark.

CHAPTER

21

As Reverend Gilder spoke the final words over Jack's coffin, Ramsey, his head bowed, stood under the tent and mouthed his own prayer. He hoped Jack had found peace.

When he raised his head, the reverend was already pressing Leigh Ann's hand, patting her on the shoulder.

Ramsey saw her look across the preacher's shoulder toward him and he smiled. He walked to her as the pastor moved to speak to others in the sparse group assembled for the graveside services.

She smiled when he stepped up before her. "Thank you, Mark, for coming. I thought you said Ray was sick?"

Ramsey glanced at his brother, who was speaking with Reverend Gilder and Robert. "He thought a lot of Jack, Leigh Ann. Said he would go back home and get into bed after the funeral. Are you going back to your house, or your mother's?"

"Mother's. For a couple of days, so she can help me take care of the twins."

"That's a good idea."

"Miss Leigh Ann," Ray said as he stepped up beside them. "Jack always was a favorite of mine. Can still see him and Mark and Robert playin' high school football. That was before you knew 'em. But that's how I remember him."

"Thank you, Ray. Mark told me you were under the weather."

"Touch of flu. I'll be okay by tomorrow."

"It was nice of you to come. Thank you." With a last polite smile for Ramsey, she turned and walked to meet her waiting mother.

Ray looked after her for a moment, then turned back to his brother. "Mark, I was standing over there listening to the preacher and thinking about Jack. Caught myself finding it hard to believe he could have killed anyone. Nothin' in his background would lead you to believe he'd turn out doing somethin' like that, would it?"

"I don't believe he did."

"I hope you're right—hope you can prove it. It'd make me feel a damn sight better about my judgment of people."

Ramsey was listening to Ray, but he was watching Leigh Ann as she climbed into the limousine provided by the funeral home and the attendant shut the door behind her and the twins.

She could say her marriage was no longer any good and that she had been to see a divorce attorney, but the paleness she had exhibited throughout the service said there were feelings still present.

Ray coughed and Ramsey turned back to face his brother. "You better be going on back to bed."

"Yeah, in a minute. You really believe Dr. Richardson set you up on purpose?"

"Know he did. I even know when he decided on it. Remember when you shook your head when I questioned his professionalism? That was when he *suddenly* recalled this one guy I should go speak to. I can still see the little smile he had. He was picturing me getting my head torn off when I met with Red. I think you need to check him out. I mean as far back as you can. If just our questioning got him mad enough to try and set me up for a beating, he's got a screw loose somewhere. I'd like to know something about his background."

Ray narrowed his eyes. "You're not taking the long way round to tell me you think he might have somethin' to do with his own daughter getting killed?"

"I don't know what to think. All I know is he's moved south to make a living and he doesn't like it here. When he said 'redneck,' it wasn't ignorance on his part; that's how he feels about this area. So what I'm thinking is, if he hates it so much, why does he stay? I'd like to know a little more about him."

"Okay, I'll do some checking." He coughed again, and shook his head. "God, I got to get home and lay down."

"Go on. I'll check on you later."

"One last thing. Heard from the F.B.I. this morning. They found the publication those page fragments came from. Not your normal porno trash. It's one big raping, torturing, and killin' story from beginning to end; some of the raping done after the killin'. It's really sick."

After the killing, Ramsey thought. "Necrophilia."

"What?"

"Necrophilia—sexual abuse of the dead. Dr. Jones mentioned it."

"F.B.I. agent didn't call it that. Said it's called a snuff magazine. They're put out for people who get a kick out of torture and killin' being mixed in with sex. He said it's mostly full of the kind of drawings you found, but also has several actual photographs of mutilated bodies. Agent says if the photos are not the real thing, whoever rigged 'em up ought to get a job in Hollywood. He said the most surprising thing about kids having access to a copy was not how rare they are, but that the magazine goes for about a thousand bucks a copy on the underground market. He said most likely one of the kid's dads has a porno collection, a serious one, and it came from that."

"Ray, we have to find those kids."

His brother nodded. "I think that's gonna happen now. Had a grave dug up at Davis Memorial last night; candles and stuff left sitting around. Could have been the same kids that are drawing all the symbols—and they could be the same ones were camping. Mayor and sheriff's both meeting with the Chamber right now." He began coughing again, had to bend over this time. He held up a hand before Ramsey could say anything. "I'm going, I'm going."

"Okay. I think I'll run out to the subdivision for a while. Then I'll come by and check on you."

Ray straightened, took a deep breath. His face was red. "What are you gonna do out there?"

"Something has been running through my mind. Both Dr. Richardson and his wife say the girl seldom dated, didn't seem to care much about dating. You say the kids at the school backed it up. Yet, she not only made it with Jack; Leigh Ann says she obviously was trying to instigate it from the first week she moved in."

Ray shrugged. "So she didn't like kids. Was attracted to older men. Not the first gal who ever felt like that."

"I've been wondering if there might be another older man; someone in addition to Jack?"

"Don't look for anybody to be steppin' forward bragging about it."

"What if she was—another married man. Assume that, and you could end up with someone worried about her telling on him. Could cause a lot of problems with the guy's wife."

"I can't see somebody killin' a gal to stay out of the dog house with his wife."

"What if he was married to somebody who he had a pretty good idea would be divorcing him if she found out? A woman who controlled the purse strings. A woman real well off, and he didn't want to risk losing that?"

"Mark, we can sit here and think up stuff all night; anything's possible. Bottom line, in any murder, is if you don't have an obvious suspect, and you don't come up with a fingerprint or eyewitness right off the bat, you end up grasping for straws. If somebody doesn't start running his mouth, bragging, that's usually the end of it. The way I see it, there's only one possibility left—if Jack didn't do it, that is. That'll be when we find out which kids were camping and it turns out one of 'em saw somethin', like a car parking up on the road."

Ramsey looked at his watch. "I'm still going out and look around the neighborhood, maybe even speak with some of the neighbors. There's some real nice homes on that street. Wonder if all of them are jointly owned, or if any of them are just in the wife's name?"

Ray smiled a little and shook his head. "You have to be the most impetuous ass I've ever known. You think of somethin', then you've gotta do it right then. Instead of wasting your time talking to people who are probably gonna tell you their personal finances are none of your business, just wait until tomorrow. I'll get the city attorney to look up each deed on that street—the whole damn subdivision if you want."

"Yeah, be sure and do that. But I think I'd like to meet the neighbors anyway, get a feel for them. Find out if any of them remember seeing anybody over at her house when her dad and mother were at work. Something else, too. Leigh Ann said when the girl sunbathed she put on an exhibition for Jack. I've been wondering if maybe the neighbor on the other side of the doc's house might have been watching, too."

CHAPTER

22

After turning into Belle Colline Heights, Ramsey noticed Leigh Ann's Lincoln parked at her mother's home. A little less than a half mile later, he turned onto the cul-de-sac leading to Leigh Ann's house and slowed his car.

In addition to her home there were a total of four other houses on the cul-de-sac whose occupants would have a direct view of Dr. Richardson's front yard and driveway. But there was only one where the occupant had a view of the Richardsons' backyard—where Julie would have lain sunbathing. Ramsey drove his car into the driveway of the New England-style two-story.

An American flag hung from a staff protruding from a polished brass bracket next to the door of the home. An equally shiny plate on the door proudly proclaimed:

CHARLES L. BAKER, LT. COLONEL, U.S.M.C. RETIRED.

A small, light-complexioned black woman dressed in a yellow dress and who appeared to be in her late sixties answered his ring.

"Yes?"

Ramsey showed his identification and badge.

"Sorry to bother you, ma'am, but if you don't mind I'd like to ask you some questions. They're in reference to the Richardson girl's murder."

A puzzled expression replaced the polite smile with which the woman had greeted him. "I'm not sure I understand. I thought when Mr. Mueller . . . I mean I've heard talk that the investigation was closed after he . . . after his unfortunate death."

"This is just procedural. Sort of for, uh, statistical data."

Her expression was still puzzled, but she nodded. "Okay. But I really don't know anything I can add to what I already told your other officers. We watched television until almost nine-thirty and then retired to our bedrooms. The next morning I went for my walk. I always do that—every morning. But I walk the other way, don't go up toward the Richardsons' or Muellers'. Don't guess I'd seen anything if I had. They say they found her back behind her house, just inside the park . . ."

"Yes, ma'am."

"You know everyone feels sorry for the Richardsons. But I feel sorry for Mrs. Mueller, too. She's such a nice lady. And now those two little children without a father. My husband grew up under similar circumstances, you know. His father was killed when he was six. But he turned out to be a marvelous man. His mother, she's the one who deserves all the credit. She did an excellent job raising him. I think Mrs. Mueller will, too. She just dotes on those two children. You see her taking them somewhere all the time. Keeps an eye on them, too— that's what's most important."

He nodded.

"I talked to her that morning. You know, before any of us were aware that anything had happened. Saw her down at her mother's while I was out walking. She was letting Mrs. Stout's poodles out. That's her mother—Mrs. Pauline Stout. She was on vacation. She just wouldn't hear of her dogs staying in a cage, and didn't want them running loose outside, either—afraid they'd get run over. The whole time Mrs. Stout was gone, Mrs. Mueller was running back and forth for those dogs. Morning, noon, and night; have to let them out a few minutes, and then put them back up. If I were her I'd have caged them until the day my mother got back. Mrs. Stout would've never known. What harm would there be in it?" She shook her head, then raised her eyes back to his. "Do you have any children?"

"No, ma'am. I'm not married."

"Well, you wouldn't understand then. I'm glad all my children are grown. Much as I miss them not being around all the time, I appreciate the rest. And don't tell anybody I said so, but I'm glad Mother likes living in Chicago so much. Lives with my sister Hattie, you know. Comes down here a month each summer, and a couple weeks for Christmas. Now don't misunderstand me, I love her, too—love her to death. But with my having to take care of my husband and all, and at my age—well, there's only so much a body can do. I used to have to run just like Mrs. Mueller. Down there letting the dogs out to exercise, and then having to run back to get her kids fed and dressed for school—hadn't even had time to get herself dressed yet, still wearing her robe and all. I know what it's like. Run, run, run. I once—"

"Ma'am, I apologize for interrupting, but I have to get on around to the rest of the neighborhood." He had come to see her husband—size him up. "Is Mr. Baker in?"

"Yes, sir, he's in the living room watching television."

"Do you think he'd mind if I spoke with him for a minute?"

"Of course not." She stepped back from the door and motioned with her hand for him to come inside. "I'll take you to him."

"Thank you. I can wait here."

"No, it would be best for you to go to him. He's confined to a wheelchair—wounded in Vietnam. Don't make anything over it, though; he doesn't like for people to do that. What is your name again? I couldn't read that thing you showed me without my glasses."

"Mark Ramsey."

He followed her through the foyer into the living room.

Sitting bent over in his wheelchair in front of the television and dressed in a robe, the woman's husband was of a much darker coloring than she. Much older, too. His snow-white hair was closely cropped. He glanced over his shoulder as they walked into the room.

The woman spoke. "Honey, this is Mr. Ramsey. He is with the city police. He wanted to ask you some questions about Julie—for statistical purposes."

The man moved his hand to the controls on the wheelchair, and swung it around to face Ramsey.

"Certainly. Fire away," he said in a hoarse voice.

Confined to a wheelchair it was certainly unlikely he would have had anything to do with a murder that would have caused him to have to be several houses from his own in the middle of the night. There was one other possibility, though. "Your wife said you no longer have any children living with you."

"No, sir," the man said. "Have three grown sons, all in the Corps."

"Have any of them visited you recently?"

"No, sir. All three are stationed overseas. Last Christmas was the last time any of them were furloughed home. I can provide you with the phone numbers of their unit commanders if you wish to verify that."

Ramsey smiled politely. "That won't be necessary, sir . . . One more thing. Would either of you have noticed any young men visiting the girl?"

The man's white eyebrows knitted together in thought for a moment and then he shook his head. "You know, I don't believe I've ever seen a young man at that home, either swimming with the young lady or even visiting. Oh, I'm sure there have been, but I never noticed." He glanced up at his wife. "Have you, Loretta?"

The woman shook her head.

Leaving the Bakers' home, Ramsey crossed the street to a two-story redbrick. Walking to the front entrance, he pushed the doorbell button several times without response. He glanced at his watch. Seven-thirty. Looking up the street, he noticed Leigh Ann's driveway was empty.

Stepping from the porch, he angled across the yard to the house next door, a nearly identical two-story, but with the brick painted white.

A few seconds after his knock, the front door opened as far as its safety chain would allow. A woman peered through the opening. "Yes?"

Ramsey held his identification where she could see it. "I'm with the city police. I'd like to ask you a couple of questions about the Richardson girl's murder."

"The police have already been by."

"This is just part of our follow-up investigation. Statistical purposes. It'll only take a minute."

"My son said that I shouldn't let any strangers inside the house.

"I understand. Do you mind calling the city police department and giving them my name and description? They'll verify who I am. I'll wait here."

"Your identification said Ramsey?"

"Yes, ma'am, Mark Ramsey."

It was four or five minutes before the door reopened. She was a dishwater blonde, short and slightly built, dressed in a simple sundress.

Her name was Sylvia Mohler. She wasn't married, did have a son in his twenties, but the boy had been in Biloxi at a statewide fraternity party the night of the murder.

She had previously explained all this to the police, she said, and they had verified where her son was that night. She had never noticed any boys over at Julie's home. But then she had never had any reason to notice. She was able to inform him that the people from the two-story redbrick next door had been in Europe on vacation since before the murder occurred.

The next home on the street was the big stucco contemporary directly across from Leigh Ann's. Its windows were curtainless.

There was no response when he rang the door bell. He walked to the big picture window at the front of the home. Cupping his hands on the side of his eyes, he peered inside. No furniture could be seen.

The final home with a view of the Colonial was the wooden ranch-style at the head of the cul-de-sac.

It turned out to be occupied by a big-busted blonde, who, after inviting him inside, asked him if he was thirsty. She had either bourbon or Scotch. She had obviously already had several of one or both herself. She knew nothing.

Ramsey left her standing on her porch, smiling after him as he walked back down the street toward his car. He noticed the old black man come out of his home and pull his wheelchair up near the edge of his yard.

"Son!"

Ramsey angled across the street to the man.

"Yes, sir?"

"Officer Ramsey. What is your rank, son?"

"Just Mark will be fine, Mr. Baker."

The old man nodded. "I would like to apologize. Loretta was aware of a boy visiting Miss Richardson during the day when the doctor and his wife were at work. She was only hesitant to confide in you because she was afraid she would sound like a busybody. I told her, land sakes, woman, we're talking about a murder here. This statistical information the police officer is gathering might help to prevent a murder somewhere else. I'm sorry she wasn't forthright with you from the beginning, but she did feel like she was prying. You know women are like that."

"Yes, sir. Did she know who the boy was?"

"No. He drove a black Corvette." The man looked across his shoulder and pointed toward an empty lot down the street and off to the left.

"That lot adjoins the lake. Lots of kids fish down there.

Worries my wife half to death. She's always afraid somebody is going to fall in the lake, especially when it's young kids. She saw some young ones in there swimming one time and called your department; just knew they were going to drown. She says the boy parked his Corvette down there; walked to Julie's house. In fact, she says she saw him do it twice."

How many black Corvettes were there? "Do you think she might remember him well enough so that if we had a police artist come here she could help him sketch a recognizable likeness?"

"Oh, I doubt if she could do that. She's not very observant—age, you know. I doubt if she could tell you much of anything about him. But the boy living over there could tell you who he is."

Ramsey glanced to where the man was pointing—to the home where the boy who had been at the statewide rush party lived. "I don't follow you."

"Loretta says the same boy who visited the young lady has visited young Rex several times—stayed the weekend a couple of times."

There was a car in the driveway which hadn't been there when Ramsey had first visited the home.

"He just drove in," the old man said. "The Toyota's his."

"Thank you, sir. Thank you very much."

Ramsey turned and walked back across the street to the house.

It was the boy who answered the ring. Dressed in blue jeans and a sweatshirt, he was tall and solidly built. Well groomed, his thick black hair was cut slightly above his collar. He had a polite smile on his face.

"I'm Officer Mark Ramsey, with the city police department."

The boy nodded. "Mother told me. I'm Rex Mohler."

"Do you mind if I come in?"

"No, sir." The boy stepped back.

"Where's your mother?"

"She's in the living room."

"Do you mind if we go in there?"

The boy nodded and gestured with his head for Ramsey to walk ahead of him.

The woman stood when they entered the living room.

"Ma'am, I wanted to ask your son some questions. I wanted you to be aware I was. He doesn't have to answer if he doesn't wish."

"I told you he was at statewide!" she snapped.

"Mother," the boy said, a reassuring smile coming to his face. "It's his job."

"There's a friend of yours who drives a black Corvette—been by here to see you. I think he probably spent the night a couple of times."

"Jeffrey Giordano," the woman said.

Ramsey continued to direct his questions to the boy. "I believe he had been by to see the Richardson girl before. Do you know anything about that?"

"Jeffrey's married," the woman said.

"Mother—yes, sir, he's been over there."

Ramsey looked toward the woman. "And he's married?"

She nodded.

"Mr. Ramsey," the boy said. "If you start questioning him you're going to ruin him."

"Son, maybe if you'd explain."

"He was a junior when I pledged at State. We became good friends. He got married second semester that year, dropped out and went to work selling for a company in Mobile. When he's working the territory in this area, he stays with me sometimes. One night, right after I came home from school last month, we went down to the Youngers' house. It's empty. Youngers' moved. They have a basketball hoop in their backyard. We were back there shooting and Julie walked over.

"She and Jeffrey began talking. She was really making a come on. I came on back over here. I'm engaged and Dawn—that's my fiancée—she'd already met Julie; told me to stay away from her. Dawn was coming over to eat with me. I didn't want any part of being around the girl when she drove up.

"When dinner was ready, Mother asked where Jeffrey was and asked me to go down to get him. About that time he walked in the door. He had that look on his face. I knew what had happened. They had gone into the Youngers' house, climbed in through a window and he had laid her."

"Rex!" the mother exclaimed.

The boy smiled politely in his mother's direction, then continued. "Jeff claimed it was really the other way around, that she made him. Anyway, he's been in the Youngers' house with her a couple of times since. I think probably been in her own home with her when her father and mother weren't there. I know you feel like you're going to have to talk to him. But I sure wish you wouldn't. You're going to destroy him. His wife's jealous worse than Dawn."

"I'm afraid we don't have any choice, son. We have to speak with everybody she dated, see where they were that night."

"You mean about the possibility of his being involved?" The boy shook his head. "That couldn't be, sir. I can prove it. You don't have to talk to him for that. When I was down getting ready for statewide in Biloxi, I was bored, nothing to do. Dawn had to stay in Jackson. I called him in Mobile from the motel that Wednesday night, used the fraternity's credit card. You can get the time I called off the bill. It was a little after midnight. We talked about old times. I guess until one-thirty or two. No, it was later than that. After I hung up I went out to get some breakfast and I remember it was a little after three when I arrived at the restaurant. He knocked on my motel door, and woke me up at eight the next morning. I'd only had about four hours' sleep. He was on his way to Hattiesburg to meet with one of his company's distributors. We sat around and talked until about ten, then he left. Is there any way I can take a lie detector test or something?"

"You mean for him?"

The boy nodded. "Yes, sir, I'll be glad to, if it would mean you all wouldn't be talking to him. And I can get you the phone bill to show you what time it was when I spoke with him during the night."

"Tell you what, go ahead and call your friend. Tell him to make a sales trip up here in the next few days and stop by and ask for either me—Mark Ramsey—or the police chief. We'll talk to him that way. Unless something unusual pops up we can probably get by with that and not have to ask his wife anything."

"Thank you, I sure appreciate that—I know he will."

As Ramsey emerged from the home, the old man in the wheelchair was on his porch, lowering his flag for the night. He waved. Ramsey waved back, then opened his Cadillac's door and slipped inside behind the steering wheel.

He dialed his brother on the cellular phone.

"No need to call the city attorney tomorrow, Ray, there's not any couple out here that it would make any difference if the title were in the woman's name. At least not in any of the houses close to the girl's. Did find out about a guy who's been dating her, but I don't believe it's going to do us any good. He lives in Mobile and I think he's going to have a pretty good alibi. He'll be coming up in the next couple of days, and he's not going to mind volunteering for a polygraph. His name is Jeffrey Giordano. He'll ask for you or me."

"Your voice sounds down, Mark. Getting tired of dead ends? You forgot that's mostly what investigating is? Not all the time. Occasionally you get lucky. Boom, you got it—somethin' that puts you on the right track, maybe even gives you the answer. But ninety-nine percent of the time you end up like you just did, tired, disgusted, and with nothin'."

"Not nothing. I'm more convinced than ever she didn't resist Jack. Maybe I'm just the macho bastard Honey said I was, but I don't believe the act itself meant enough to her for her to resist; at least not to the point of getting herself stabbed."

"Honey?"

"The girl from Tulane."

"Oh, yeah."

"This Giordano kid . . . Only a few minutes after meeting him, Julie was in the hay with him. It's obvious she wasn't big on having to be in love, or even liking a guy. I know she could have been particular, felt strongly about her right to decide. But I just can't picture her feeling strongly enough about it to get killed. I just can't picture it."

"In a way it'd be better if it was Jack who did it," Ray said. "I been thinking about it. Rape's more a man enjoying the brutalizing than the sex. A person already inclined to such a bent, then crossing into murder, could find the charge irresistible—be planning on experiencing the same feeling again."

CHAPTER

23

Sliding into his bed shortly before midnight, Ramsey lay quietly, keeping his eyes closed. But it did no good.

Something was bothering him, a sensation he couldn't quite grasp. A feeling like he had forgotten something he was supposed to remember. He had been like this before, and he knew when he was that trying to sleep was useless. His mind wouldn't rest until he realized what was worrying him, and why.

He slipped from beneath his covers, stepped out of the bed, and walked toward the kitchen.

There was a fresh gallon of milk in the refrigerator. Annie, the maid, she probably got tired of seeing the sour milk. She often did things like that for him. He lifted the carton out, filled a glass with the milk, then mixed in a heavy dose of liquid Hershey's Chocolate. After stirring the mixture, he put it in the microwave.

Warm milk, he remembered reading somewhere, had something in it that helped you become drowsy. His mother had always fixed him a cup of warm milk laced with chocolate when he was a little boy and had trouble sleeping.

The dog digging. Unearthing a symbol that Dr. Jones said was used to protect a gathering place or an important place. *An important place!* That was what had been in the back of his mind. Had the two-by-four been placed on top of something important—something buried under the piece of wood? The killer had left the contraceptive in the sinkhole. Had he left anything else, something the kids had found, then buried?

About as much probability of that as of Haley's Comet hitting the earth tonight, Ramsey surmised. But if there wasn't anything down there, why was the dog digging? He wouldn't have been digging for a piece of wood. He would have had to have smelled something, or sensed it, wouldn't he? But what?

This was crazy. But he wasn't going to pass up any possibility. He couldn't. He damn sure wasn't going to lie awake all night wondering, either.

He reached for the telephone sitting on the countertop, lifted the receiver, and quickly punched in the number.

"Hello."

"Fay. This is Mark. I'm sorry to call so late, but I need to speak to Ray."

He could hear the rustling of the covers, and Fay's voice as she said something to her husband.

A few seconds later he heard her say his brother's name again, this time in a louder and sharper tone.

"Hello."

"Ray, Dr. Jones said the piece of wood had something carved on it which meant it was to protect an important place. What if there's something buried under where it was?"

"Do what?"

"What if there was something buried under the piece of two-by-four; deeper?"

"Yeah, possibly. I thought you said—" Ray began coughing

and it was a few seconds before he could speak again. ". . . I thought you said the ground was hard under it."

"Maybe something's been buried there for a long time, the two-by-four added later, to protect whatever it was. Ground's mostly sugar sand and clay there. It would've set up pretty fast."

"Okay. I'll send somebody out in the morning to check on it." He coughed again. "If I'm still alive, that is. Whatever it is I've come down with, you don't want. I got to get back to sleep —if I can."

"Yeah. Sorry. I just got anxious thinking about it."

"If there's anything there, Mark, one more day won't make any difference. Call me in the morning."

Ramsey replaced the receiver, leaned back against the counter, and stood quietly, thinking. After a few seconds he shook his head, pushed himself away from the counter, and strode toward his bedroom.

After dressing hurriedly, he went to the garage storage room and lifted a shovel from its rack, silently cursing his impatience as he did so. Why was he always like this? He wasn't impetuous, he was crazy, that's why.

He laid the shovel on the backseat of the car, then opened the driver's door and slid inside. There was a flashlight already in the trunk. Both his .38 and the snub-nosed revolver Ray had given him were in the glove compartment.

As he followed the gravel road which led from his home to its intersection with the highway fronting his property, his eyes were drawn to the lightning on the horizon.

A big storm was building. The quick repetitive flashing reminded him of a documentary he had seen on Mississippi Public Television about the siege of Leningrad. The German eighty-eight millimeter guns had lit up the sky in vibrating frequency.

The small pasture where he kept his two horses needed moisture badly. The grass had not gotten any rain from the fickle storm that had passed overhead several days before— the night Julie had been murdered.

That storm had moved to the east, dropping only enough moisture to splatter clear spots in the dust on his car. This storm would probably do no more. The prevailing winds were west to east and the dark clouds building in the sky were already miles to the northeast.

In northeastern Davis County, Mississippi, Mary Lou Bickerstaff felt a little wobbly as she slid off the barstool and started across the floor of the small private club. But she didn't worry. She had Betty Amis at her side, and Betty, a nondrinker, would do the driving. In their late forties, the two had been spending their weekly Friday night outings together for nearly ten years now and Betty had always taken care of her.

They had begun their friendship three months after Mary Lou's husband was killed when he hung a chisel plough on a white oak stump and flipped his tractor backward on top of himself, and three days after Betty's husband left her a note saying he was headed to Nashville. For what? Betty never had understood, and grown weary of him, too, had never tried to find out.

They had both picked the same club that night, Mary Lou to drink away her pain and Betty to be soothed by the country band. There had only been one empty table left and they had reached it at the same moment, smiled, and sat down together. Remembering all these things made Mary Lou happy and sad at the same time, and she gave Betty an extra-big smile.

Arms around each other's shoulders, the two women stepped from the club out into the night, weaved their way slowly across the gravel toward the shiny baby-blue Ford sitting at the side of the parking lot.

Helping Mary Lou into the passenger seat, Betty glanced up at the heavy thunderclouds building over the area and worried about hail. She had just bought the Ford, the first brand-new car she had ever owned. Hail wouldn't do.

"Ma'am."

Betty turned to stare at the lanky young boy who, dressed in a T-shirt, blue jeans, and high-top tennis shoes without socks, had seemed to appear out of nowhere, and now stood staring shyly at the ground.

"What in the world you doin' out this time of night, Johnny?" she asked. She glanced at her watch. "It's nigh on to twelve o'clock. Guess I've just been a wastin' my time talkin' to you all these weeks." She turned and ducked her head close to the car window.

"Mary Lou, look here what we got. He mows my grass and I make it a special point least once a week to talk to youngsters workin' for me; try to explain the need for 'em to be growin' up proper. Payin' 'em while I'm talkin' to 'em, too. Teachin' 'em and payin' 'em to learn. With what yard help's costin' nowadays, they're makin' better than two-fifty an hour just for listenin'. Wish I'd known somebody like me when I was a growin' up." She turned back around to face the boy. "Well?"

Despite his young age, the boy was taller than Betty, though she was a good-size woman, almost five foot nine. She didn't have to stoop to put her nose close to his mouth and sniff. "You haven't been drinkin', have you? I'll sure 'nuff call your daddy right now if you have." She straightened. "Well? What's the matter, boy? Your tongue too thick to talk? Let me look at those pupils."

Johnny, his head tilted slightly to the side, staring at the ground, shifted his eyes back toward hers. "I was playing pool down at Skinner's, and the other kids just up and left."

"Oh, Lordy! And I mean for a young'un barely touched fifteen to be out playin' pool, not 'bout your friends up and leavin'. You would think someone with a daddy such as yours would be brung up better."

"Betty!" Mary Lou yelled from inside the car. "Just shut up and let the boy have a ride. I'm getting sick."

Betty stepped to the back door and opened it, gesturing with an impatient jerk of her head for the boy to climb inside.

"Thank you, ma'am."

After fifteen minutes of driving, Betty glanced over her shoulder to the backseat. "Boy, I've been sittin' here figurin', and with what gas and wear and tear on my car comes to,

you're gonna be owin' me some free mowin' time. I'm goin'
near 'bout two miles out of my way, four miles round trip,
carryin' you back to that fancy subdivision you live in."

"Belle Colline Heights," Mary Lou said. "There's a
plumber lives in there I believe's got the hots for me."

"Mary Lou! Watch your mouth. And I know what the subdivision's name is."

Mary Lou glanced back at the smiling boy. "You think he
ain't heard talk about the hots before? Kids now days know
more than you and I did when we wuz married."

"Still don't make no difference. You're not supposed to be
talkin' such in front of young'uns."

"I don't mind," Johnny said from the backseat.

"Well I do," Betty stated emphatically.

"In fact, it sort of turns me on."

Betty, her eyes glaring, looked back over her shoulder.
"Hush your nasty mouth, boy."

Mary Lou laughed loudly, slapping the dashboard with her
open palms.

"Fact is, I'm sorta getting the hots right now."

"Boy!"

Mary Lou roared.

They were now less than a mile from the main entrance to
the subdivision.

"There's a gravel logging road turns off into the park right
up there" came the insistent voice from the backseat. "Why
don't you pull off on it?"

Mary Lou, laughing so hard tears were running from her
eyes, glanced back over her shoulder. She stopped laughing.
Her eyes widened.

"Betty, he's got a knife!"

Betty, staring into the rearview mirror, had already seen it.
Her mouth was hanging open.

Johnny suddenly sat forward, slid his left hand around to
cup Mary Lou's chin and jerk her head sharply backward, his
right hand placing the knife against her throat. "If you don't
pull off onto that road, I'm gonna slit her good."

Mary Lou turned pale. "Johnny," she said. "Ohhh! Betty, he cut me!"

The boy's narrow, cold eyes stared across to Betty. His hand pulled Mary Lou's head further back, holding the knife out for both women to see.

"God, Betty, please do what he says."

Betty slowed, then guided her Ford off onto the gravel road.

"No," the boy said. "Don't stop. On down the road until I tell you."

She pressed the accelerator too far to the floor, the Ford's rear wheels throwing gravel.

"Hots starting to get to you?" the boy asked. "Makes you want to hurry, doesn't it." He moved the knife, but stayed leaned forward close to Mary Lou, his empty hand beginning to stroke the side of her pale cheek.

Betty only stared straight ahead now, her hands shaking on the steering wheel.

Mary Lou touched trembling fingers to the side of her neck, felt the spot of sticky wetness. "Oh, God," she moaned.

They passed an old trailer sitting off the side of the road to the left, then drove a mile farther.

"Stop here! See the dirt road? Pull into it."

It wasn't a road at all, just a narrow thirty-foot clearing running into the trees at the side of the road.

After Betty guided the Ford into the opening the automobile was well concealed from the logging road. Only its rear end could possibly be noticed by anyone passing by.

"Get out!"

Johnny pushed both women ahead of him through the tangled briars at the end of the short cleared stretch, into the tall pines, then fifty feet farther out into a clear meadow.

"Ms. Betty, I think I'm going to bang you first."

"Noooo!"

As Betty's eyes grew bigger, her head beginning to shake back and forth, Mary Lou started backing away. The boy looked away from Betty toward her friend.

"Sit down!" he screamed.

Mary Lou reached an arm behind herself, sitting awkwardly backward on the grass.

The boy, a smile coming to his face, turned back to face Betty again. Stepping closer to her, he moved the point of the knife to her throat. With his other hand he reached to the neck of her blouse, gathered a handful of the material and yanked hard, ripping the garment open down its front.

Mary Lou screamed and scrambled to her feet, turned and ran toward the strip of pine trees separating her from the blue Ford.

"Get back here, you fat bitch!"

She had almost reached the trees when the boy caught up with her, jabbed the knife down hard into her back.

With a loud scream she threw both hands back over her shoulder to grab at the pain. Johnny jerked the knife out and jabbed it again. And again. She sank to her knees and crumpled forward on her face.

Betty, ripped blouse flapping out to her sides as she ran, was dashing toward the pines now, angling away from where the boy stood smiling down at Mary Lou. Johnny ran to cut her off.

Mary Lou, her eyes open wide, her face pressed into the wet grass, could feel the warm wetness spreading across her back. "Oh, dear Jesus!"

She pushed herself to her knees, tried to stand, but her legs gave away and she fell back to her hands and knees again. "Oh, dear Jesus, ohhhhh." She began crawling toward the edge of the woods.

From off in the trees to the right, Betty screamed, a long, shrill scream of pain, and then came her repeated short cries of agony. Then nothing.

Mary Lou tried to crawl faster, but she was growing weaker, her head spinning. Summoning all the strength she had left, she pulled herself through a patch of wild blueberry bushes and past the trunk of a thick pine. She heard the boy moving, coming back through the trees to her right.

She altered her course to the left, lowered her body,

bumped into something, moved her head to the side to go around it, and it moved with her. She saw the white loafers, raised her face to the khaki slacks. A quizzical expression came to her face. She specifically remembered Johnny was wearing blue jeans and tennis shoes.

The ice pick slammed into the base of her skull. Her body lost control. Her chin fell to rest on the toe of a white loafer.

CHAPTER

24

Thirty minutes after leaving his home, Ramsey guided his car to the side of the gravel logging road and parked on its grassy shoulder. Reaching into the glove compartment, he pulled out his long-barreled .38 rather than the revolver Ray had given him. He was more familiar with his own pistol.

Removing the shovel from the backseat of the car, he then moved around to the trunk and began searching for his flashlight. He found it jammed down into the spare-tire well. The batteries were weak and the flashlight only gave a faint glow. But it would be adequate.

Thorns snagged his khakis and scratched his legs as he forced his way through the vine-tangled undergrowth at the side of the road and into the trees. If he recalled the lay of the park correctly, he should be right in line with the sinkhole and about a hundred yards from it, much closer than the three hundred or so yards he would have had to traverse if he had entered the trees from the subdivision.

He found keeping his bearings was more difficult than he had thought it would be. The dim glow of the flashlight barely illuminated the ground in front of him. The small crescent-shaped sliver of moon perched above the forest was no help at all—the thick canopy of leaves and limbs strained out what light the heavy clouds sailing east hadn't already absorbed. But he continued to plod ahead, trying as nearly as possible to keep moving in the correct direction.

A few minutes later his determination was rewarded. He recognized the tree he had noticed the first time he had visited the sinkhole—an oddly shaped cedar, its double trunks twisted around each other in corkscrew fashion.

The hole should be no more than seventy-five to a hundred feet to his left. He turned and walked in that direction, moving less than fifty feet before his way was barred by a thicket of stunted bushes tangled in morning glory vines.

Now he had only to circle around the edge of the thicket to the winding entrance down into the sinkhole.

He heard the faint noise of a motor and he stopped and stood still.

The noise was coming from a truck or an automobile moving along the gravel logging road. The vehicle slowed in the vicinity of his parked car, then picked up speed again, resuming its pace along the road.

A half dozen steps farther he found the break in the thicket. His flashlight, already dim when he had first turned it on, wasn't helping much. He switched it off. He would save what battery power he had left in case he had need of it.

After giving his eyes time to adjust to the dark, he followed the narrow, twisting path to the edge of the sinkhole.

He heard a scampering noise in front of him, fumbled for his flashlight as something brushed by his ankle and was gone. He left the flashlight on.

Walking to the center of the sinkhole, he played the flashlight beam back and forth over the ground.

The shallow depression the dog had scratched was no longer there.

There had not been a rain since the last time he had visited the place, so the dirt could not have washed back level.

Had the kids had been back again? He supposed any of the subdivision's children could have been there to play since he last visited the spot.

What did it matter? He was there now and nothing would be gained by leaving without checking what he came for. Using pressure from his foot to test the ground, he found where the shallow hole had been when he felt the unpacked dirt give.

He pulled the uncomfortable revolver from his waistband and placed it on the lip of the sinkhole, illuminated the spot for a moment with the light, then placed it on the hole's rim. Pressing the point of the shovel into the soft ground, he began digging.

After removing a foot of dirt—past the level of the dog's efforts—the ground was still soft. Its bottom had been packed hard that first time he had seen it. Whatever, or whoever, had recently filled the hole had first dug it deeper.

Feeling a nervous sensation sweep over him, he glanced over his shoulder. He reached to the lip of the sinkhole and felt for the pistol.

It wasn't there.

His hands quickly swept the lip of the hole—found the flashlight. He switched it on. The revolver lay a couple of feet away.

Shaking his head, he took a deep breath and released it slowly, almost chuckled when he noticed his rapid heart beat. Placing the flashlight next to the pistol, he began digging again.

His shovel hit hard ground. No? He pressed the blade against the bottom of the hole. Hard—but spongy, too. Kneeling, he felt around where he had been digging.

Felt the hair.

Lurching backward to his feet, he fumbled again for the light, found it, and shined it into the hole. He couldn't distinguish anything. Dropping to his knees, he moved the flashlight into the hole.

It was dark hair.

He leaned closer—saw the pointed ear. What in hell? He lowered his face almost even with the top of the hole and strained to see.

Peter!

He sagged back on his heels, his stomach twisting.

Who in God's name would do . . . ? Not the kids. Surely not kids.

He took a deep breath and leaned back to the hole again. Using his hands now rather than the sharp steel of the shovel, he began removing the dirt around the boxer's head.

In a couple of minutes he had cleaned enough of the dirt away that he could reach under the animal's stiff forelegs. Grasping the bulky chest, he pulled. The loose dirt gave way and he lifted the lifeless form from the hole and laid the animal on its side.

Brushing the dirt from its face and from its coat, he studied the dog. Other than finding a small spot of blood on top of the head, he saw no wound. He stood, and as he did, he heard a rustling in the bushes several feet outside the sinkhole.

Fumbling along the lip of the depression, he again found the .38 and took it into his hand. Switching off his flashlight, he stood quietly in the dark. All he could hear were the crickets, and the occasional yelping of a tree frog.

A couple of minutes passed and he began to relax. He slid the revolver inside his waistband this time, placed the flashlight in his hip pocket, then stooped and lifted the deadweight of the boxer. Leaving the shovel behind, he made his way up the steep slope and out of the hole.

Halfway to the logging road he heard the vehicle again—some vehicle—coming down the road in the opposite direction from the earlier one. Then it stopped and he heard no further sound. He was too far away from the road to tell whether the engine was idling or had been switched off.

Lovers doing some late-night parking?

From the sound, the vehicle had stopped near his car. He thought of its fancy wire hubcaps.

Suddenly something was crashing through the brush—coming straight at him!

His heart jumping, dropping the dog, he fumbled at his waistband for his revolver.

No, it wasn't coming toward him.

The crashing was going away now. Fading . . . the rhythmic jumps now distinguishable.

A startled deer!

He took a deep breath, brushed his hair back off his now-damp forehead, and once again slipped the revolver back inside his waistband. Lifting the dog from the ground, he resumed his trek toward the crest of the hill.

Minutes later he was at the edge of the woods with only a few feet of tangled underbrush to cross before the logging road. He could see the dim outline of his car.

He was suddenly blinded by bright lights beamed into his face.

"What do you think you're doing, buddy?"

He froze.

"He's got a pistol in his belt, Rick, watch out!"

"Hell, that's Mr. Ramsey."

The lights moved from his face, and he could see.

The two park rangers walked toward him.

"What in tarnation you got there, Mr. Ramsey?"

Johnny lay back against the headboard of his bed. He was staring across his bedroom at the older boy who, stoned, now starting to shake his head, was sitting on the floor slumped back against the wall next to the door.

The boy raised his face, started to speak, but didn't. Instead, he shook his head again and then dropped his gaze, where in his limp hand he held the bong loaded with hashish. It had gone out. He felt on the floor around his hips trying to find his lighter.

Johnny was sick of the sniveling—sick to death of it. But the older boy was bigger. Soft and flabby, but bigger. Big enough that when faced with the prospect of his own death, he might be more than could be handled. But not after a few more hits off the bong, and a couple more drinks of Scotch.

There was plenty of time. Johnny's dad wouldn't be coming in—he was shacked up with that slut he had hired as a receptionist at his office. He said she was eighteen, but Johnny bet she wasn't over sixteen, maybe even younger than he was.

He wondered if his dad had hit her yet. He always ended up hitting them. Johnny had seen it happen the first time when he was eleven years old—and seen what happened later. That one had liked it. He had peered through the crack in the door while she had crawled across the floor to his dad. And he had kept watching.

Some had not liked it—there had been a couple of problems with the police when they lived in Atlanta. But Johnny's way —it didn't matter whether they liked it or not.

He looked at the boy feeling for the lighter. It was originally going to be the both of them together—*their way*. They were going to do all kinds of things together. Just the two of them, the boy had said. In fact, the boy had been the one who had first suggested really doing it. But then, tonight, when they had, to the two old sluts, the boy had become hysterical.

Never again, Johnny thought. He would never again be foolish enough to carry along a witness to his pleasures. It was too dangerous. Besides, he didn't want to share the experience again. He wanted it to be just his. There were some of the things he did to the old women that had made him feel awkward knowing someone else was around, even with the boy on his hands and knees throwing up most of the time. The self-consciousness took away from the pleasure.

Low pleading cries of mercy were emanating from the video playing on the TV screen, and he turned his head to watch the soldiers raping the old woman. But he had watched the scene so many times before, it wasn't really all that exciting anymore. Or maybe, he thought, after having experienced the real thing, felt real flesh tear and heard the real screams, nothing else could ever again be exciting.

The boy next to the door whimpered his sorrow at not being able to find his lighter. Johnny reached to his bedside table, opened its drawer, and lifted out the lighter he kept there. He pitched it toward the boy. It bounced on the hardwood floor and slid up against one of the boy's white loafers. Johnny stared a minute at the red stains on the shoes, raised his eyes to the dark flecks on the boy's khaki trousers. The change of clothing the older boy had brought was still in Johnny's closet. He would have to get rid of that, too.

The boy raised his head. Johnny pointed to the lighter. "Next to your shoe, Paul. You about ready to go riding?"

The boy found the lighter, used it at the bowl of the pipe, his cheeks hollowing with his deep sucking.

"Paul, I said are you about ready to go riding?"

The boy looked up, gave the appearance of having some difficulty in focusing his vision. "I don't want to."

"You have to be home before dawn, before your old man gets in from work. You need to quit that stuff for a while and go riding first—get some fresh air."

Paul shook his head. "We're going to hell," he mumbled.

Johnny didn't mind. That's where he wanted to go. And he didn't mind waiting for Paul a little longer, either. Another half hour or so and the boy would come with him whether he wanted to or not. He would be past resisting by then. Johnny leaned back against the headboard again. The video was getting to the part he liked best—where the soldiers grabbed the woman who looked like Mrs. Mueller.

CHAPTER

25

Ramsey arrived at the police station a little after ten the next morning, having first visited the well site to check on the drilling progress.

Ray and the black police sergeant were standing behind the counter in the outer office. They were speaking with a short, solidly built blond-haired woman who appeared to be in her early thirties.

Ray's secretary, Lila, was at her desk even though it was Saturday morning. He engaged in small talk with her until the blonde had finished and walked past him toward the building's front door. He walked to the counter.

Ray was staring after the woman. "Remember her?"

Ramsey glanced over his shoulder after the woman, then turned back to shake his head.

"Her name's Karen Gill. She graduated from high school a

couple of years after you did. Real nice lady. Right now a worried one.''

"Why?''

"Her son's birthday was today. An aunt was supposed to have brought a cake over to her. When she didn't, Karen went by to pick it up and the aunt wasn't there; bed hadn't been slept in.'' He turned toward the sergeant who was busily filling out the missing person report. "What was the aunt's name?''

"Betty Amis.''

"Yeah,'' Ray said, turning back to face his brother. "Karen's fearin' the worst. Might be right. If it was a kid I wouldn't get up in the air about it, not for a while anyway. Youngsters are always running away from home. A middle-aged woman, though, living alone with no other kin. A woman like that doesn't miss her grand-nephew's birthday party. At least not without a real good reason.''

He lifted a sheet of paper off the counter and handed it to Ramsey. "That's the veterinarian's report. The boxer was killed by a small puncture wound to the head. The weapon was somethin' not very big around, and hard. Not like a screw-driver—was sharp. Vet says it might have been an ice pick.''

"Discover anything else in the hole?''

"Had it dug out with a backhoe, the whole bottom, deep as a grave, nothin'. If the dog was digging after somethin', it was gone by the time they put him there. I told the mayor what Dr. Jones said. Dog might not have been mutilated, but it damn sure was killed by those kids. We're pulling out all the stops. Sheriff Toney's got deputies going door to door. Highway patrol is gonna send some help. We're gonna find out who they are if it takes a month. I want to know which one of 'em's father has that porno collection, too. Ask the man where he was the night the Richardson girl was murdered.''

Ramsey shook his head in disgust. He had been hoping, praying, that something would be found in the hole, or that Ray would inform him that one of the kids had suddenly come forward. Something, *anything*—not just continued dead ends.

"Ray, I don't want to sound like I'm quitting before I even get started. But I don't know what to do next."

"There isn't anything. I told you that before you got started. But you needed to do what you said you were gonna do—try. You did, leave it at that."

He didn't want to leave it at that. "Maybe when you find those kids—"

"That's gonna be done. But you know what the chances are of 'em having seen anything. You been over to see Leigh Ann this morning?"

"Going over there when I leave here, why?"

"I've just been thinking. Two days after she buries her husband, here's me calling her up informing her she's gonna have to explain to her kids their pet's been killed. Not a real good time for her."

Not only Ray's words, but even his tone was sympathetic. Ramsey stared at his brother.

"I know," Ray said, nodding his head. "I know. I may not be real high on the gal, but she's a human being; and I expect she's feeling pretty low right about now."

When Ramsey arrived at Leigh Ann's, she poured him a glass of tea, then the two moved from the kitchen to sit on the living-room couch.

"Leigh Ann, I haven't accomplished much of anything. I'm beginning to wonder if I'm going to be able to."

She nodded. "I was thinking about it last night. We might not ever know. There might always be people thinking Jack killed Julie, but I'm not going to walk around in this town with my head down. And I'm not going to move away, either—not after four generations of my family have lived here. This is my town, my place, where I intend to be buried. Besides, I owe it to Jack's memory—let people realize that I know he didn't kill the girl."

The doorbell rang.

"Excuse me a minute," she said as she rose from the easy

chair. He watched her as she walked from the room, then turned back to sip his tea.

In a minute she was back. She had a small, sweet smile on her face.

"It's the boy mowing the yard. He's thirsty. I forgot all about the poor thing. And after him coming over and volunteering to mow my yard for half his normal price. Wasn't that nice?

"I called his father—they live in the subdivision—and told him how much I appreciated the boy's gesture." She moved on into the kitchen, speaking back over her shoulder as she walked.

"I'm going to fix him a glass of tea. It'll just take a minute."

When she came back through the living room with the glass, Ramsey stood. "I just wanted to stop in for a moment. See how you were doing. I'm going on back out to the well. If you need anything, call me on my cellular phone. Can't raise me there, call my office and they can contact me by radio."

"I appreciate your coming by, Mark. Maybe one of these nights you'll come over and eat dinner."

"We'll do that some time."

He followed her to the door, nodded idly at the young boy, who accepted the glass from her.

"Thank you again for coming by, Mark. It really helps me to see you."

As he walked to his car, she remained on the porch, waved at him when he glanced toward her. Sliding behind the steering wheel, he glimpsed movement at the edge of the park. It was the pulpwood cutter's son.

The boy stepped from the trees and walked down the property line between Leigh Ann and the Richardsons' homes.

Ramsey stepped back out of his car and waited as the boy angled toward him.

"Mr. Ramsey," the boy said in a soft, subdued tone.

"Yeah, son."

"Will you ask them to let my paw out? Please? He's sorry for what he done."

Ramsey had no idea Luttle was still locked up. *No money to pay his bail.* The kid had been staying by himself?

"Would you be doin' that for me, Mr. Ramsey? I sorta need him back at home pretty bad. I been checkin' on and off for two days tryin' to catch you down here."

The boy was dressed in a pair of old blue jeans and a faded but clean short-sleeved dress shirt. Probably selected the best things he owned before he came to make his plea. The child's lips were not held tight now. His eyes were no longer cold, instead had a whipped look. Ramsey couldn't help it; he felt sorry for the boy.

"If you get my paw out of jail, I'll tell you who the kids are. I'll even show you where they've got their clubhouse, if you care any. It's only a piece up from my trailer."

Ramsey's heart was suddenly knocking. "Wait right here a minute, son." He hurried back where Leigh Ann stood in the doorway. "Call Ray right away. If he's not at the station, tell them to patch you into his car radio. Tell him I'm with Luttle's son, that's he's going to tell me who the kids are who were camping out. Tell him to meet me over at the trailer and bring the boy's father with him. Make sure he understands to bring Luttle with him."

As Ramsey and the pulpwood cutter's son drove away, the lanky boy pushing the lawn mower stopped and glared after the car. He moved his eyes to Leigh Ann as she stepped back inside the house and closed the door.

CHAPTER

26

The pulpwood cutter's son had Ramsey drive a half mile past the trailer before telling him to stop.

The boy nodded off toward the left side of the road. "It's down in the draw," he said.

It was a more difficult passage than Ramsey would have expected. Most of the hills in the park were low ones. It was unusual for any of their gentle slopes to rise or fall at more than a ten- or fifteen-degree angle. The slope of the hill he now followed the boy down was much steeper. Occasionally he had to grab the trunk of a tree to stop his progress from becoming too rapid. Twice his feet slid out from under him to send him scooting on his buttocks until he could dig his heels into the ground. But he would have rappeled down Mount Everest to know anything at all about the boys.

At the bottom of the draw, its entrance hidden by a combination of live cedars and leafy limbs cut from oak trees, the clubhouse was actually a shallow cave in the side of the hill. The camouflaging was done well, the branches recently cut with the leaves still dark green.

Moving some of the limbs aside, the boy entered the cave. Ramsey followed, squeezing through the narrow opening between a pair of plywood panels. He was greeted by nearly total blackness, and the stench of rotting meat.

The boy struck a wooden match against his leg, then bent to light a kerosene lamp sitting on a small wooden table. The interior of the cave brightened.

Its total depth was not more than twenty feet; its width, ten or twelve feet, narrowing rapidly in a pie-shaped wedge toward the back.

In addition to the kerosene lantern and the table, there was a Boy Scout cooking kit, two metal folding chairs, and an old wooden rocking chair inside the confines of the cave. He saw where the terrible smell was coming from.

Placed on the floor against the wall to one side, intermingled with candles and small containers of incense, were several jars. Some of them were small, the size of canning jars. A few were of the big commercial-size variety. Nearly all of them had small pieces of rotting meat floating in various-colored liquids. Bloated, dark-green flies sat on the rims.

The shape of the contents of one of the bigger jars caught Ramsey's eye. He stepped closer. A softball-size, helmet-shaped mass, he guessed it the brain of a large animal; a sheep or a calf—maybe a big dog.

The ninety percent of the mass below the level of the clear liquid was still recognizably gray, though darkened and partially decayed. The part of the brain above the level of the liquid was black, beginning to disintegrate. He could see maggots working inside the rot. He stepped back to the center of the cave.

The boy had moved to the narrowest part of the back of the cave and dropped to his knees. In a minute he had scooped a layer of loose dirt aside, producing a small metal lockbox. He carried it back to Ramsey. Placing it on the floor, the boy pointed at it.

"I've seen this twice," he said. "They take pictures when they do things like what they done to Peter. They shouldn't have killed him. I was teachin' him how to tree squirrels."

Ramsey bent to open the lockbox. Inside it was a video tape.

"You're gonna turn Paw loose now, aren't you?"

"Yeah, son, when you tell me the kids' names. What did you say's on this tape?"

"Devil stuff; when they kill things. When I told Paw about it, he said don't never be comin' down here no more. We got a machine you can play that on if you wanna see it. It shows a frog and a chicken."

The white LTD was parked at the Luttle trailer when Ramsey and the boy arrived there. Ray was leaning against it. Behind him, the pulpwood cutter sat in the passenger seat.

As Ramsey stepped from his car, his brother moved to meet him.

Ramsey held the piece of paper out. "He gave me three names; said you'd recognize one of them. Said you'd locked up the kid's father before."

Ray studied the paper, then nodded his head. "Yeah. He must of meant this Jerry Horton." He looked down at the pulpwood cutter's son. "Is that Gerald Horton's son?"

"Yessir, sure nuff is."

"Don't know the other two," Ray mumbled as he stared at the names. "Son, do you know these other boys' dads—Johnny Keller, Hal Garrett?"

"Johnny's paw is a doctor. Don't know nothin' about Hal's dad."

Ray's brow furrowed. "Doctor? I don't—Wait a minute. There's a dentist named John Keller. He lives in the subdivision."

"Yes, sir. Johnny's paw lives down there."

Ray shook his head. "Dr. Keller's gonna skin his kid alive.

Never would have figured his son being involved in somethin' like this. Son, what does the other kid look like? This Hal."

"Some taller than me, same kinda hair, lot of zits."

"You know where he lives?"

The boy shook his head. "Don't know where none of 'em live, 'ceptin' Johnny."

Ray raised his face to Ramsey's. "Well, Mark, I can have 'em all picked up and brought down to the station, or we can go by and visit with 'em one at a time. We have 'em picked up, there's gonna be lawyers and parents talking to each other. Talking to 'em one at a time we'll catch 'em cold; have a better chance to learn somethin' right off."

Ramsey held up the video tape. "Let's look at this first."

Luttle spoke from inside the LTD. "Son, that be out of the cave?"

The boy nodded. "Only way I was knowin' how to get you out of jail, Paw."

"It's okay," the man said softly, and nodded at his son. "Chief Hopkins, I've done seen that tape. Told my boy to stay away from them kids. They ain't no good. But I told him not to be sayin' nothin' neither. He did and they come after him for it, I'd had to be a killin' one of 'em. I'd be appreciatin' it if you don't tell 'em it was my son what told you about the cave."

Ray stared at the man for a moment. "Mr. Luttle, you didn't have any right to be holding back who they were. What if they know about a car or truck parked up here the night of the murder? I ought to lock you up for obstructing justice."

"Mr. Ramsey!" the boy exclaimed, the alarm obvious in his voice. "You promised you'd be lettin' my paw go. You promised."

Ramsey looked down at the boy and nodded. "I did." He turned toward his brother.

Ray nodded his assent. "Mr. Luttle. You pull somethin' again like what you did over at Miss Leigh Ann's, I'm not gonna just lock you up. I'm gonna see you sent to Parchman. I've had enough of your crap in this town."

The man nodded. "You won't hear no more outta me," he promised.

"Ray, there's some jars in the cave. I believe at least one of them has a brain in it." When he saw his brother's eyes narrow, Ramsey added, "An animal brain . . . I think."

Ray nodded and stepped to the window of the LTD, reached inside for the radio mike.

Ramsey turned back to the boy. "Son, you said you have a video-tape player in the trailer?"

The boy looked to his father, and the man answered. "I bought it fair and square down at the truckstop from a driver passin' through. Got a receipt for it."

Leaning inside the window to speak into the microphone, Ray's face was only a few inches from the man's. "What did you give for it?"

"Eleven dollars, Chief, fair and square."

After Ray contacted the police station, he handed his brother the mike. Ramsey explained to the dispatcher how to find the cave. A squad car would deliver the jars and their contents to the crime lab in Jackson.

Entering the trailer, the man led them to his small bedroom. Ray sat on the edge of the bed while the boy inserted the tape in the VCR. Ramsey stood in the cramped space between the bed and the wall. The father, fingering a chew into his mouth, peered through the doorway.

The first scene was slightly blurred, but cleared quickly. It was a closeup shot of a small green frog sitting on a section of two-by-four. The etched symbols on the wood could be seen clearly.

"That's the same chunk of wood you found," Ray mumbled. "Or another one just like it."

Ramsey flinched when the ice pick jammed down hard, pinning the frog to the two-by-four. The pick's handle vibrated with the creature's frantic movements.

The movements grew weaker, finally ceased altogether. The frog quivered a couple of times before lying still. The pick handle quit moving. Ramsey noticed his brother shake his head.

At the end of the scene there was a brief moment of clutter, then a chicken standing beside a bush appeared on the screen. The camera came in for a closeup. The chicken turned its head toward the lens.

A gloved hand jammed the pick down hard into the chicken's back and it sprang wildly forward into the bush, fell backward to the ground. Scrambling to its feet, the pick sticking from its back like a warning antenna on a bicycle, the chicken scrambled a few quick steps to the left, then the right, finally toppled to its side. Wings fluttering, legs kicking, it gradually stopped moving.

Fuzzy white clutter appeared on the screen once more, then it was night. Part of a fence focused into view. Then a calf. A dark figure was placing a rope around the animal's neck.

Ramsey strained to recognize a feature of the figure, saw that whoever it was wore a black ski mask and had it pulled down over his face, was peering through a pair of slits.

A break occurred in the scene and the action changed to the calf being led along the side of what appeared to be a barn, and on around the building's corner.

"I ain't been seein' this," the pulpwood cutter's son said.

In the next scene the camera moved in for a closeup. The calf's head seemed to grow grotesquely out of proportion due to the angle of the shot.

Then the camera pulled back for a wide-angle view. The calf's head reduced to the right proportion.

There was momentary clutter, then the calf again, then the flash of a Kyzar blade cut through the air and the sharp tool dug deep into the calf's neck.

The animal convulsed; its front legs stiffened. Its knees buckled and it crumpled forward, its jaw skidding on the ground. Remaining a moment in that position, the calf then rolled onto its side, quivered, and lay still.

"Those little bastards," Ray mumbled.

"I ain't been seein' none of this," the pulpwood cutter's son repeated in openmouthed awe. "Tape only showed the frog and chicken when I swiped it the first time."

It was daylight in the next scene and Ramsey saw Peter, backing up. The boxer's forehead was wrinkled and his eyes were intent on the camera lens.

"Aw, no," the boy said.

The dog whirled and darted into the bushes. Ramsey didn't realize his shoulder muscles had tightened until he felt them begin to relax.

It was night again on the tape. Leafy limbs were in sharp focus. Past the branches everything was blurred and dark. The camera moved forward through the leaves and Ramsey saw the dark smoke curling from the smoldering campfire.

The sinkhole.

The camera tilted forward, focusing down past the rim onto the bare back of a man. Julie's face could be seen above his shoulder. Her eyes were open wide in a blank stare, her mouth was gaped, slack. Ramsey felt his back crawl.

"Jesus!" Ray exclaimed.

The man in the scene suddenly turned his head in the direction of the camera, his face clear. White clutter once again appeared on the screen.

Ray pushed himself forward off the edge of the bed and hit the VCR's reverse button. Waiting until the man's face was in view once more, he pushed pause. The man was white, had dark hair, was impressively good-looking. Comparing him to the girl, he seemed to be of average height, had wide muscled shoulders, and well-built lean arms.

"Have you seen him before, Mark?"

Ramsey hadn't and shook his head, but he had seen something else. He stepped up beside Ray and pushed the reverse button. Waiting a couple of seconds, he pushed play. He waited again until the tape had reached the place where the man had captured their attention by turning his face toward the camera. He pushed the pause button, pointed to the screen.

"Look at her eyes, Ray."

They were open, and blank.

"Keep looking." He pushed play.

Her eyes closed slowly, then opened again.

"See, she's not dead."

He pushed the buttons and replayed the scene again from where the man's back came into view. Rewinding the tape yet another time, he ran it forward once more, this time in slow motion.

"Ray, is it rape or voluntary?"

His brother shook his head. "I can't tell. We'll get a print of the guy's face made off of it."

Ramsey pushed the play button, and the scene changed from slow to regular motion. The white fuzz reappeared and continued for a moment.

There was Peter again, this time straining against a rope looped tight around his neck and held taut by someone standing behind and out of sight of the camera lens. Feet scooting against the ground, the wide-eyed boxer was being dragged in for a closeup. Ramsey turned away and walked from the bedroom. The boy did, too.

CHAPTER

27

When they stopped in front of the small aluminum-sided home, a medium-built, red-haired man dressed in blue coveralls was in the front yard mowing the lawn.

Ray looked toward Ramsey. "That's Gerald Horton. He's the only one of the fathers I'm gonna have any leverage with. It's not much—marijuana with intent to distribute. He was the sheriff's guest for six months."

"Still on parole?"

Ray shook his head. "No, but he's gonna act polite; don't want to be irritating me."

The man had looked up when they stopped and was halfway across the lawn on his way to them when we emerged from the LTD.

"Chief." The man had both hands in his coverall pockets and didn't offer to pull one out to shake hands.

"Mr. Horton," Ray said, nodding politely. "Your son in?"

The man's eyes slitted. "He been in some kind of trouble?" His hands came out of his pockets and rubbed nervously together in front of him.

" 'Fraid he has, Mr. Horton. How much trouble is gonna be up to the district attorney—and how much hell the Humane Society raises. But that's not what I'm here about."

The wrinkles on the man's forehead deepened. "Humane Society?"

"He belongs to some kind of club. Group of kids that have been killin' animals."

The wrinkles disappeared and a one-sided smile came to the man's face. "You've got to be joshing." The man's hands relaxed, moved back to hang by their thumbs from his pockets.

"That's what he done. But like I said, I'm not here for that. I want to ask him a few questions about anybody he might have seen when he was camping out a week ago Wednesday night."

The man didn't respond immediately. When he did, there was a new, colder tone to his voice. "He was here last Wednesday night; wasn't camping out nowhere."

Ray's tone changed, too, and his face tightened. "Mr. Horton. I can put him under arrest for what he's already done to those animals, read him his rights and carry him off down to the jail; take my time about questioning him. Can take you along for lying, obstructing justice—talk to you about what you've been up to lately. Or you can just invite me on into your house to talk to him, friendly like. I'll give you my word I won't be asking him anything that might go against him later regarding the animal killin'. I'm not interested in that right now. It's up to you how you want to do it."

The man stared for several more seconds and then, his shoulders slumping, he nodded. He turned and started toward his house. They followed.

"Jerry!" the man yelled as they walked into the home.

"Yeah!"

"Chief Hopkins is here to see you!"

"Yes, sir."

In a moment the young boy stepped from the hall into the

living room. About five five, pale-complexioned and red-haired like his father, the boy was overweight and noticeably soft. His skin almost appeared puffy. He glanced nervously at Ray and Ramsey and then at his father.

"Yes, sir."

"Chief Hopkins here says you've been involved in some animal killing."

The boy's eyes widened. He immediately started shaking his head. "Not me. No, sir."

"That's not what I came for, son," Ray said. "I want to ask you a couple of questions about what you might have seen when you were camping out in the park a week ago Wednesday night."

"I didn't—"

The father shook his head. The boy's eyes cut to him and then back to Ray again. "Okay. I was camping out. But I didn't have nothing to do with killing no animals."

"Mind if we have a seat?" Ray asked.

"Go ahead," the man said, and walked to an old easy chair at the side of the living room. Ramsey and Ray moved to a faded yellow couch. The boy remained standing.

"What time did you get down to the sinkhole?" Ray asked.

The boy looked toward his father and the man nodded. " 'Bout dark."

"Stay all night?"

The boy glanced again for his father's okay, and the man nodded again. "No, sir, we left around eleven."

"Who is *we*?"

The boy, expressionless, glanced toward his father once more.

"Hal and Johnny."

"Their full names."

A glance again. "Hal Garrett and Johnny Keller."

"What did you all do?"

The boy looked toward his father once again, and so, now, did Ray.

At Ray's continued cold stare, the man rose. "You mind if I take my boy out to the other room for a minute?"

"That'd probably be a good idea, Mr. Horton."

Ramsey exchanged glances with his brother as the man and his boy walked from the room.

"Like father, like son," Ray mumbled. "Ten to one the kid ends up in Parchman before he's twenty-five."

It was several minutes before the two Hortons returned to the living room. The man took up his seat in the easy chair while his son continued to stand in the middle of the floor.

The boy cleared his throat, and his face tightened slightly. "I know about the girl being murdered. Hal does, too. But we were scared to say anything because we were down there that night. If it wasn't for that, I would've already come and told you about what we saw."

"What?" Ray asked.

"We saw this guy come down through the woods."

"You know who he was?"

"No, sir."

"What did he look like?"

"I don't know."

"You don't know?"

"It was dark."

"Big? Little? What color hair did this guy have?"

"Hair wasn't real light. He was bigger than the girl; couple inches."

"What girl?"

"The one that got killed. The doctor's daughter."

"It was light enough for you to recognize her, but you don't remember anything about him?"

"She came up from that old house to meet him. We knew it was her."

"Tell me exactly what you saw; from the beginning."

"After the girl came out of her house, we saw the guy coming down through the woods. They met up at the edge of the park and came back to where we camp out."

"She came with him voluntarily? He wasn't having to make her?"

"No, sir."

"You're positive he wasn't forcing her?"

"They were talking and laughing, carrying on."

"You said they came to where you camp out. You mean the sinkhole?"

The boy nodded.

"Where were you all then?"

"We were hiding and watching. They didn't know we were anywhere around."

"What did they do in the hole?"

"Made out."

"Voluntarily?"

"Oh, she liked it sure enough." The boy smiled a little.

"You were close enough to see that, and don't remember anything about what the boy looked like?"

"We didn't see 'em making out, Hal and me. Johnny's the one that snuck up to the hole. He told us what they done."

"Johnny didn't happen to have a video camera with him, did he?"

The boy's face tightened slightly, and his eyes narrowed. "Yes, sir, he did."

"And he used it to film them?"

"Was going to. There's bushes and vines and all kinds of stuff thick around that hole. He thought with the wind kicking up so hard he could crawl up on them without them being able to hear him. But just as he got where he could see good and had started filming, the guy looked back over his shoulder toward the edge of the hole. Johnny thought he had been heard; so he skedaddled."

"Then Johnny came back to where you and Hal were?"

"Yes, sir."

"What did you do then?"

"Left."

"All of you?"

"Yes, sir."

"Together?"

"I cut across the park; Hal and Johnny went down the logging road."

"Why did you split up?"

"For me, going straight through the park is a lot closer to here. It's near about three miles out of the way around the logging road to the highway."

"It was storming that night; dark. It didn't bother you walking through those trees?"

Ramsey had wondered the same thing.

The boy smiled, stood a little straighter. "No, sir, Mr. Hopkins. Didn't bother me none."

"You said Hal and Johnny went down the road?"

"Yes, sir."

"Do you know if they went straight home?"

"They split up. Hal went on home. I don't know about Johnny. I suppose he cut across the woods back into the subdivision. He lives there."

"Why don't you know what he done?"

"I just don't."

"How do you know what Hal done?"

"He told me the next day."

"And Johnny didn't say what he done?"

"I haven't seen him."

"Haven't seen him since that night?"

"No, sir. Hardly ever see him until he calls to set up a gathering."

"Is that what you call your meetings?"

"Yes, sir."

"How many other than you three attend these gatherings?"

"Just us."

"I mean anytime. Not just that night."

"Just us."

Ramsey knew what his brother was getting at. The two kids both claimed they had nothing to do with the killing of the animals, yet it appeared there could have been two people involved in the videotaping, especially with the calf.

"Nobody else belongs to your club?" Ray asked.

The boy smiled a little. "No, sir."

"What did I say funny?" Ray's tone was suddenly sharp.

"Nothing." The boy dropped his gaze to the floor.

"What did you smile about?"

"Nothing, Mr. Hopkins. If I did, I wasn't meaning to."

"It was when I called your group a club. That kind of name is kid stuff, isn't it? What do you call yourselves?"

"Nothing. We don't call ourselves nothing."

Ray was silent a moment. "Tell me how to get to Hal's house."

Outside in the white LTD, Ramsey turned to his brother. "Why didn't you ask him about the grave desecration?"

"He would have denied it whether he was involved or not. We don't have anything to make him feel like we know he was in on it. We'll talk to him again. Maybe we'll learn somethin' from one of the others that we can use."

Ramsey nodded, laid his head back against the seat a moment, then turned his face toward his brother again. "Ray, killing the animals, retaining some of the body parts—had to be for some kind of ritual. Julie's body was arranged almost ritually."

"You thinking that fat little smart aleck and his buddies did the killin'? Not a chance. At least not that one. He doesn't have the balls—guarantee it. Possibly one of the others. I'll let you know after we finish talking with 'em."

Ramsey shook his head. "No, I'm not thinking about any of them being the killer. What I'm wondering is if one of them came back after the other two had left, found the girl's body. Had him a ready-made real human corpse to work on; something better than just looking at pictures in a porno book."

CHAPTER

28

"This is the address," Ray said as they parked in front of the small wood-sided house where Hal Garrett lived.

After they had crossed the lawn and knocked at the entrance to the house, it was but a few seconds until the door opened. A middle-aged, sandy-haired man, a pleasant smile on his face, stood in the doorway.

"Yes?"

"I'm Police Chief Raymond Hopkins, this is Officer Mark Ramsey."

"There's not any kind of problem with Eloise is there?"

Ray shook his head.

The tense expression that had come to the man's face at Ray's identifying himself disappeared, and he nodded. "Good, she's my sister, lives on the east side of town. I figured something might have happened to her. How can I help you, then?"

"Do you mind if we come inside?"

"No. Certainly not." The man's voice remained pleasant, but his expression was now one of curiosity.

Inside the living room he pointed toward the chairs sitting on each side of the small fireplace and moved to seat himself on the couch across from them. He still retained the quizzical expression.

"It's not about the railroad ties, is it? Stealing them's one thing, but putting them across the tracks is dangerous. I was in an engine last year that was knocked slap off the track by some ties. I've been a railroad engineer for nigh on to thirty years now and never seen the problems like we have been having the last few years. Drugs."

Ray shook his head. "It's about a club your son belongs to. To get straight to the point, some of the kids in this club have been doing some animal killin'."

The man's eyes widened. "I don't understand. You don't mean you think Hal is involved in something like that?" He smiled faintly, and shook his head. "No. Not Hal. Not my boy. Someone's badly mistaken. Just a minute." The man rose from his seat and walked rapidly from the living room.

In less than a minute he was back with his son in tow. "This is Hal."

The boy was thin and had reddish-blond hair. He had a black eye and there was a nasty bruise on his forehead. His face showed he was scared. Either the father had already explained to him who was waiting in the living room or the boy had guessed.

The man looked down at his son. "Somebody told these gentlemen you're involved with some boys who've been killing animals. I wanted you to tell them you're not."

The tears immediately started flowing from the boy's eyes and he began shaking his head.

The man's eyes widened at his son's response. "Hal, I can't believe that."

The boy kept shaking his head. "I didn't kill any animals, Daddy. It wasn't me."

The father turned and walked to the couch, sat down, and

slumped back in it. "Ask him what you want to, Chief Hopkins. He'll tell you the truth."

"When you and Jerry Horton and Johnny Keller camped out in the park a week ago last Wednesday night," Ray said, "that's what I'm interested in right now. Not the animals. I want you to tell me everything you and the others did that night."

The boy shook his head hard, began sobbing aloud. "I didn't kill any animals!" He suddenly turned and ran from the room.

The father stood. "What kind of animals did they kill, Chief?"

"Not interested in that right now, Mr. Garrett. I just want to know what he saw the night the girl was murdered."

The man's face displayed his confusion. He shook his head. "Murder—I—murder . . . ?"

"The Richardson girl."

The man kept moving his head back and forth. "I—I don't know what you're talking about. I just came in an hour ago. I've been on the rails ten days straight. I haven't even spoken with Eloise yet. Hal was here waiting on me."

"Where was your boy while you were gone?"

"With Eloise." Much of the color had drained from the man's face. "Why would he know anything about a murder?"

"We don't know if he does. Their campsite was close to where the murder happened. We just want to know if he saw anything that might help us."

The man nodded. "I'll go fetch him back in here."

"Sure. And Mr. Garrett, like I said, I'm not here to be talking about the animals. I'm not interested in that right now. No need to kid you, there are gonna be some people who are interested. Your son's gonna be in some trouble over it. It's a serious thing, what they done. But right now my concern is if they saw anyone in the park the night of the murder. Be sure and tell him that's all I want to visit with him about."

The father nodded. "He's been raised in a Christian home, Chief; as much as I could make it raising him without a mother —and me being gone so much of the time." He paused, bit his lip, and shook his head. "You see that black eye he had? Fighting while I was gone." He shook his head again, sighed audibly. "I'll go speak with him."

In a few minutes the man and his son reentered the room to stop and stand in front of Ray. Tears were still seeping from the boy's eyes. The father's face was still pale.

"Ask him whatever you want, Chief."

Ray looked at the boy. "Maybe it'd be better if you just tell me what you all did that night and what you saw; in your own words."

The boy nodded, wiped his wet cheeks with the back of his hand. "Yes, sir. But first I want to tell you about the animals. Johnny did the killing. Me and Jerry didn't have anything to do with it. Don't even know where Johnny did it; just saw a tape about it. That's all."

"Okay, son. Now what about that night."

"We went down there a little before dark. We built a campfire in a sinkhole that's down in the woods toward the subdivision. When it got good and dark we started—we started prowling." The boy glanced across his shoulder at his father. "We were prowling around homes, sorta seeing what was going on inside them, like we always do."

Ramsey noticed the father briefly close his eyes.

"About ten a car stopped up on the logging road and a guy came down through the woods—"

"Did you know who he was?" Ray asked.

"No, sir."

"Did you see his car?"

"Yes, sir. It was parked off the side of the logging road. When I started to Aunt Eloise's I walked right past it."

Ramsey sat straighter in his chair.

"What kind was it?" Ray asked.

"An old one. Had four doors; was black."

"I mean what kind; the make and model."

Come on, kid, Ramsey thought. *Come on.*

"I don't know cars very good; just an old car. Know what its license plate read."

Ramsey could barely keep from shouting.

Ray had dropped his head in exasperation, but quickly raised it to face the boy again. "You're saying you remember the license number?"

"Wasn't numbers. It was words—*Don Wan.*"

CHAPTER

29

Don Wan was a Davis County resident. His home was on the opposite side of town from the national park. He wasn't a kid. The Mississippi Highway Patrol computer listed him as Donald Kennedy, white male, twenty-eight.

Ramsey and his brother weren't alone this time. When Ray braked the LTD to a stop at the small wood-frame house, a Sheriff's Department deputy and a pair of police officers were pulling their vehicles to a stop the next block over. They would walk to the back of the home while the two brothers approached it from the front.

Ray leaned forward, reached into the glove compartment, and lifted out a snub-nosed .38 revolver. Leaning to the side, he slipped it into his trouser pocket.

"Mark, we're probably barking up the wrong tree here. He got what he came for in the sinkhole. No reason for him to be getting upset when he walked her back to the house."

Ramsey nodded. His initial exhilaration had waned. That's what he had been thinking.

"On the other hand," Ray added. "If he *is* the one, situation could get tense in there. Be careful and stay back behind me. Don't get in my way if somethin' starts."

Ramsey felt a little smile come to his face. "Okay, big brother."

At the door to the house the two stepped to opposite sides of the door. Ramsey pushed the doorbell button.

The door opened. The young man was dark-haired and impressively good-looking—it was the same face that had turned toward the video camera.

"Mr. Donald Kennedy?" Ray inquired.

"Yes."

After seeing the face, the next thing Ramsey had moved his eyes to were the man's clothes. He was dressed in tightly fitted blue jeans and a tailored white dress shirt. There was no obvious place where he could have a gun hidden.

"I'm Chief Raymond Hopkins. We're here to ask you some questions about Julie Richardson's murder. May we come in?"

Ramsey looked to the search warrant in the breast pocket of Ray's coat, and also noticed his brother had his hand inside his pants pocket.

The twenty-eight-year-old, his smile gone and the color suddenly drained from his tanned face, nodded and stepped back from the door.

Ray walked inside first, rotating slowly as he did so in order to continue to face the young man the entire time. Ramsey stepped in behind his brother.

Ray, one hand still in his pocket, handed Kennedy the search warrant. "I have a couple of officers who are gonna be looking around your home while we visit."

The man glanced at the piece of paper, then looked out the open front door.

Ray gestured with his forehead and Ramsey stepped past Kennedy and through the living room toward the rear of the house. After opening the back door and letting the police officers and deputy inside, he moved back into the living room. His brother was still facing the young man.

"You're welcome to call your attorney if you want to," Ray said.

Kennedy shook his head. "No need. I didn't do anything."

"You could be charged later. It might be a good idea for you to call a lawyer. We can wait here or we can take you down to the station and wait for him there."

"I'll take a lie detector test. I didn't do anything."

Ray nodded. "Good. We'll be happy to let you do just that when we get through here."

"I was with her. I had a date with her. That's all."

"And?"

"May I sit down, Chief?"

Ray turned his face toward the officers standing at the back of the living room. "Go on and look through the house." He faced back toward Kennedy. "If you don't mind, I'd like to search you first. Then we can all have a seat."

The young man nodded and raised his hands above his head.

"No need for that. Just relax."

Ramsey stepped forward before his brother did. Running his hands around the waistband of the young man's blue jeans, Ramsey then knelt and felt around the man's ankles and the top of his socks.

Ray removed his hand from his trouser pocket.

The three of them moved to sit on the small couch, the young man in the middle.

"You parked your car up on the logging road," Ray said. "Take it from there."

"I came down through the woods toward Julie's house—"

"What time?"

"About ten, maybe a little afterward."

Ray nodded. "Go ahead."

"She was waiting at the edge of the woods. She wasn't really expecting me. She had met this friend of mine a couple days before and told him when her parents were going to be gone. She said she was pretty sure she could talk them into letting her stay home alone and asked him to meet her at the back of her yard around ten. She wanted him to come down through the park from the logging road because she didn't want any of the neighbors to see him.

"At the last minute he got scared and backed out because of her age. He's forty. She was irritated when I showed up, got steaming hot in fact. But that just lasted a little while. I took her back to a place where I used to camp when I was a kid and lived over in the subdivision. It's a sinkhole a couple, three hundred yards, back in the trees. I can show you where it is."

Ray nodded. "We know where it is."

"We made out there, and then I took her back to her house and left. That's all it was. I want to take a lie detector test. I'm telling the truth."

"I want you to go a little slower," Ray said. "What was she wearing when you met her?"

"Uh—blue jeans and a T-shirt. A white T-shirt."

"Was she wearing any underclothes?"

The young man considered for a moment. "Panties, no bra."

So there should have been panties found with the body, Ramsey thought. Then he thought back to the kids again and about one or more of them finding a ready-made corpse. He noticed the look on his brother's face and knew he was thinking the same thing.

"Did she have anything with her?" Ray asked.

"What do you mean?"

"Was she carrying anything with her when you met her?"

The young man thought another moment. "She had a purse. Oh, yeah, she had that cordless telephone; in case her dad called."

"What do you mean?"

"Her dad was pretty rough on her about dating. She didn't want to meet in the house even though her parents were going to be gone all night. She was afraid her dad might come back to check on her. She had the cordless phone in case he called. I told her I didn't think its range would reach all the way to the sinkhole, but she brought it with her anyway."

"Did you use any protection?"

"Yeah, a rubber she had. She always carried them."

"Then this wasn't your first time with her?"

"No, sir. Been several times with her."

"Did you notice anything in the sinkhole?"

"What do you mean?"

"Did you notice anything unusual?"

"No. Oh, there'd been some kids camping there earlier, if that's what you mean. Kids will camp there forever. I used to when I was a little boy. I been there a hundred times. There was a fire still there, smoldering. I rebuilt it. We made out by its light."

"Then you took her back to the edge of the subdivision and she went on inside her house?"

"Not exactly. After we got back to the edge of the woods we sort of started wrestling around again. Got down on the ground. Then this light shone on us. It was her next-door neighbor's car backing out of the driveway. The car lights were right on us for a minute and we just lay there . . ."

Which neighbor? Ramsey thought.

"After the car had driven off, she started teasing about us getting caught in the act. Started saying things about people watching us make out. Asked me if the thought turned me on. We got to laughing, started messing around again. Ended up taking each other's clothes off."

"Did you use a rubber again?"

"We didn't go that far then."

"Why?"

Ramsey couldn't wait. "Which neighbor?"

"What?"

"Which neighbor? Which house did the car leave from?"

"On the north. Mr. Mueller's house. The guy who killed himself."

Ray began his questioning again. "I asked you why you didn't go that far the second time."

"She said she heard something. Probably just the wind. But

she wasn't teasing. You could tell by the look on her face. She said it sounded like her dad calling her.''

Ramsey narrowed his eyes.

"Her father's voice?" Ray asked.

"Yes, sir. I teased her about her being scared of him. She told me to get dressed and get on out of there; told me to hurry up. So I did."

"What exactly did she say about hearing her father?"

"Just she heard it."

"What were her exact words?"

The young man, his brow furrowing, shook his head. "Gosh. Let me think. I just don't remember exactly. Something like, That's Dad or that's my father. That's it, she said, that's my father. I said, what? She said, that was my father calling me. Then she got all nervous and told me to get out of there."

"You left then?" Ray continued.

The young man nodded.

"What time was that?"

Kennedy's forehead wrinkled in thought. "I'm not sure exactly. I got back here around a quarter after twelve. I stopped at the Super Stop for a Coke first. Probably left her a little before twelve. Say ten till; somewhere close to that."

"What was she doing when you left?"

"Just dressing . . . Oh yeah, she forgot where she had put the phone. She was looking all around herself for a moment, frantic like, and I didn't know what she was doing. Then she leaned over and whispered, Where's that damn telephone? I reminded her she had left it back in the trees."

"So she was going after the phone when you left her?"

"Yes, sir."

"Had she finished dressing at that time?"

"I don't—Yeah, partially, had her blue jeans on. Hadn't put her T-shirt back on yet."

"Are you sure? She wasn't wearing her jeans when she was found."

"Yeah. No question."

"And you didn't hear anything later, when you were leaving; her or anybody else?"

"No, sir. I just went up the hill and got in my car and came home. I run a little truck that I sell shrimp and oysters out of over on State Street in Jackson. I left early that next morning and drove down to Gulfport. Stayed the day, and when I came back the next morning I saw in the paper where she had been murdered and raped. Since I had been with her I got to worrying about the rape part. I was afraid some of you all might try to tie me into the murder because of the sex we'd had. I know I should have come on up and told you. I would have, but I was just too scared."

"Mr. Kennedy, did you know she was pregnant?"

The young man's eyes widened. "No, sir. If she was, it wasn't me. She always insisted on using a rubber with me."

CHAPTER

30

After arriving back at the police station, Ramsey sat in Ray's office reading a magazine while Champlin administered the polygraph.

"He's clean as he can be," Ray said as he entered the office. "Or such a cold-blooded sociopath the machine can't read him."

Ramsey nodded. "I figured he'd pass. He didn't have any hesitancy in wanting to take it."

"Well, where's our next stop? Dr. Richardson's or Leigh Ann's?"

"You did speak with the people the doctor said he visited in Vicksburg, didn't you?"

"What do you think, little brother? 'Course I did. At least I sent an officer over there to talk with them."

"And somebody questioned the men who loaded the furniture the next day?"

Ray flashed an irritated look. "Yes, little brother."

"You're not very excited about the doctor being a possibility, are you?"

"I just can't imagine it," Ray said, shaking his head. "With his wife giving him an alibi it would mean both of 'em would have to be involved. No, I been thinking more along other lines. What if Julie said she heard her father's voice to get rid of Kennedy—because she had somethin' else she was planning on doing? Somethin' that had just popped into her head."

"What?"

"What happened just before she said she heard her father?"

"They were making out."

"Before that."

Ramsey thought. "Jack's car leaving."

"Right. And maybe she figured he'd be back in a few minutes, right? I mean where would you be going that time of night and be gone long? Maybe she figured he was running up to a convenience store. Wherever he went, if she wanted to meet him when he got back, she'd want to get rid of her lover first. Square one; Jack again."

"Except for one big thing, Ray. If she wanted to meet him, then he damn sure wouldn't have had to try and force her into anything. No, you can't have your cake and eat it, too. The only reason he would have to get violent would be if he wanted her but she didn't him. If she didn't want him, then our theory about her scaring off her boyfriend to meet him makes no sense. You can't have it both ways."

"She threatened to tell on him."

"Come on—to whom? Leigh Ann already knew about them. You think Jack would have given three damns if she told her father? She was eighteen—legal. What did he have to worry about—his next-door neighbor being mad at him?"

Ray nodded. "And you still don't think Leigh Ann lied about his leaving the house?"

"I'm saying he could have got out of bed without her noticing. Couldn't sleep, went in to watch TV. Maybe like you said, went to a convenience store. Had run out of cigarettes or something—I don't know. Maybe went up to work in his study, finished with whatever he was working on, and carried something to be mailed that needed to get out the next day. He wasn't going in to work the next day—Thursday was his day off. He *didn't* go in, remember?

"He was mowing the lawn that morning when he saw the dog playing with her purse. Hell, I don't know where he went, or why. But having left his house doesn't make him a murderer. In fact, if anything, it makes it less likely he could have killed her. Stop and think. Kennedy said she was almost completely dressed and getting ready to go into her house when he left her. At that time Jack was gone in his car. She would have been in her home before he got back—unless she did wait for him. And I've just been over that. If she was waiting for him, he wouldn't have had to use force."

Ray shrugged. "So we might as well have stayed in bed this morning."

"No. We know she wasn't raped now. We've narrowed the time frame of the attack down. You said the medical examiner placed her time of death between nine and one. We know she was still alive at eleven-thirty. One other thing—let's not overlook the possibility that she really did hear her father's voice. There's one thing our buddy Don Wan said that got me to thinking she really might have."

"What?"

"He said when she asked where the phone was, she whispered the question. Why would she have done that if she wasn't worried her dad was around?"

Ray was silent for a moment, and then said, "So you're suggesting the doc and his wife conspired to kill their own daughter?"

"I'm not suggesting anything. I'm just trying to take it all in, catalogue it, not overlook any possibility. Did you personally speak with the wife?"

"No. One of my officers did, but I read the report. Maybe we should talk to her. Gonna have to talk to the father. This being Saturday afternoon, we'll probably catch 'em both in together."

Ramsey nodded.

Once inside his cruiser, Ray reached for the radio mike. "Unit One to headquarters."

"Go ahead, Chief."

"Patch me in on a land line to Dr. Reginald Richardson's home."

It was a couple of minutes until they heard the phone ring-ing.

"Dr. Richardson's residence."

"Is the doctor in? Or his wife?"

"No, sir. Dr. Richardson's on weekend duty at the hospital. Mrs. Richardson will be in when she closes the library."

"The local library?"

"Yes, sir. On Saturdays she usually gets home about five."

As he replaced the microphone Ray turned his face to Ram-sey's. "With the kind of money they have, I'm surprised she works."

There was only a single automobile in the library parking lot. It sat in front of a sign that read, MRS. JOANNA RICH-ARDSON: ASST. LIBRARIAN.

Inside the library two young children sat reading from Dr. Seuss books. An old, gray-bearded black man sat slumped at a table in the far corner of the library. He was snoring. They walked to a counter in the middle of the library. A middle-aged, short blonde stood behind it.

"Mrs. Richardson?"

"Yes."

"I'm Chief Raymond Hopkins, and this is my bro—Officer Mark Ramsey."

She smiled politely.

"Hate to bother you about this again, but I need to ask you some questions pertaining to your daughter."

She held her polite smile, but Ramsey noticed her eyes sad-den.

"You and your husband drove over to Vicksburg that night and met with some friends," Ray said. "Then stayed in a motel, met with some men around seven in the morning, loaded the furniture, and brought it back, right?"

"I'm not sure of the exact time, Chief Hopkins, but yes, that's substantially correct."

"Were you and your husband together the whole time? Both at the friend's house and when you stayed at the motel; together the whole time you were in Vicksburg?"

A quizzical expression crossed her face. "Why on earth would you ask something like that?"

"I'm sorry," Ray said. "I really didn't mean it so much as a question as just repeating the facts you gave the officers."

"Oh, I understand." Her face relaxed and her polite smile returned. "Yes, that is correct. That is what I told them."

Ramsey could see his brother was struggling for words and so he asked the next question. "Did you or your husband speak to your daughter after you were in Vicksburg?"

"I informed your officers I placed a call to her a little after midnight; almost midnight straight up. I'd just watched a movie on television and noticed how late it was. But I didn't receive an answer. I didn't bother calling the next morning because we were going to be back in a couple of hours."

"You didn't feel a need to call again when she didn't answer that late?"

The woman seemed to be struggling for words now. It was a long moment before she said, "I—I meant to. But I fell asleep."

Ramsey nodded, smiled politely. "Did your husband try her again?"

"I don't know. I doubt it. He sleeps pretty soundly. No, I'm sure he didn't. Oh, I don't know."

There was a long silence. Ramsey glanced toward Ray. Ray returned the look, and looked back at Mrs. Richardson.

She shook her head. "Gentlemen, I have trouble sleeping if I don't take sleeping pills. I'd taken a couple right before I placed the call to her. I dropped off to sleep without calling her back. I didn't awake until morning. That's why I don't know what happened after I went to sleep. After I have taken my pills and fallen asleep, even a ringing telephone won't wake me." She paused; a wistful expression came to her face and her eyes moistened. "Julie used to worry about my sleeping so soundly that I wouldn't hear our smoke alarm if the house caught on fire. She used to say—" With that Mrs. Richardson was unable to go any further and she shook her head.

Ramsey gave her a moment to recover before asking the next question. "Does your husband take sleeping pills?"

The woman looked directly into his eyes. "May I ask if something has transpired that I am unaware of?"

Ramsey looked at his brother, saw Ray nod, and turned back to answer the woman. "Appears now your daughter wasn't raped, Mrs. Richardson. We've a man who says he had a date with her that night. Says he met her in the woods and brought her back to the place she was found before he left. He's taken a polygraph—a lie detector test. It indicates he's telling the truth. He said that just before he left, Julie thought she heard someone call her name. So we're questioning everyone all over again, trying to get everything straight in our minds."

Mrs. Richardson was silent for a moment. "Julie wasn't raped?"

"No, ma'am, doesn't appear that way now."

There was another period of silence. "Who is this person who says he was with her?"

Ray answered. "Wouldn't be proper for us to release the man's name at this time."

"You keep saying, man."

"He's twenty-eight," Ray said.

"Did he say who it was who called my daughter's name? That is what you said, wasn't it; somebody called her name?"

"No, ma'am, he didn't know," Ray said. "He didn't even hear it. Your daughter told him she heard it."

"You gentlemen say this person claims he met my daughter

in the woods? No one was home. Why didn't he meet her in the house?"

Ray continued speaking. "We were hoping you could help us with that, Mrs. Richardson. The man said it was because Dr. Richardson didn't like her dating."

"Certainly not having a guest over when we're out of town. But if she did anyway, would it seem likely she would have met him in the woods when there was no way we'd know if she had let him inside the house? You're not making sense, gentlemen."

"Mrs. Richardson, it would appear to me she was worried that you or your husband might come back to the house. The man she was with told us that was his impression. I was wondering if you might know why she felt that might happen?"

The woman didn't respond to Ray's question. "You know who Julie said called her name, don't you?"

Ray was silent for a moment, then said, "Yes, ma'am. She told the man she was with that it was her father."

There was another period of silence, a much longer one. When the woman finally spoke, her tone was cold.

"Gentlemen, I hope you are not thinking that her father was somehow involved in her death. That would be disgusting. He might only have been her stepfather, but in the six years we've been married he couldn't have shown any more love to his own flesh and blood than he did to her."

The two brothers glanced at each other before Ray spoke again. "You're positive that your husband was in the room the whole night?"

The woman's cheeks immediately flushed red. "I have nothing further to say to you. Your questions are sickening. I can't believe you'd dare to infer something like that."

Ray shook his head. "Ma'am, we don't mean to—"

She couldn't control her anger any longer. Ramsey saw her cheek tic just before she screamed at them, "Get out! Get out of here immediately!"

CHAPTER

31

Driving away from the library, Ramsey leaned back in the LTD's passenger seat and thought for a moment, then turned to his brother. "A stepfather who's only known the girl for six years. His wife, knocked out on sleeping pills, really doesn't know whether he was in the room all night or not. It's only an hour-and-a-half drive from Vicksburg to their house. He's got to be a potential suspect now, especially with Don Wan saying the girl thought she heard her father's voice. But for some reason I just can't picture him doing it. Even if you assume a father—"

"It's happened before," Ray interjected. "Even blood fathers."

"Okay, assume he did it and you have to say it was premeditated. He waited until his wife was asleep and slipped up here and killed the girl, and then hurried back to Vicksburg. For

what reason? None of the standard motives fit—greed, jealousy, revenge."

"We don't know if they do or not. We've had no real reason
to check."

"What are you thinking might fit?"

"Nothin' in particular. But we're gonna have to start back at
the beginning now and check all the possibilities. Greed, for
example. I can tell you now we aren't gonna find that there's
been a recent big insurance policy taken out on the girl. Too
obvious. But it's the type of thing we're gonna have to check
out. There's a lot of other things we need to go back and look
over closely now. Things that weren't done before because
there was no reason to."

"You're going to think I'm crazy, Ray, but I wish you'd do a
little background on the wife, too. Something bothers me
about her; something she said or did when we were speaking
with her. Something."

Ray nodded. "Maybe it's not what she done, but what she
didn't do. Until she got upset over me asking her if she was
sure her husband was in the room all night, she was like a
piece of ice. Didn't show any emotion when she heard her
daughter hadn't been raped. That, instead, a boyfriend had
banged her in the woods. She was cool and thinking all the
time. Being careful with what she said, if you ask me."

When they arrived at the John H. Douglas State Hospital,
they were greeted by strict security precautions—a steel, hy-
draulic-controlled barricade across both the entrance and exit
lanes and three armed, uniformed men on duty inside the
small guard house between the lanes.

Since the mass breakout from unit R-14 the year before, and
shortly after that the near escape of Marcus Minnefield, the
mass murderer, several hundred thousand extra dollars had
been allocated to the security budget.

During the attempted breakout Minnefield had been killed
by the sheriff, who was a few days later killed by a former
private investigator trying to hide the tracks of a murder he

had committed. The entire sordid mess had made the national news and a movie was now being made about it.

The guard, who stepped out of the guard house to greet them, asked for their credentials despite the marked LTD. After carefully examining both ID's, the man smiled politely, stepped back, and nodded across his shoulder to the men standing inside the guard house.

The steel barricade took several seconds to rise, then Ramsey and Ray drove through.

Dr. Richardson's office was on the third floor of the administration building and he saw them immediately upon their arrival.

"My wife has informed me you are now saying a man is claiming I was there that night." The doctor's tone was sharp, and he hadn't risen when they walked into his office.

"We didn't say that," Ray said.

"Let's not stand on semantics. If he heard my voice, I was there. He didn't! Now what is it you wish to speak with me about?"

"We want you to go over what you did that night in Vicksburg."

"And I'm not going to," the doctor retorted snappily. "I'm tired of answering the same questions over and over again. I will tell you that I will be happy to submit to a polygraph. The sole condition will be that the questions are to be restricted to only whether or not I murdered my daughter. The words stick in my throat and make me nauseous, but I will do that gladly.

"However, I will only, and I repeat, *only*, submit to the exam if the murder is the only question at issue. It is the only question of any importance—if you can term such a ludicrous question important—that you would have to ask anyway.

"If that is not acceptable to you, then you will get nothing, except a lawsuit if you dare suggest to anyone that I was in any way involved with my daughter's death; even make the slightest inference. Now leave my office and don't bother me again, unless and until you're prepared to administer a polygraph under my stated terms. Good day." The doctor stood. His face was flushed, his jaw set hard. *If looks could kill*, Ramsey thought.

"Dr. Richardson," Ray said, "we're only—"

The doctor reached to the telephone on his desk and pushed a button.

His secretary's voice immediately came back through the speaker. "Yes, sir?"

"Get my attorney on the line. Immediately!"

"Yes, sir."

Walking out the front door of the administration building, Ramsey looked across his shoulder toward his brother. "Being a psychiatrist, he knows you can't run a test that restricted; can't just ask did you kill her?"

"It wasn't just an outburst on his part," Ray said. "You know his wife had to have called him as soon as we left the library. He had plenty of time to think up what he was gonna say. If I had the slightest idea what he was planning on gaining, I'd say he was setting us up to where he could claim he offered to take a polygraph." Ray paused, was silent a moment, finally said, "Why? Who would care that he offered? I'm getting more interested by the minute in the doc."

They had no sooner settled in the LTD when the voice came over the radio:

"P.D. to Unit One."

Ray reached for the mike. "Go ahead."

"Chief, mayor's looking for you. Said you were due at his office half an hour ago."

"Christ," Ray said, looking at Ramsey. "The meeting with the Chamber president. I'm in trouble again." He pressed the mike button. "Tell him I'm on my way."

After replacing the mike, he shook his head. "Free meal, too, Chamber footing the bill. President was gonna drive us over to Jackson to eat." He shook his head in disgust with himself. "I'll take you back to your car."

"Ray, if you don't mind I'm going to run on over to Dr. Keller's while you're gone. His boy still might have seen something the others didn't. And I want to know who his buddy is, too, if he has one."

"Buddy?"

"Both of the other kids say they didn't have anything to do with killing any of the animals. Both said neither one of them was even around when it took place. They blamed it all on Johnny. Remember when the tape showed that calf being killed? It's possible Johnny was alone when he shot that—there were a couple breaks in the tape and he could have been moving the camera and setting it up in a different place between each scene. But there very well could have been somebody along with him, too."

"Go ahead, but Dr. Keller's a good friend of the mayor's. This could be one of those times that if you don't do everything just right, you could cause me more trouble than I can handle."

"I'll keep it in mind."

"I'm gonna leave you my car. It'll make you look a little more official than you'd look pulling that Cadillac of yours up in Keller's driveway."

Ray reached for the car's radio. "Unit One to P.D."

"Go ahead, Chief."

"Tell the mayor my car's heating up again. We're going to have to use his if we're still planning on going to eat."

"Roger."

CHAPTER

32

Dr. Keller lived in one of the bigger houses in Belle Colline Heights, a two-story French Provincial stucco. Ramsey parked the LTD in the driveway and walked to the front door.

The man who answered the doorbell was tall and slim. He wore a smoking jacket over dark slacks and held an unlit pipe in his hand. His face was expressionless.

"Dr. Keller?"

"Yes."

"I'm Mark Ramsey, city police." He lifted his case to show the shield and his identification.

The dentist only glanced at it perfunctorily. A brief, polite smile crossed his face. "You're too late. An officer was by here; wasn't fifteen minutes ago."

"I'm not sure I know what you mean."

"You're not here to collect for the police fund?"

"No, sir."

The smile was replaced by a puzzled expression.

"Dr. Keller, there were some children camping in the park on the hill behind the Richardson girl's home the night she was murdered. We've been informed your son was one of them. With your permission, I would like to speak with him."

The thin face tightened. "Somebody's informed you wrong, Officer. I'm sorry, but Johnny wasn't anywhere that night, other than his bed in this house."

"Would you mind if I questioned him about it?"

"Officer, it's not like I don't know what I'm speaking about. I stayed up late that night; some book work I was behind on. I checked in on him before I went to bed." The man's tone was sharp.

"I'm not doubting that at all, Doctor. But I would still like an opportunity to speak with him."

Ramsey experienced the man's cold stare for a moment. Then, his rigid features softening somewhat, the dentist nodded. "Very well. If you'll wait here for a minute." The man stepped back inside his home and closed the door.

It was several minutes before Keller reopened the door. His polite smile was back.

"My attorney will be here in a few minutes. He requested you wait outside the house until he arrives." Still smiling, the dentist closed the door again.

It was a full thirty minutes before the attorney's blue Mercedes pulled into the wide driveway. It stopped next to where Ramsey was leaned back against the trunk of his brother's LTD.

"Mr. Ramsey," attorney Bennie Evans said as he came around the back of his car. "How are you doing?"

Ramsey had known who it was as soon as he saw the sleek automobile. A roly-poly, dark-haired, dark-skinned, five-six package of arrogance, the attorney was despised by most everyone who knew him. And was the first person those same people turned to when they got into legal trouble. Bennie Evans was damn good at what he did.

The attorney, his famous fixed smile on his face, held out his hand in greeting. The hand was sticky and, after shaking it, Ramsey glanced briefly at the man's old-fashioned flat-top. The black hair glistened with something.

"I'm doing fine, Bennie. You're Dr. Keller's lawyer, too, huh?" Ramsey rubbed the flat of his palm against the side of his trousers.

"Been his attorney for years. Consider him a personal friend. So you're the police officer over here wanting to speak to his son?"

"Yeah."

"Oil business that bad?" In between speaking, the smile always came back the same.

"I've been helping Ray on the murder investigation."

"What investigation, Mr. Ramsey?"

"The Richardson girl, Bennie."

"I thought that case was closed."

"It isn't."

"I see. May I see your identification, please?"

Ramsey reached into his back pocket, pulled out the case, and handed it over.

The attorney studied it closely. "The date here indicates you've been an investigator for about six months. My guess is Ray backdated it. That's assuming you started on the case right after Leigh Ann probably asked you—right after Jack was arrested. Is the backdating supposed to make it look like you're not playing cop for one specific reason?"

"Bennie, is my ID sufficient?"

"Sufficient to make you an outstanding member of your brother's little force, yes. Not sufficient to give you the right to be harassing people." The attorney handed the case back, and Ramsey looked for oily spots before returning it to his back pocket.

"I need to ask the doctor's son a couple of questions."

"Regarding what?"

"The questions are for the doctor's son."

"And I'm his attorney."

"The boy's? Does he need one?"

For a brief moment Bennie's lips curled into a genuine smile. "Not that I know of," he said, the fixed smile back in place. "What's the problem with telling me what you're wanting to speak with him about?"

"We have two witnesses who say he was camping in the park behind the Richardson house the night of the murder. I want to speak with him about that."

"That's what Dr. Keller told me over the phone. He says Johnny was home that night; doesn't really want you bothering him."

"Bennie, I'm going to speak with the boy if I have to arrest him and take him down to the station first."

The attorney's eyes narrowed. "That's a pretty threatening statement. Arrest him for what?"

"Well, for starters, I have the same two witnesses saying he has been killing animals for fun."

"You have to be kidding . . . No, you're not, are you? Wait here a minute and let me speak with the doctor and his son. I'll be right back." The attorney turned and strode toward the house. The door opened as he stepped onto the porch, and he entered the home without breaking stride.

Ramsey turned to lean against the trunk of the LTD once more.

It was at least fifteen minutes before the door to Dr. Keller's home opened once again. The attorney emerged and walked toward Ramsey.

"Are charges going to be filed regarding the alleged animal killing?" Bennie asked.

"That's not up to me."

"Well, until I know, it wouldn't be very professional of me to let you question the boy, now would it?"

"I'll give you my word I won't ask anything about that. I just want to know what he did and saw the night he camped in the park."

"I'm afraid I'm going to have to say no."

Ramsey walked around to the driver's door of the LTD and slid inside, reached for the radio microphone.

"Unit One to P.D."

"P.D., go ahead."

"Chief Hopkins still at the steak house?"

"I believe he's on the way back with the mayor."

"Can you patch me in?"

"Hang on a minute."

It was less than a minute.

"Unit One."

Ramsey lifted the mike to his mouth. "Go ahead."

"Hang on a minute, I'm patching you in. Go ahead."

"Mark?"

"Yeah, Ray. I'm over at the doctor's. He called Bennie Evans and they won't let me speak with the boy."

"Did you tell them what it was we were interested in finding out right now?"

"They're not going to let me speak with him for any reason, Ray."

"They won't, huh? Meet me up at the courthouse. I'll be there in a few minutes. We'll get a warrant and go back out and pick him up."

"A misdemeanor animal cruelty charge isn't going to bother Bennie."

"You can tell him I can promise him more than that. Might also mention to him that if we find out the kid saw anything that night and is hiding it, I'm gonna do my best to figure out a charge for that, too. Goes double for the father if he knows anything."

Ramsey smiled, wondering what the mayor must be saying to Ray now. He reached to turn the radio volume on high, glanced to each side to make sure the LTD's windows were lowered. "Will you repeat that again, Ray?"

"I said to tell Bennie if he plays games with me, his client's gonna regret it. I'll be out there with a warrant before Dr. Keller gets his son tucked in tonight."

"I thought that's what you said, Ray, thank you." He switched off the radio and turned to face the attorney who was now leaning inside the passenger window.

"Ray's tough, isn't he, Bennie?"

"That's bullshit. Borders on blackmail, too. But Dr. Keller needs to be aware of your brother's threats. I'll go inform him."

"You do that, Bennie."

After twenty minutes of waiting, Ramsey reached inside the LTD and flicked the siren switch, let the shrill whine fill the air for several seconds before switching it off.

The home's front door opened.

"Just a minute, please!" the attorney shouted.

Fifteen more minutes passed before Bennie and the dentist emerged and walked toward the LTD.

"Dr. Keller would like to speak with you."

"Sure."

"Mr. Ramsey, my son says he was camping that night. His room was dark when I looked inside. I guess I was mistaken in what I thought I saw. I don't want you to think I would have intentionally mislead you. I have a reputation to uphold in this town."

"Yessir, and now can I speak with your son?"

The attorney answered. "The boy might have seen someone there that night; and might can identify him. But with an animal cruelty charge hanging over his head I'm afraid I need to be speaking with the D.A. instead of you; try and see if I can work out some kind of trade that will resolve this situation amicably."

"If he saw Donald Kennedy; that's not news."

The attorney smiled and shook his head. "I don't have the slightest idea who you're referring to."

"Who are you talking about, then?"

"I think it's time for us to go see the D.A," the attorney said.

When Ramsey drove the LTD up to the front of the police department, Ray and Sheriff Toney were standing outside waiting.

Ramsey smiled as he walked up to his brother. "Didn't get the mayor upset, did I, Ray?"

"Like you give a damn. But, no. He's a big-time pet lover. Told me to let him know how this goes tonight."

In a few minutes the blue Mercedes with Bennie and Dr. Keller inside arrived. They all walked into the building together. District Attorney Warren James, a tall, slim man who had done poorly in private practice but found his niche in politics, was already inside.

Everybody shook hands all around and then, after pointing the dentist and his attorney to the conference room where they would meet, the D.A. turned back to the others.

"I need to have an initial conference with Dr. Keller and Bennie to see what they're offering, and in exchange for what. It shouldn't take but a couple of minutes. If you gentlemen don't mind waiting, I might need to ask you something."

"We'll be right here," Ray said. "Oh, yeah, Warren, Mark and I think there might've been two kids involved when the video tape I told you about was being made. The other two boys we talked to say they didn't have anything to do with it. I believe them. See if you can get the kid to say if anybody was with him."

James nodded. "I shouldn't be but a couple of minutes," he repeated.

A full thirty minutes passed. When James finally did walk back into Ray's office, his expression was somber. "I'm going to have to call the judge down here and see if I can't work out some kind of deal. The kid saw somebody."

Ramsey looked toward his brother. "Did you tell the D.A. about Kennedy?"

Ray nodded.

The district attorney shook his head. "It's not him. It's somebody else."

CHAPTER

33

It had grown dark by the time the conference between the judge, District Attorney Warren James, Dr. Keller, and his attorney Bennie Evans had ended, and the sheriff, Ray, and Ramsey were invited into the room. Dr. Keller had already left.

"He's gone to get his son," the D.A. said.

It was nearly an hour before the pair returned. The boy stepped into the conference room with his eyes cast down at the floor. His father followed him inside.

"Johnny," the D.A. said, "I'm District Attorney Warren James. This is Sheriff Toney, Police Chief Hopkins, and . . . Officer Mark Ramsey. They're going to be sitting in while you give your statement. The lady at the end of the table is a stenographer. When you have finished with what you have to say, she will prepare a transcript for you to look over and see if there is anything you might have left out. We've spoken with the judge. He's agreed that in exchange for your telling us everything you witnessed the night the Richardson girl was murdered, you won't be prosecuted for your actions in regard to the animals. Do you understand this?"

"Yes, sir."

When Johnny lowered his face again, Ramsey saw the slight smile that flitted across the fifteen-year-old's lips.

James turned toward the boy's attorney. "Are we ready to start now, Bennie?"

"Whenever you are. I—" The attorney stopped, his face tightening. He stared at the boy a moment and then looked at his father. "Dr. Keller. I'd like to speak to you and Johnny outside for just a minute. If you other gentlemen will excuse us for just a moment." He turned and walked toward the office door. The dentist and his son followed.

A few minutes later, when the three walked back through the doorway, Bennie had a relaxed smile on his face. But the dentist's cheeks were noticeably red.

Ramsey guessed what had transpired. Bennie, his mind occupied with making positive the agreement with the judge protected the boy as to anything he might have done to the animals, had not thought to ask Johnny if he had anything to do with killing Julie. That Bennie had suddenly decided it would be prudent to ask, showed he held the boy's character in the same regard as Ramsey did.

The attorney directed the boy to a chair at the table, and then seated himself. Pulling a tape recorder from an inside coat pocket, he switched the machine on and sat it upright on the table. District Attorney James turned on his recorder, then addressed the boy:

"Begin when you arrived at the park that night, Johnny. Take your time and don't leave anything out, whether you think it important or not. We'll be the judge of that."

The father's cheeks continued to glow.

Nothing Johnny would say could ever be used in court against him. Ramsey hated that the boy was now so lightly being taken off the hook for his cruelty. He would especially hate it if nothing concrete came out of the information the boy was going to give. Johnny had obviously been the leader and instigator of everything the kids had done; the most guilty of them all. Yet, having had the agreement completely explained to him by his attorney, he now sat straight in his chair, cocky. He looked directly from one set of eyes to the other as he began speaking. Ramsey shook his head, noting as he did Johnny staring at him. The corners of the boy's lips flicked up into a half smile. The youngster was enjoying his mastery of the situation.

Johnny said nothing Ramsey had not already heard until the boy reached the point in his statement where he left Hal on the logging road.

"I went back down in the woods. They had come out of the sinkhole and were at the edge of the trees. They were making out again. Then they stopped and got up, and started talking. I couldn't hear what they were saying because the wind was blowing so hard. They started getting dressed and then the guy started into the woods. He was coming toward me and I had to hurry back up the hill. I hid behind some bushes until he went past. Then I went back down the hill. I got mixed up coming down. It's easy to do in those trees at night. I came out a couple of houses down from hers on the other side of that old black guy's house. A dog started barking and I moved back up the hill a little ways and cut over and came down to the edge of the girl's yard. I saw a light on in one of the downstairs rooms. So I went and looked in the window."

The footprints in the flower bed. Johnny was not quite as tall as Jack, but the boy's feet were big. At this thought, Ramsey glanced at his brother and saw Ray returning the look. They nodded at each other.

"Then there was this man walking fast toward me. I just happened to look over my shoulder and saw him coming. I started to run. But then I saw he was going on past me and I just stood there behind the hedges without moving. It was her father and—"

District Attorney James interrupted the boy. "You're absolutely sure?"

Everyone in the room was staring intently at Johnny.

"Yeah, positive."

"Wasn't it stormy and dark that night?"

"No, sir. Not then. There had been a shower just before that, but it had cleared off. The moonlight was real bright right then. It was easy to see."

"And you knew the doctor well enough to be certain of who it was?"

"Sure. I've mowed his yard several times."

Mowed his yard! Johnny was the boy Leigh Ann had handed the glass of tea to. Ramsey remembered the face now. He had only half noticed him at the time.

"He went on past me and around the side of the house and past the house next door. I stayed behind the bushes for a pretty good while. When I was sure he left I started back toward—"

Ramsey interrupted without thinking. "Where was his car?"

The boy looked at him. "How am I supposed to know something like that?"

"Did you hear a car motor?"

"It was storming."

"I thought you said it had quit?"

"Quit raining—it was still thundering."

"Did you see any headlights?"

"No."

"You're positive?"

"Yeah, I'm positive. There had been a car earlier—leaving Mrs. Mueller's house. I didn't see one after that. There wasn't one."

"Let the boy finish with what he was telling us," the D.A. said.

Johnny stared for a moment at Ramsey, then turned back to face the D.A. "When I started back toward the park I found the girl. She was lying there on her back, dead."

Ramsey was wondering something else. "How did you know she was dead?"

"He'd stabbed her, she was bleeding, lying still; she was dead."

"Are you sure?"

"Yeah, I'm sure."

"How are you sure? Did you listen to her heart, feel her pulse?"

The father stood. "What is this?"

"Sit down, Dr. Keller," the district attorney said. "Mr. Ramsey, please leave the questioning to me."

"Okay, Warren, ask the boy if he touched the girl." *Her T-shirt had been rearranged after she was dead—or while she was dying.* Ramsey stared hard at the boy.

The D.A. was glaring, and Ramsey didn't care. "Well, did you? Did you touch her?"

Ray turned toward his brother. "Drop it, Mark."

The father was red-faced, staring, his lips moving silently.

The boy boldly continued to return Ramsey's stare.

The district attorney stood. "The judge's order makes Johnny available to us whenever we want to question him. We can get into more detail later. Right now I think it's time to pick Dr. Richardson up. Sheriff."

Toney shook his head. "I think this one ought to be Ray and Mark's," he said.

District Attorney James nodded. "I'll have the warrant back here in a few minutes."

Thirty minutes later, Ray guided his LTD to a stop in Dr. Richardson's driveway. At the same time Sheriff Toney and one of his deputies parked their cruiser at the curb in front of the home. There was also an arrest warrant for Dr. Richardson's wife. She was being charged with obstructing justice by giving a false alibi.

"Have you got your pistol on you?" Ray asked.

Ramsey shook his head. Ray leaned over to the glove compartment, took out the revolver inside, and handed it to his brother.

"I'm gonna let you take the lead on this, Mark. You're the one who got us here."

"That little bastard molested her after she was dead, Ray. I can feel it. I'd bet my life on it."

"If he did, there's nothin' you can do about it. Get it out of your mind. Main thing is who killed her."

"Okay, so let's make an arrest." He reached for the door handle.

Crossing the yard, he saw the second-floor hall light shining through the glass door of the upstairs balcony. The first floor was dark.

At the front door, Ray stepped to the left side and Ramsey moved to the right.

They both heard the loud scream from inside the house.

Ramsey glanced at his brother, then reached for the door-knob. The door was unlocked. He pushed it open and leaned around the facing. There was a dim light coming from a table lamp in the living room. Holding his revolver in front of him, he stepped inside the house. A male voice cursed loudly in the living room. Ramsey hurried across the foyer.

Mrs. Richardson, holding her hands protectively in front of her face, lay on the couch. Dr. Richardson, his fists clenched and his face twisted in rage, stood over her. Then, seeming to sense the presence of the two brothers, he raised his eyes toward the foyer.

Mrs. Richardson glanced in the direction her husband was staring. She scrambled to her feet and ran toward them.

"IT WAS HIM!" she screamed hysterically.

CHAPTER

34

Ray was shaking his head when he walked through the doorway into the small lounge of the police station. He had a cigar clamped in his teeth. He pulled a seat from under the metal table and sat. "I don't know. Hell, I just don't know. The wife's story seemed to wrap it all up. Then Richardson's attorney presented a written statement from the doctor denying it all—sounded convincing, too."

Ramsey frowned and shook his head impatiently. "What?"

He had been waiting in the lounge for better than two hours. District Attorney James, already fearful of what Richardson's attorney was going to try and make out of Ramsey's involvement in the murder investigation when the case went before a jury, had asked him to wait in the lounge. So he had sat there the entire time the others had listened to the woman's story. He didn't know that the doctor had also given a statement.

Ray lit his cigar before he spoke again. "If the doctor is the killer, the credit belongs to you. If you hadn't kept at it, unraveling everything piece by piece, we'd never got to the point where we told Mrs. Richardson that Julie thought she heard her father's voice. She took it from there."

"She wasn't involved then?"

Ray shook his head. "No, she wasn't. Her husband fed her a story he knew she'd believe based on what she knew about his background. What's that child-molesting word he called Jack?"

"Pedophile?"

"Yeah, he was somethin' like that himself, I guess. And had a temper to go with it. His wife used to be his nurse. She said that several years ago, before they got married, a teenager he was treating made a pass at him and he accepted, got her pregnant. The girl threatened him; wanted abortion money and a lot more, too. He lost his temper and ended up beating hell out of her.

"She brought assault charges against him. Don't know what it cost him, but the charges were eventually dropped. But dropped or not, somewhere in New York there's the case file that shows our good doctor not only was capable of messing around with underage girls, but that he was capable of violence against them, too. The wife knowing about the file, she wasn't surprised when he told her she needed to tell everybody that he was with her all night in Vicksburg . . ."

"To forestall any detailed checking into his past."

"Right. People previously involved in sex crimes are gonna get pulled in and questioned anytime something like that comes up in their area. Civil liberties people don't like it, but if you've done something like that once, you're going to be a prime suspect forever. That's true in every police department in the nation. Doc would've known that. Wouldn't be at all surprised if that's why he's moved around so much—trying to shake off anybody knowing where he's at."

"Where did his wife think he was?"

"Thought he'd gone to Memphis. When they were in Vicksburg they sent a couple of antique chairs back to Memphis to be refinished by a guy whose work they liked. After they moved over here, they decided to redo their house before they brought the chairs back; also left some more of their furniture stored in Vicksburg.

"They'd just finished with the house and went that day to get the stuff. Next time he had a chance to take off, they were gonna go after the pieces in Memphis. When they got back to the motel in Vicksburg that night, he told her he really couldn't afford to be taking off so much. Told her that he had decided to drive up to Memphis right then and pick the chairs up; get it all over with. So he did, or so she thought.

"He pulled in the next morning unshaven, worn out, and irritated; especially irritated, she remembers. But the furniture didn't have bugs on it, and that's what she'd been worried about."

"What in the hell are you talking about?"

Ray smiled. "Turns out our wife is a thinker. After her husband left she got worried about bugs getting on the chairs. He was taking 61 up the river to Memphis, gonna pick up the two chairs and come back the same way with 'em. They were big, fancy chairs. It was obvious he could only get one in the trunk. The other was gonna have to ride tied down on top of the car.

"Him being a man, she knew he probably wouldn't even think about what bugs splattering on the material would do to the chairs. August, driving down 61 along the Mississippi River, bugs splattering on your windshield get so bad you can't see without turning on your windshield wipers. When he got back that morning, she was relieved to see he did think of it, had visquene wrapped around the chair.

"Then she noticed there were almost no bugs on the visquene. Just a passing observation at the time, didn't make anything of it. Finding her daughter murdered when she got back over here, the lack of bugs on the visquene was the furtherest thing from her thoughts. Until a couple of days ago. It popped in her mind then that he might not have gone to Memphis.

"Nothin' to do with her daughter's death, mind you. No, that didn't even occur to her. She was thinking about another woman.

"She called the man in Memphis; the one who had finished and stored the chairs for 'em. He told her the doctor had picked up the chairs a few weeks before, when he had been at a convention there.

"She knew then that the chairs probably had been stored in Vicksburg ever since. That he had used going after 'em as a reason to have eight or nine hours someplace else. Remember, she's the one that took him away from his first wife. At the same time she was doing that, he was also knocking up a patient. She knew his appetite. There wasn't any doubt in her mind he had met with a woman that night. But who? His not wanting her to tell the police he was gone from the motel made even more sense then. Not only to hide his background, but to keep from having to prove where he really was, expose to her that he was with another woman.

"With her daughter's death she just wasn't up to confronting him right then, so she didn't say anything. Then we came by and told her about her daughter thinking she heard her father's voice. Started asking questions about her husband. We were obviously only interested in her daughter's murder, could care less about his steppin' out. That made her start wondering what we were getting at; what we did know. Of course we didn't know anything. But she became convinced we did.

"Her mind got to churning. She thought about her first husband—Julie's real father. She divorced him after she caught him molesting Julie when the girl was just a small child, only in the third grade.

"Thinking back to that incident, the possibility of what might have been going on between the doctor and her daughter hit her like a ton of bricks. Other things that had happened started making sense to her.

"She remembered back to a scene when the doctor and her daughter had engaged in an argument in the backyard. It had gotten so out of hand the doctor had slapped the girl and she had slapped back. When the wife ran outside, neither of them would say what the argument had been over; wouldn't even discuss it with her. Then the next day her husband bought the girl the diamond watch band I told you about being on her body—cost eleven hundred dollars. The mother got to thinking it might have been a bribe, to keep the girl from telling on him.

"Next thing that went through her mind was how strict her husband was in his limiting the girl's dating. He had explained to his wife that after suffering the experience she did at the hands of her father, the girl needed to be carefully protected. He said if she was exposed to young boys' crude groping attempts at sex, there was a real possibility the girl might be driven in either of two ways, both bad—to becoming a slut, or to becoming so distrusting of males she would not ever be able to enjoy a normal heterosexual relationship again. He said he had seen such reactions before. The wife said she didn't like the restrictions on her daughter, but she went along with it because he was a psychiatrist and she believed him.

"But now, with her fears growing about her husband's real motive, thinking back to what her first husband had done, she saw the doctor's strictness in a different light—jealousy. She was about to go out of her mind with her fear building each time she thought of somethin' else. His strictness—jealousy. His sexual appetite—married, dating her behind his first wife's back and getting a teenage patient pregnant all at the same time.

"The wife couldn't stand thinking about it anymore. She confronted him with it. There was no way she could be sure, she told us. Said if he'd just denied it, that probably would've been the end of it.

"But he didn't. He just up and admitted it. He admitted all of it, from when he started molesting her daughter a year after they had been married right up to getting the kid pregnant. Then, being afraid the girl was gonna tell on him, he planned it all out and came back that night and killed her. That's when the wife said she told him she was gonna go to the police and he started beating her; told her he was gonna kill her, too."

Ramsey shook his head. "Wait a minute, Ray. I can go along with everything else, but he didn't tell her he killed the girl; didn't tell a woman he had killed her daughter. No, no way he did that."

"Why not? If she was mad at him over molesting the girl, gonna go to the police, he could see he was in big trouble. If he wanted to scare her into being quiet, what better way than tell her he'd already killed her daughter, and if she said anything she'd be next."

Ramsey shook his head again. "I could even see him killing his wife to keep her quiet. But not telling her he killed her daughter and expect her not to do anything about it. No, I don't believe it."

"He knew how she'd react better than we do."

"What does James think, Ray?"

"He's got a witness that says she heard a confession. He's gonna bring murder charges."

"I said, what does he think?"

Ray shrugged. "Who knows?"

"What do you think?"

"If I was the doctor, I'd of never admitted killin' the girl. But I'm not him. And I've seen some real strange happenings in my years in this kinda work. Besides, taking what our old friend Don Wan said and adding it to Johnny's story, it makes sense that the killer would've been someone who lived right close to where the girl's body was found."

"Explain."

"Okay. Between the time Don Wan left and Johnny saw the doctor, couldn't have been over ten, fifteen minutes at the most. She had to have been killed within that span of time. You know somebody didn't just come running up out of the blue and stab her. Whoever it was had to come up on her, talk or argue at least for a little while, then kill her, then get gone— all before Johnny was back down the hill where he could see who it was. To do all that and get gone without being seen—

going quickly back into a nearby house seems awful logical to me. The three closest houses to where her body was found were her own home, the old retired colonel's home, and Jack and Leigh Ann's. Considering the colonel's confined to a wheelchair, he's not much of a suspect if you're looking for somebody able to move fast. That leaves the doctor or his wife, and Jack and Leigh Ann—" He smiled. "And Jack was gone in his car."

"Come on, Ray."

"Thought that'd get a rise out of you. You see my point, though—doctor's a reasonable bet, or else there was somebody who oughta be running track who was out there."

"What does the doctor say?"

"He said he didn't do it. What would you expect him to say?"

"I mean the details. You said his attorney let him make a statement."

"In a nutshell, he said that soon after he married the woman, Julie made a pass at him and he realized her real father's molesting had warped her sexually; made her promiscuous. Said that he had been trying to help her ever since, but wasn't getting much results. Said he had even tried to bribe her to get her to behave—said that's what the watch he gave her was for, she'd begged for it for a long time.

"He said that when the girl didn't want to go to Vicksburg he had a good idea of what she had planned. He even told his wife what he thought the girl was planning and the wife got hot, said she was sick of him always suspecting the girl. He said they constantly argued over that—the wife refusing to accept the fact that her daughter had a problem.

"During the convention he had already picked up the two chairs in Memphis, dropped them off in Vicksburg because the house wasn't ready yet. Hadn't thought to mention it to his wife. Decided to use the excuse of saying he was gonna go after the chairs so that his wife wouldn't know he was going back to the house.

"He says he was coming back to catch the girl screwin'

around, that's all—he was going to put a stop to it once and for all. At least have absolute proof he could tell his wife. But after the girl was murdered, he was afraid to admit he came back; even to his wife. Then, when she started questioning him about the girl, he decided to tell her he had gone back to the house, and why.

"But she didn't believe him. He said she went crazy, accused him of going back to the house to molest the girl; said he had been doing it all along. He says she's made up the whole story of his confessing to punish him. He admits he was in the house and admits he walked past the back corner of the house like the Keller kid said, but insists he was coming from inside the house, not from the park. That's it, according to him."

Ramsey shook his head. "Drive back fifty miles to catch her meeting a boy?" He shook his head again. "Maybe drive back if he was molesting her, planned on spending the night with her. No, I don't believe his story, either."

"We're in agreement there, little brother, and neither does the D.A."

"Who's representing Mrs. Richardson?"

"Attorney out of the Wilkinson firm in Jackson, and good."

"Will he let her undergo a polygraph."

"D.A. asked. Her attorney wants to give her a couple of days to get her wits back together, and then he'll let us know."

"After she takes a private test and her attorney knows whether she's telling the truth or not."

Ray shook his head. "No, I don't think so. James is gonna drop the obstruction charge against her in exchange for her testimony against her husband. She wouldn't have anything to gain by submitting to a polygraph. Even if she's telling the truth, why take a chance her responses might not look good on the machine, maybe lose her deal with James?"

Ramsey shook his head. "Ray, we're not ever going to know for sure whether he killed the girl or not."

"Twelve people are gonna claim they do."

CHAPTER

35

Eddie Tullos cut back on the small outboard motor's throttle and his fourteen-foot flat-bottom aluminum boat glided to a stop a few hundred feet off the Hinds County shoreline of the Ross Barnett Reservoir—the nearly twenty-mile-long, thirty-three-thousand-acre lake that the City of Jackson draws on for its water supply.

Tullos looked once again to an ancient oak sitting on the nearby shore and back over his shoulder to a pair of man-made landmarks rising from the Rankin County side of the lake. The boat was perfectly triangulated. He nodded toward the bow of the craft and Joe Bob Mitchell, unsteady with the weight of the single scuba tank on his back, rose to his feet and donned his face mask.

The two were catfish grabbing. It was now Joe Bob's job to dive and examine their fish houses—the cypress boxes they had strategically submerged along the reservoir's bottom in order to entice the big yellow flathead common to those waters. Seven of the fish, ranging in size from twenty to thirty pounds, already lay in the bottom of the boat and the two men still had four houses yet to run.

Joe Bob, the end of a long rope in one of his gloved hands, a six-foot-long piece of metal conduit in the other, closed his lips over his mouthpiece and stepped out into the warm water.

The visibility didn't improve when the bubbles formed by his entry into the water dissipated; he could barely see three inches in front of his face. But that didn't surprise him. He had been in the reservoir's silt-laden waters before when the only way he could distinguish his fingers was to press them against his face mask.

The water only a few feet deep, his flipper-covered feet almost immediately touched the sandy bottom. A couple of gliding steps and his leg bumped into the box he would check.

Built from rough-cut one-by-ten planks, the narrow, nine-foot-long traps had only a single opening, a circle approximately twenty inches in diamater at one end of the structures. It was the perfect spawning den for the mating catfish. And it was surprising the size of the fish that could make their way into the boxes' entrances. Joe Bob had once squirmed from one of the houses, a four-foot-long, sixty-pound cat, three inches wider than the entrance it had come through.

Sitting down on the sandy bottom, Joe Bob slid his legs into the trap's opening, then probed inside it with the barbed-wire-tipped piece of conduit. Immediately a large catfish slammed into his stomach.

Joe Bob raised his knees and trapped the wriggling fish against the bottom of the box, then stuck his hand inside the gaping mouth and threaded the end of the rope through the gills.

Before tying the rope off, he was careful to take up all its slack, pulling down hard on the float attached to it. When he leaned back to let the fish swim out of the box, he wanted to be positive that the rising force of the float would pull the creature away, unable to come back to him. If it had a mate still trapped inside the box, that would be what it would try to do. Joe Bob had once seen a man with most of the skin missing from one side of his face where a cat had come back to try and rescue its mate.

Leaning back and letting the captured fish move past him and be pulled toward the surface, Joe Bob experienced a light touch at the top of his scalp. He flinched and raised his forearm in protection. But he wasn't touched again. A swipe of the fish's tail as it rose past him, he decided.

He probed inside the box once more, but received no response. Leaning back to push himself out of the box, he again felt fleeting pressure on his scalp. Forehead wrinkling in puzzlement inside his face mask, he raised his hand to investigate. He felt something like seaweed—except the freshwater Ross Barnett Reservoir didn't have seaweed.

Grasping a handful of the fine material, he pulled it down to press it against the front of his mask. It looked more like hair than seaweed—long blond hair. He quickly leaned back his head to glance above him and a face pressed against the outside of his mask, wide eyes staring back into his.

In the boat above, Eddie Tullos's attention was drawn to the sudden rush of air bubbling up beside the boat. An instant later Joe Bob burst to the surface, coming a full half of his length out of the water before crashing back into it and grabbing frantically at the side of the boat.

In less than two hours a search and rescue team from the Reservoir Volunteer Fire Department was back at the scene. Using the big treble hooks kept on board to drag for drowning victims, they snagged not one, but two bodies. It took a strong effort to pull the corpses to the surface, both of them being wrapped in barbed wire, the wire in turn anchored to cement building blocks.

The first thing noticed by the two firemen who managed to cut the barbed wire and lift the bodies into the craft, were the multiple stab wounds. Then they saw that each woman was covered with numerous bite marks.

* * *

A little over two hours later Ramsey stood in the Davis County Morgue, his eyes intent on Betty Amis's niece, Karen. She had accompanied the medical examiner to the far side of the building and was waiting for him to pull back the sheet from the body lying on the stainless-steel gurney.

"Okay?" Ramsey heard the doctor ask the niece, and she nodded. The sheet came back. Karen's hands flew to her face and she screamed.

The two police officers who had accompanied her to the morgue helped turn her around and led her toward the door at the far end of the building. The doctor, a large, ponderously built man wearing a gray knee-length surgical gown, looked after them for a moment, then turned back to the gurney, replaced the sheet, and rolled the stainless-steel table into the refrigeration unit, closed the door. He motioned to Ray and Ramsey and they moved across the tile floor toward him.

"Sorry to make you wait," he said as Ray and Ramsey walked up to the opposite side of the dissecting table he had moved to. "Had to get that ID out of the way first."

"Dr. Petrie, this is my brother, Mark Ramsey."

The doctor nodded his greeting, then reached down through the neck of his gown to produce the largest cigar Ramsey had ever seen. He clamped it in his teeth and lit it before turning his attention to the body lying between them.

"Cause of death in each case was the stab wounds," he explained. He pulled the sheet back.

Mary Lou Bickerstaff's pale and swollen body lay on its back. Only her head, propped up by means of a T-shaped plastic device placed under her neck, didn't rest against the table's stainless-steel surface. Her eyes were open, their pupils dilated and fixed. There was a noticeable stench. Dr. Petrie was puffing hard on his cigar, the acrid blue-gray smoke swirling about his face and curling up into his nostrils.

He pointed to a wound on the left side of Mary Lou's neck. "Here," he said, and then repeated, "and here" as he pointed to a second wound at the top of the right shoulder.

He pointed to a third puncture. "Wounds were all made by the same weapon; a knife with an unusually narrow, thin blade —like a stiletto, nothing like the kind of wide, thick-bladed weapon you say was used on the Richardson girl. But that's not why I told you I didn't think whoever killed these two women was the same one who killed her. I'm basing that opinion on the bite marks." He pointed to the ugly bruise on Mary Lou's left cheek, the imprints of the teeth clearly visible.

He moved his finger down the body, always keeping his gloveless hand a couple of inches from touching it. "Here, here, and here—bit her seven times altogether. There's eleven places on the other one. Whoever did this gets his kicks by biting. The Richardson girl wasn't bitten a single time. That leads me to believe that you're dealing with two different killers."

He reached to the side of his mouth and removed the cigar, thumped it, letting the long gray ash drop to the tile floor. "Why are you so interested in the comparisons between this case and the Richardson girl's anyway? Her father starting to fall through the cracks?"

"Might be," Ray answered. "His attorney says he's passed a polygraph. It was done by a private firm, but they're willing for the D.A. to administer one now."

Dr. Petrie nodded. "So what's the D.A. thinking?"

Ray shook his head. "Don't know exactly. He can't be as sure as he was before the offer to take a polygraph. But I imagine he's still leaning toward prosecution. The county's up in arms what with most of 'em already decided he molested the girl, at least."

Dr. Petrie nodded. "Well, nothing's for certain when you're dealing with someone crazy enough to commit murder, but, like I said, I would be surprised if it turns out that whoever killed the Richardson girl was the same guy who got hold of these two women. My opinion is you're dealing with two different killers. In fact, I'd bet on it."

CHAPTER

36

Inside the cramped working quarters of his drilling company's portable house trailer, Ramsey was standing at a desk speaking on the telephone with Leigh Ann. She had called because she had heard a rumor that the district attorney had offered to accept a plea bargain of second-degree murder from Dr. Richardson.

Ramsey shook his head. "Even if Richardson's guilty I don't think his attorney will go for it. Quite frankly, the only thing the D.A. has going for himself now is that the lie detector test the doctor took isn't admissible. That, and the fact there are a lot of people living in this county who think Richardson at least molested the girl and needs to pay for that—whether he did or not."

"You said 'even if he is guilty,' Mark. You don't think he is?"

"I don't know. But I don't believe he told his wife he killed the girl. That's just not what someone would confess to. And with his wife now having admitted she tried to kill him, I think whatever chance there was of the jury believing her about him saying he did, is gone, too."

"What do you mean, tried to kill him?"

"She came after him with a butcher knife. That's why he had hit her just before we got there."

"You didn't say anything about that before."

"Didn't know. Doctor didn't say anything about it until his attorney announced it yesterday to the reporters. Ray thought it was just some kind of bull. Then last night the wife admitted to it; said she went after him with the knife after he confessed to molesting the girl. He still claims he didn't admit anything, that the wife was just so sure he had done the molesting that she went crazy, tried to kill him, will do anything to see him dead—including lie about his confessing.

"Stop and think about it, Leigh Ann. Whether or not he actually molested the girl, if the wife was sure enough in her own mind that he did—sure enough to the point that she tried to kill him—then she certainly isn't above lying, above doing anything to see him punished. You can bet Richardson's attorney will make that point clear to the jury. Then all the D.A.'s going to have left is Johnny saying he saw Richardson leaving the house. The man's already admitted to that and gave his reason for it. It's to the point now I wouldn't want to bet on a conviction short of them finding the murder weapon with the doctor's fingerprints on it."

"What good would even that do?" Leigh Ann asked. "You said all the police know is that it was a wide-bladed knife, like a hunting knife—lots of people have them. I don't see how his owning one would make any difference—unless it still had her blood on it. You know that's not going to be the case."

"It was more than just a hunting knife, Leigh Ann. It had an abnormality—the tip broken off. The forensic lab made an impression of the blunt end where it lodged in a bone. If they ever find the knife it'll be easy to prove it's the right one. But Richardson's house has been searched twice now and, like he's said from the first, there wasn't a hunting knife of any kind in the house—nothing that thick and wide-bladed."

"What you're really telling me," she said, "is not that he might get off, but that you think he will. That's just not right. I—" She sighed in disgust. "This thing has been all mixed up since it began, and now—I don't want to talk about it anymore. It's depressing. What else can we—How does your well look?"

"You could have found a better subject than that if you were trying to lighten up the conversation. I thought by now we'd already be in the formation we were after. But we're not. That means what we're looking for is deeper than we thought, and that's bad—less chance now of it being productive when we do get into it. Of course that comes as no surprise. We've had more go wrong with this hole than any we've ever drilled."

Robert, his short, stocky body dressed in mud-stained overalls, looked across his shoulder from where he stood at the far side of the trailer monitoring a bank of drilling instruments. He gave a sarcastic chuckle. "What do you mean, *we*, Mark? When have you been out here?"

"What did Robert say?" Leigh Ann asked.

"Just being his usual smart-ass self. We'll know what we have, if anything, pretty soon. One way or the other it'll all be over in the next twenty-four hours." He glanced at his watch. "There's nothing much I can do here for a the next few hours but stand around and wait. You too tired to catch a midnight breakfast somewhere?"

"I'm starved."

"I need to look at some of the tailings we've drilled out first. It could be another hour or so before I can get loose. That too late?"

"I'll be waiting."

He switched off the cellular phone and stepped across the trailer to look down at the chromatograph, the instrument recording the drill bit's rate of penetration.

Robert shook his head. "We're almost at planned total

depth. We going to hang it up or go a little deeper if we're not in the formation by then?"

Ramsey knew he had been asked a question, but *what* hadn't really registered. He was thinking about something else. He raised his face to his geologist.

"I'm going to pass on looking at those tailings for right now. Going to run on out to Leigh Ann's. Maybe I can get her to come back to the house with me after we eat. It keeps bothering me that the Keller kid was over there mowing her yard—volunteered. That little bastard hasn't got a charitable bone in his body. And he's still the only one we know for sure was around Julie that night. He gives me the creeps."

"You believe there's any chance he could have been the one who killed Julie?"

"I wish they'd give him a polygraph, but that's not going to happen. First of all, what he claims has been corroberated by the doctor himself—that he was at the house. Second, Bennie never has let a client take a polygraph. He says they're too easy to read wrong. But all I know is that until a little more is settled I don't like Leigh Ann even being in the same neighborhood with the kid."

Robert shook his head. "If it was me staying over at that house alone, you wouldn't have to ask me to go home with you more than once. And not just because of that kid. Her husband committed suicide; her next-door neighbor might have killed his own daughter; and then his wife tried to kill him. Bunch of weird area kids killed her dog. Jesus, you couldn't tie me up tight enough to keep me in that neighborhood at night, much less her house; not if you gave me a pack of guard dogs."

Ramsey nodded, sat silently for a moment, then picked up the telephone directory and looked in the Jackson residential section for Dr. Roosevelt Jones's number, found it, and punched it into the telephone.

The doctor answered on the first ring.

"Dr. Jones, this is Mark Ramsey. Sorry to bother you so late."

"You didn't awaken me. What can I do for you?"

"Are you aware of the tape we found—the one taken by the children who killed several animals?"

"Yes. Chief Hopkins called earlier tonight about it."

Ramsey smiled and shook his head. His brother had probably already asked what he was about to. "There were also two women from this county whose bodies were found in the reservoir. They had been murdered and had numerous bite marks on them."

"Yes. Chief Hopkins said as much. If you are asking my expert opinion in the same field you questioned me about earlier, I would say almost categorically that there is no chance that any kind of cult practitioners—these children you refer to or otherwise—had anything to do with the murder of the two women. Even if you were referring to hard-core members of the worst kind of deviant, twisted cults, even then the murders would not have been committed in the fashion they were. A murder committed by such a group would have at the very least been done in some kind of ritualistic fashion, body parts excised or blood drained—for some black magic purpose, not just a brutal murder committed apparently for no other reason than the satisfying of a blood lust.

"In the simplest terms possible, it is my opinion that what you are faced with in Davis County is an old-fashioned everyday maniac, a particularly frenzied one judging by the repetitive stab wounds, and one sexually driven—the bite marks are a certain sign of that. Future victims might be sexually abused in a variety of ways, by rape or some other method—whatever the killer is obsessed with at the time of the attack. But they will almost without exception be bitten—it's what a biter does when he's turned on.

"Now having established the type of killer you are facing, we can go a couple of steps further. This can be the first time this particular person has ever killed anyone or he can be an old hand at it.

"If it is his first killing he could be so shocked at the aftermath of what he wrought that he never repeats it again. I wouldn't count on that happening.

"Second, the killer could be a repetitive type—a serial murderer if you like—but one who can control himself for long periods of time, and it might be months or even years until he strikes again.

"Finally—and I would say this the most likely scenario given the fact that he killed two women at the same time and did so with such brutal frenzy—he will turn out to be the type of killer who for a short time strikes with great frequency.

"I say for a short time because such a killer is almost always quickly apprehended. He is too far out of control to be prudent, think much about his being caught, only reacts to whatever stimuli that triggers him.

"His next attack might be when the moon is the same as it was during his first attack, or the weather similar, or maybe simply when he observes somebody who gives rise to his sexual frenzy.

"His next attack might occur in a place as far distant as another section of the country or as close by as in the same neighborhood these women occupied. There have even been cases of such frenzy-driven killers striking the same family twice at separate times in the same home."

CHAPTER

37

After finishing her telephone conversation with Ramsey, Leigh Ann, a reflective expression across her face, remained seated in her easy chair for a few moments before finally rising to her feet and walking from the living room to her bedroom.

The eyes that had been peering through the window behind the chair moved with her.

In the bedroom, she sat down in front of her dressing table and slipped off her shoes. Standing, she unzipped her skirt and let it drop to the floor. She unbuttoned and removed her blouse. Glancing into her dresser mirror, she noticed the reflection of the big French doors across the room.

She walked to the doors and pulled their curtains. Unhooking her bra, she dropped it on the bed, then moved into her closet to select what she would wear when she went with Ramsey to eat.

Johnny, dressed in blue jeans and a dark sweatshirt, and wearing surgical gloves and a ski mask with eye and mouth openings, stepped away from the French doors and walked silently around the house.

In the shadows at a front corner of the house, he leaned forward and peered toward the front door. None of the outside fixtures were on, but the light from the streetlamps lit the front of the house well. It would be easy to be seen. But there was nobody to look.

The garage of the home at the end of the cul-de-sac was empty. The home directly across the street was the vacant Younger place.

A dining-room light glowed from the interior of the house catty-cornered across the street. But the son's car was gone and the woman was always in bed by nine.

The people who lived in the last house with a view of Leigh Ann's front entrance were still on vacation.

Johnny strode quickly to the window at the left of the front door.

Using his knife, laid flat and eased under the bottom of the screen and then wiggled, he popped the hooks from around their screwlike catches.

Lifting the screen from its hinges, he carried it to the dark corner of the house and laid it in the bushes. In case anyone should look that way, he did not want it to be leaning against the wall or lying on the ground.

The piece of cardboard placed over the broken windowpane was held in place with masking tape. He quickly cut through that. Snaking his arm through the opening, he undid the latch, raised the window, and quickly stepped through the opening to the inside of the house. He lowered and locked the window.

Slipping off his low-cut tennis shoes, he moved across the foyer in his bare feet to the edge of the living room. He could see that Leigh Ann's bedroom door was closed. He could hear the shower running in the master bathroom. He moved back to the base of the stairs and hurried up them.

Upstairs, he glanced inside the first bedroom. The glow from the night light showed the children's twin beds empty. He stepped into the room.

A framed head-and-shoulders photograph of Leigh Ann sat on the bedside table nearest the door and he picked it up. His lips widening into a smile that disappeared behind the ski mask, only his white teeth remaining visible, he removed the photo from the frame. After folding it in such a manner as to not leave a crease across her face, he slipped it into his back pocket.

Back downstairs, he walked through the dining room and into the kitchen, where he removed the telephone receiver from its wall mount next to the living-room doorway.

Pressing his palm tight against the earpiece, he muted the shrill, beeping noise until it had ceased.

Leaving the receiver hanging from its cord, he moved through the living room toward Leigh Ann's bedroom door. He tried the knob. The door was only shut, not locked. He entered the room.

The bathroom door was locked. He heard the shower quit running. Hurrying to the walk-in closet, he switched off its light, stepped inside, and pulled the door closed behind him.

A moment later the bathroom door opened and Leigh Ann, a yellow towel wrapped around her body, stepped back into the bedroom and walked to the foot of the bed where she had laid out her clothes.

When she finished dressing, she turned to study herself in the dressing-table mirror. She shook her head, reached to the buttons on her blouse, and began undoing them. After dropping the blouse on the foot of the bed, she moved to her closet and opened the door.

Johnny was in her face, grabbing her and forcing her backward and over onto the bed.

She screamed and hit at the ski-mask-covered face above hers.

The knife flashed.

"Noooo!"

"Lie still!" The blade jammed down into the bed next to her head.

"Mmmmoohh—"

"Shut up! Shut up, now!"

Eyes wide, she moved her head in little short jerky nods.

"Your nipples are hard, aren't they?"

"Ooohhh!"

"I don't have to see them to know. I didn't believe it when I first read about it. But it's true. Fear excites women."

The voice. It sounded like— She shook her head. "Oh, please—please don't hurt me."

He moved his hand to her brassiere strap and slipped it off her shoulder.

She began repeatedly shaking her head. Tears welled in her eyes.

He moved his hand to the swell at the top of her breast. She clasped his wrist and stopped his hand.

He moved his knife to the front of her face and she released her grip.

His hand beginning to knead her soft flesh, he leaned across her body, his face moving down toward her side, and he bit her.

"Oohhh!"

"Be quiet!" He rose above her again, staring down into her eyes. "Turn over."

She barely shook her head. "Please, I beg you."

"Turn over!"

She shuddered and shut her eyes, rolled to her stomach.

His mouth moved to the top of her shoulder blade, and she felt his warm breath on her skin, and he bit her again, harder.

"Oh, God! Pleeease stop!"

As he lifted his face from her back, she glanced around her shoulder to stare at the black mask, could see his slack mouth. His breathing was loud. He stared down toward her buttocks, then leaned toward them. Her eyes moved to his hand. The knife was held loosely.

She slapped back at it, knocking it flying from his grasp, and she lunged away from him, rolled across the king-size bed to the far side. He dove after her, got his hands around her ankle and dragged her back toward him. She yanked her leg loose and tucked her legs back away from his grabbing hands.

He came to his knees on the bed and came across it toward her. She thrust out hard with her legs, slamming her feet into his chest, knocking the wind out of him and sending him tumbling backward off the bed onto the floor.

She jumped to her feet in the middle of the bed, hurtled off it, and dashed through her bedroom door.

Running through the living room, she yanked a straightback chair from under a table and propelled it tumbling back behind her.

At the front door she fumbled a moment with the deadlock, slid it back, flung the door open, and dashed out into blinding headlights. She screamed and ran toward the black Cadillac.

The boy stopped, stood framed in the doorway.

Ramsey threw open his door and jumped from the car to the pavement.

Johnny turned and disappeared back inside the house.

Leigh Ann threw herself into Ramsey's arms. "Help me!" she screamed.

"It's okay."

"Help me!"

He tore her arms from around his neck. "Leigh Ann! It's okay! Use the phone in my car to call the police." He pushed past her and dashed for the front door.

Inside the house, Ramsey saw tennis shoes lying at the edge of the foyer. He glanced up the staircase, then hurried into the living room. Hesitating a moment to scan the room, he then moved quickly across the carpet past the overturned chair and to the master bedroom door.

He heard Leigh Ann scream.

He turned and ran back to the front door and out it onto the porch. Leigh Ann pointed toward the area between her house and the old Colonial.

"He came through the garage! Ran behind the Richardsons'!"

CHAPTER

38

Ramsey rounded the near corner of the old Colonial and stopped in the Richardsons' backyard. The figure wasn't to be seen. Ramsey started to move forward toward the far side of the house but hesitated when he noticed the metal hinge latch open and laid back on the inclined doors down into the cellar.

He walked to the doors and lifted on their handles.

Locked—from the inside.

He stood thinking for a moment, then leaned and grabbed the top edge of one of the doors and pulled hard. It began to give, and he pulled with all of his strength.

The thin planking splintered and he fell backward to the ground. He pushed himself back to his feet, reached his hand to grasp the top of one of the broken boards, placed his other hand at the far top edge of the door, and yanked hard. The hinges gave and the broken section of door lifted off. He threw it to the side, stepped over onto the steps, and moved down them.

Though shrouded in spots with dark shadows, the cellar was illuminated fairly well, bright moonlight streaming in through both the wide horizontal windows peeking above the ground on each side of the cellar and the gaping door space behind him.

There were no interior stairs leading down from the house above. Anyone locking the cellar from inside would have to still be there. He moved his gaze slowly around the area.

Several pieces of old furniture sat against the wall to his right. More furniture, covered with sheets, lined the wall to his left. The sheet draped over a long couch was pulled askew, the largest part of the white covering billowing out over something behind the couch. He moved toward it.

A shovel was propped against an old rotting support pier. He took it in his hands, holding it angled across his chest as he approached the couch.

Leaning to gather a corner of the sheet in his hand, he pulled it back.

An old chest of drawers stood there.

He turned, started back across the cellar toward its other side, his eyes darting back and forth as he walked.

Then he stopped, his brow furrowing with his thought.

Mrs. Swilley had told her class there had to be a hidden passageway in the house.

The floor was dirt. Both side walls and the front of the cellar were constructed of mortared stones. The only wooden wall was the one at the back. Several rows of shelves were built into it, innumerable bottles and jars sitting on them. He moved up close to the wall and slowly walked along it.

He laid the shovel on the ground and reached out to grasp one of the thick braces running vertically between the shelves. He pulled. It was solidly anchored. Moving a few feet down the wall to the next brace, he pulled again. It gave. He tugged on it once more, then pushed against it. It would move an inch in either direction.

Grasping the brace solidly with both hands, he bunched his muscles and yanked.

Bottles and jars fell off the shelf and crashed to the floor. A several-foot section of the shelves swung open like a door and the figure stepped forward, his hand coming down hard.

Ramsey didn't have time to raise his hands in defense, a metal pipe smashing hard into his head. His knees buckled, but he managed to keep his feet. He reached to try to stop the second swing, partially deflected the blow, the pipe glancing hard off the side of his head.

Dazed, he fell backward to the floor.

The form hurdled over him, crossed the cellar, went up the stairs and out the door.

Ramsey pushed himself to his feet, took a step, and went back to one knee. Shaking his head in an attempt to clear his senses, he pushed himself to his feet again, stumbled to the steps, and up them out of the cellar.

The figure, running hard, was near the rear of the Richardsons' yard, and then disappeared into the thick trees.

Ramsey, his head clearing rapidly, sprinted toward the park.

Entering the trees running as fast as he could, Ramsey couldn't hear anything but his own footsteps. He stopped.

The sound of flight was coming from deeper in the park and back slightly to the right. Ramsey turned and ran in that direction. Immediately he was slapped in the face by a low-hanging oak branch, then tripped on a tangle of vines, lost his balance, and went sprawling to the ground.

Another wave of dizziness passing over him, he rested for a moment on his hands and knees. He could still hear the sounds of the running and he pushed himself on to his feet, started forward again, this time slower, pushing back the whiplike branches with his forearms.

On and on deeper into the park he moved, his senses fully recovering, able to see fairly well when the light of the half moon wasn't completely cut off by heavy limbs overhead. Another couple of hundred feet and he stopped to listen again.

The running was ahead of him and slightly back to the left—farther away now.

Ramsey quickened his pace.

After another couple of hundred feet he stopped again.

Silence.

He moved forward once more, this time walking, trying to make as little noise as possible, straining to hear.

Another hundred feet and he stopped again.

He still heard nothing.

He saw the double cedar, the two trunks twisted around each other in corkscrew fashion. He looked to his right, and walked slowly in the direction of the sinkhole.

A sound off to his left.

He stopped.

Another—a single step.

He moved in that direction, taking long slow steps, pausing every three or four strides to listen.

Another step—barely perceptible. And now another.

A deer?

He looked on the ground around him, his eyes searching, saw a broken limb lying in the shadows. He picked it up, pulled his arm back, and threw the branch as far ahead of him as he could. It hit a pine trunk fifty feet away and fell into a tangle of morning-glory vines.

He heard one step . . . A second step. Then there was the sound of branches being brushed aside. Too clumsy for a deer. Ramsey dashed forward, dodging under low-hanging limbs as he ran.

He could now hear the plodding steps ahead of him even over the sound of his own feet, and then there was the sound of vines being ripped apart.

He hurdled a stunted bush, and then stopped.

The cow, bathed in an eerie circle of moonlight that shone through an opening in the thick foilage above, gave a quick glance over its shoulder toward Ramsey, then lunged forward, tangled vines again giving way and ripping under the animal's strong legs.

Ramsey took a deep breath and exhaled audibly, turned, and started back toward the sinkhole.

He stopped again when he heard the distant slamming of car doors. Now came the muted exchanges from back toward the subdivision.

Ray entered the park running, his flashlight's beam shining ahead of him, his snub-nosed revolver held at the ready. A hundred feet to each side of him, two other officers entered the trees.

Ramsey stood at the entrance to the path leading to the sinkhole. He strained to hear. A good part of the moon's illumination was able to shine through the sparse overhead limbs, and he could see down the shadowy trail to where it turned back toward the depression. He started down the path, walking slowly, taking quiet, careful steps.

As he neared the turn in the trail, the moonlight began to dim. He glanced up through the drooping, overhanging limbs to see a heavy cloud starting across the face of the moon. Then he barely heard the movement ahead of him and he quickly stopped.

His muscles taut, he narrowed his eyes, tried to see through the increasing darkness, then blackness.

He heard a second movement—behind him this time. A footstep?

His throat tightening, he turned sideways in the trail, pressed his back into the thick bushes to that side, glanced back and forth into the blackness to each side of him.

He felt the movement against his ankle, and jerked his leg away from the furry body. The same thing that had happened the night he had discovered Peter's body in the sinkhole.

Whatever it was moved on out the path.

Ramsey turned in that direction, squared his shoulders and waited, listened intently for another step—thought he heard one.

"Aiieeee!"

The scream came from near the entrance to the path.

Ramsey lunged in that direction.

The cloud cleared the moon. Johnny, his mask removed, his bare foot bleeding, slammed at the ground with the piece of iron pipe in his hand. The angry, aged boar coon, his fur bristled, dodged the blow and hurried on out the path.

Ramsey slammed into Johnny's chest, driving the boy backward and to the ground, the piece of pipe sailing harmlessly into the bushes.

"Mark!" The sound of Ray's voice reverberated through the trees, and flashlight beams began to play down the path. "Mark! Where in hell are you?"

"Over here!" His senses fully recovered, and much stronger than Johnny, it was no trouble at all for Ramsey to hold the struggling boy to the ground until Ray made his way down the path.

CHAPTER

39

Leigh Ann, having donned a blouse and slipped on a pair of shoes, her hands clasped over her mouth, was waiting at the side of the Richardsons' yard when Ramsey stepped out of the park.

She ran toward him. "Thank God!" she cried.

Ray, followed by the white police officer who had come to Leigh Ann's the day of the Luttle incident, pushed the hand-cuffed boy toward the white LTD at the end of the Richardsons' driveway. Another squad car, red lights flashing, was speeding down the street toward the house.

As Ray reached to open a rear door of the LTD, the boy jerked away and collapsed to the ground. "No! I want my father!"

Johnny's next sound was a scream of pain as Ray grabbed a handful of hair and yanked him back to his feet. Opening one of the LTD's back doors, Ray sent the boy sprawling headfirst onto the backseat and slammed the door.

Ramsey, his arm around Leigh Ann and walking toward the door, spoke back over his shoulder to his brother. "Call a doctor."

Leigh Ann shook her head. "No."

"I just want him to check you over."

She shook her head. "I didn't let him touch me."

"To calm you down, Leigh Ann. You need something." She was still trembling.

"No."

Ray walked up behind them. "You sure, Leigh Ann?"

She nodded.

"Okay," he said. "Mark, we'll wait until tomorrow to worry about getting a statement. If she decides she needs a doctor, let me know." He glanced at the ugly bruise at the top of Ramsey's forehead. "You think you ought to have a doctor look at that?"

Ramsey shook his head. "No. It'll be okay. I don't want to leave her right now."

"Chief," the black police sergeant called. He was walking toward them after coming from the back of the Richardson house. "Look at this." He held an object out to Ray.

It was a watch.

"Look on the back," the sergeant said.

"I'll be damned," Ray said. He held the back of the watch out for Ramsey to see.

Engraved in block lettering was: TO BETTY, FROM YOUR LOVING NIECE, KAREN.

"I found it in that cellar room the kid was hiding in," the sergeant said. "The little son of a bitch kept a souvenir from killing those women." He held up a bracelet. "Two souvenirs. There's no markings on it, but I'll bet a month's pay it belonged to the other woman."

Leigh Ann's color had returned by the time they entered the house. The sudden short tics which had been working at the side of her face subsided soon after he had sat her on the couch and sat close beside her.

"Leigh Ann, where are the twins?"

"Thank God they're at Mother's. God, if they'd been here I'd never have resisted or tried to run." She shuddered and turned her face toward his. "Not left them alone in the house with him—" She burst into sobs and he moved his arms around her back, pulled her close.

She rested the side of her face against his chest and shook her head. "I'm sorry," she said in a choked voice. "I can't help it. I keep feeling like I'm going to start screaming."

"It's all over. You won't ever have to worry about him again. Nobody will ever have to worry about him again." He leaned to press his lips against her head.

She lifted her head from his chest. "Will you stay here tonight? I don't think I can if you—"

He pulled her back against him. "I'm here for as long as you want."

She nodded, snuggled her head against his shoulder, wrapped her arms around his arm, and was quiet for several seconds. Then she lifted her head again. "I look awful, don't I?" she said.

He smiled, almost chuckled at her question. "You look fine."

She shook her head and dried her tears with the back of her hands. "No, I look terrible. I can feel it."

"You look fine." He pulled her back against him, held her for several seconds, then lowered his head toward hers.

"Leigh Ann, I think there's a good chance Johnny might be the one who killed Julie, too. I've been thinking about it for two days and I don't believe the timing was right for either Jack or her father to have killed her."

Leigh Ann had lifted her head from his shoulder as he spoke. Now she had a quizzical expression on her face.

"What do you mean?"

"Think back to where 'Don Wan' left Julie. Johnny said that when he saw Don Wan coming toward him, he turned and ran up the hill, hid off to the side and let the guy pass, then came back down, ended up at the wrong house and went back up, crossed over, and came down again. He was out of sight of Julie for, what, ten minutes, fifteen at the outside. It doesn't really make any difference, because the main thing is, he was never far enough away that he wouldn't have noticed a car's headlights coming back down the road.

"And he said—I specifically asked him—he said he never saw a car after Jack had driven off. The way I asked him, he thought I was referring to the doctor's car leaving. That's how I meant it at the time. But I got to thinking—if he didn't see a car after that, then Jack hadn't returned yet, either. He couldn't have killed her.

"As far as the doctor being the murderer, I'm not as sure about his innocence as I am Jack's. But I just don't think it would've been possible for him to kill her, either.

"Remember how bright the moon was that night? At least during that particular time of the night—right after the shower had passed over. Johnny said it was because of the moonlight that he was able to make out that it was the doctor who went past him.

"Being that bright, how come Johnny when he came walking into the backyard, didn't see the doctor stabbing his daughter? Or, if the doctor had already killed her, but hadn't come back toward the house yet, how come then he didn't notice Johnny walking across the yard? They couldn't have been more than fifty, sixty feet apart. If Richardson had noticed Johnny, then he certainly wouldn't have walked right past him a few minutes later.

"I think the doctor's telling the truth. He was in the house and stepped to the back door to look out in the backyard, called Julie's name. Getting no response, he went back inside the house. When the phones rang he got unnerved and left the house, went past Johnny hiding at the window.

"After Richardson was out of sight, Johnny started back into the woods and came upon Julie—still alive. He had watched her while she was having sex with Don Wan. He admitted to that. He saw them start making out a second time; got turned on.

" 'Course we'll never know for sure, and I don't guess it really makes any difference. Except for one thing. Jack's name isn't going to be cleared."

A quizzical expression once more marked her face. "Why, if—"

He shook his head. "The D.A. won't even bring up Julie's murder, Leigh Ann. With that watch and bracelet, and the teeth impressions I'm sure they're going to match up to the bites on those two bodies, he has two murders he can prosecute Johnny on with indisputable evidence. He won't take a chance of confusing the jury by throwing in a third murder he might have a hard time proving.

"Bennie's sure to plead insanity as the boy's defense for killing the two women. After they see the kid, and get a look at the pictures of the women's bodies, the jury might even go along with it.

"Even if the boy tells Bennie about Julie, Bennie will never mention it. Her death was too conventional; might hurt the insanity defense.

"So on the one hand the prosecution won't bring up Julie's murder because of not wanting it to interfere with the two sure convictions. On the other hand, the defense won't bring it up because the way Julie died doesn't make the kid seem insane enough. So whether Johnny killed Julie or not, I think—"

Leigh Ann's eyes narrowed at his pause. "What?" she asked.

"Something I just thought of that I need to tell Ray."

Hurrying to the wall-mounted telephone in the kitchen, he lifted the dangling receiver to place it back in its cradle. Waiting a few seconds, he lifted the receiver to his ear, heard the dial tone, and punched in the number.

"Davis County Sheriff's Department."

"This is Mark Ramsey. Chief Hopkins is on his way down there with a prisoner. As soon as he gets there will you tell him to call me? He knows where I am."

"He's walking in the door now."

Ramsey thumbed his fingers against the kitchen wall as he waited.

"Yeah, Mark."

"Ray. You need to get somebody out to search that boy's room for the knife that killed the Richardson girl. If it's there now, it might not be after Dr. Keller hears his son's been arrested."

"I've already contacted the D.A. He's seeing to a search warrant right now."

"Mark!" Leigh Ann exclaimed, and came to her feet.

He looked in her direction.

"Mark, the knife; he had a knife. God, I thought he was getting ready to kill me one time; he stuck it down into the bed next to my head. I knocked it out of his hand. It's in the bedroom."

"Ray, hang on a minute. Don't hang up. Johnny had a knife. I'm going to go look at it."

Leaving the receiver dangling by its cord, he walked quickly toward the bedroom.

Inside the room he surveyed the carpet, didn't see the knife.

Leigh Ann stepped up beside him. "He did, Mark. I don't know where it is now, but he did."

Ramsey walked toward the closet and looked on the floor inside it; then he pulled the door back from the wall.

The knife lay next to the baseboard.

Slowly, a smile came to his face, grew broader. He reached for the telephone on the nightstand.

"Ray, it's the right one—the point's broken off. It's the knife the little bastard killed Julie with. Get some officers out here right away."

He replaced the receiver, turned to where Leigh Ann was still looking at the knife, and took her in his arms. Squeezing her to his chest, he kissed her on the side of the head, the cheek, then on her lips. "That's it!"

Leigh Ann, crying happily, hugged him as hard as she could.

CHAPTER

40

It was a little after nine the following morning when the telephone rang. Ramsey leaned across Leigh Ann to lift the receiver. Her eyes came open, and he reached down to press his lips to her forehead before leaning back against the headboard and speaking into the receiver. "Hello."

"Mark."

"Good morning, big brother. And how is your day going today?"

Ray chuckled before speaking. "You want to tell me what's got you in a good mood, Mark, or you want me to guess?"

Despite his brother's lighthearted assumption, there had been no lovemaking during the night. Leigh Ann had shuddered and moved away from Mark's first touch. Johnny's earlier visit had certainly not been the right mood-setter. But she had begun to relax just before dawn, and had slept soundly ever since.

Ray chuckled again at whatever he was thinking. "If it's not too much of a problem, Mark, you all need to be rolling out. D.A. wants you to come on down and give your statements."

Leigh Ann pushed her covers back and swung her feet to the floor. He saw the egg-shaped bruise just above the top of her nightgown. "What's that?"

She glanced at him as she felt back over her shoulder. "It's where he bit me." She winced when her fingers touched the spot. "I've got another one."

His brother was saying something. "Just a minute, Ray."

Leigh Ann slipped a strap off her shoulder, lowered the gown, and pointed to a similar-size purplish mark high on her side.

"This one hurt so bad I was sure he'd bitten a plug out of me. But it didn't break the skin." She raised her gown, pulled the strap back over her shoulder, and stood. She pointed toward the bathroom.

"I'm going to take a quick shower." She leaned back to briefly touch her lips to his forehead, then walked around the end of the bed.

His brother was saying something again, and Ramsey raised the receiver to his ear.

"Ray, that little bastard bit the hell out of Leigh Ann—bit her twice."

"Yeah," his brother answered. "He's a biter all right, just like Dr. Jones told me: Once a biter always a biter. Every mark on those women were his. Judge let us take dental molds early this morning. We were hoping some of the marks wouldn't be his; give us a lead to who else was with him—if there was anybody . . . Mark, if he broke the skin you probably ought to run her by the hospital and let 'em take a look at her; nothin' nastier than a human bite—festers up quick."

"It didn't. I—" Ramsey, his forehead wrinkling at his sudden thought, glanced toward the bathroom door.

"Mark, how long until you can make it down here so I can tell the D.A.?"

Ramsey remained with his thought.

"Mark, did you hear what I asked you?"

"Yeah. Give us an hour."

"Gonna want you to ID the knife, too—as the same one you saw in the bedroom. There weren't any prints on it."

"I'm sorry. What did you say?"

"Hell, Mark. Can you pay attention to me for a minute?"

"What did you say about the knife?"

"There weren't any prints on the knife. You and Leigh Ann will have to identify it as the one he left in the house."

"No prints?"

"He wore gloves, remember?"

"Yeah." Ramsey glanced at the bathroom door, pictured in his mind the bite marks on Leigh Ann.

"Ray, can I call you back in a little while?"

"Well—yeah, I guess. Oh, one more thing you'll be interested in. We searched Dr. Keller's house. Seems his kid got it honest. Keller's bedroom closet was loaded with videos and books you wouldn't believe—not to mention enough drugs to get him with intent to distribute. Bennie bailed him out ten minutes after we got him downtown, but there's no way he's gonna beat the charges."

"Yeah. Good. I'll call you back in a little while." Ramsey replaced the receiver and leaned back against the headboard again.

Once a biter, always a biter.

It wasn't only Dr. Jones who had made a statement like that. Ramsey remembered Dr. Petrie saying there were two killers in Davis County, the one who had killed Julie and the one who had killed the two women. *In fact, I'd bet on it*, he had said. He had based his statement solely on the fact the two women had been bitten and that Julie hadn't.

Now Leigh Ann had been bitten.

Johnny had bitten the two women. He bit Leigh Ann. Why hadn't he bitten Julie?

What difference did it make? The main thing was he had been caught, wouldn't be killing again.

But the thoughts wouldn't quit coming.

Two killers, Dr. Petrie said. But that wasn't right. There was indisputable evidence that he was wrong in that assumption. The watch and bracelet found in the cellar of the old home, the dental impressions taken that very morning—all verified that Johnny had killed the two women. The knife he had brought with him the night before was the proof that he had also killed Julie.

The knife he had brought with him the night before.

It was a different-type knife than had been used on the two women.

So he had two knives—no telling how many he had.

But why were there no fingerprints on the knife he had brought with him? Ray had said it was because Johnny had worn gloves—but the gloves would have been to keep from leaving any prints in the house. Johnny was bound to have handled the knife in the past. Why would he have bothered to clean his prints off it before he came after Leigh Ann? He damn sure wasn't planning to leave the knife behind for someone to find.

Ramsey shook his head. What was wrong with him? Had he been trying to find out who killed Julie for so long that his mind wouldn't accept the fact that the killer had been found—the only killer. As far as Johnny biting during two of his attacks but not when he attacked Julie—who could predict with certainty the actions of a crazed killer?

And as far as two different knives—he had used his narrow-bladed one on the two women and his wider one on Julie, was planning on using it on Leigh Ann, had jabbed it into the bed next to her head.

Ramsey glanced to the other side of the bed. He swung his legs out from under the cover, stepped to the floor, and walked around the bed.

Leigh Ann had put on fresh sheets. He reached and pulled the bottom one loose, lifted it and looked down at the place where the knife had penetrated.

There was no way to tell the width of the blade from the

puncture it had left, actually a rip, formed from the knife being thrust at an angle into the sheet.

Ramsey glanced at the bathroom door, the sound of the shower still running inside the room, then he walked from the bedroom on his way to the front door and some fresh air where he could think. Or where he could force himself to stop thinking.

Outside the house he looked up into the clear sky. *Come on, Mark,* he said to himself. *You've been in high gear on this case for so long you can't slow down. It's over with. Let it go.*

Turning back toward the front door, he noticed where Luttle had smashed the windowpane. The cardboard and tape Leigh Ann had used as a patch was sliced through and pushed back from the window. The screen was missing. *Where Johnny had broken into the house?*

Ramsey moved to the window and stared at the cardboard for a moment, then dropped his eyes to the bottom of the window. Then he knelt.

There was a faint impression in the dust on the windowsill— where Johnny had slipped his knife under the screen and wriggled the blade back and forth to pop the catches loose—an impression that looked for all the world like it was made by a narrow-bladed, stilettolike knife.

Ramsey's stomach twisted.

CHAPTER

41

Leigh Ann, wearing a white terry-cloth robe, was standing in front of her dresser mirror brushing her hair when Ramsey stepped into the bedroom.

"Where did you go?" she asked.

When he didn't answer she glanced toward him. Noticing his stare, her forehead wrinkled quizzically. "What?"

"Why wouldn't you make love with me last night, Leigh Ann?"

"What?"

"You heard what I asked."

The creases in her brow deepened and she shook her head. "I told you, Mark. It wasn't the right time for me with what I'd just gone through with Johnny."

"What was your reason going to be the next time . . . and the next? You knew me better than I knew myself, didn't you?"

"Mark, what are you—"

"You were going to divorce Jack, right? That's what you told me the day I asked you about the argument you had outside of Dennery's. You were going to be free as soon as all of this was over. You figured my knowing that would be just enough to get me on the hook, right? That little scene with me in the bedroom just before then, right after Luttle came by, that was to give me a taste of what I had been missing, remind me in case I'd forgotten. If Ray hadn't rung the doorbell, how would you have stopped it before we went too far? Oh, easy; you would have suddenly realized it just wasn't right for you to be acting like that with poor Jack in the trouble he was in— wouldn't have been the right time—later, maybe? Or would you have gone further? How far would you have gone to keep me working hard at proving Jack didn't do it, keep you apprised of everything that was going on?"

"Mark, you're scaring me. What's wrong? Why are you acting like this?"

"What did you do with the knife Johnny had after you put the hunting knife in its place?"

Her mouth came open. Color noticeably drained from her face. She shook her head. "What? I—"

"When I drove up last night and you ran out to my car, you were in your skirt and bra. When Ray and I came back out of the park with Johnny, you had put a blouse on. You had already been back in your bedroom and switched the knives by then."

"No!" she exclaimed. "Why are you saying—I don't know what you're saying. I didn't—"

"Yeah, you did. But you didn't do enough. You didn't know about Johnny's knife leaving a mark on the windowsill where he had jimmied the screen. It's there, Leigh Ann, easy to see. It's obvious which knife he brought into the house with him— not the one you suddenly remembered he had."

"Not the one? I—" She shook her head in dismay. "I don't . . . Two knives. He must have had two knives. Why would you think I had anything to do with—He had two knives. He had to have. He threw the other one away when he was in the park, I—Mark, I can't believe you would think that I would—"

"Yeah, I thought, Leigh Ann, thought until I got sick to my stomach, thought I was going to vomit. You having the knife, you alone in the house that night, me remembering you calling Julie a whore the first time you mentioned her to me, said she put on an exhibition to attract Jack. It had to be you who killed the girl. You had the knife all along, who else could have killed her? You went into a jealous rage and you killed her.

"Then I suddenly realized it didn't make sense for you to have switched the knives to protect yourself. No one suspected you. You would have left well enough alone if it was you who had killed Julie. But it wasn't you, was it? It wasn't you who did it, and it wasn't you who people thought did it—would keep thinking did it. No, that was either Jack or the doctor, and I had told you on the phone that the doctor was willing to take a lie detector test. That was going to shift the blame back to Jack, wasn't it? And you couldn't stand everybody thinking that, could you?

"So, how was it possible for Jack to have done it; driven back and killed her in the little time possible? He didn't drive back. He never left. That was you who left in the car.

"The fight you had outside Dennery's continued after you got back home, didn't it? You left and went to your mother's. That's why you were in your bathrobe when Mrs. Baker saw you. You had spent the night there and didn't have any clothes with you except for the nightclothes you were wearing.

"If you had really gone down there to take care of your mother's dogs, you would have dressed first, wouldn't you? You wouldn't think of leaving the house without being properly dressed, would you? Not under normal circumstances. When you went down there, was it because you were mad or because you were scared—scared he was going to beat you?"

She had begun shaking her head, and continued to move it back and forth as she spoke. "He was sweet. He wouldn't. He was sweet, Mark. You know that. He loved me."

"When he hit you at Dennery's—how many times had that happened before. If your mother knows, she'll tell us, won't she? If she knows, she hates him for it, doesn't she? If she doesn't tell, we'll eventually find someone else who will, someone who knows about it."

She was now absolutely white, and began to sway. He stepped to her, took her by the arm and walked her to the bed where she sat down, dropping her face into her hands.

She remained that way for several seconds before raising her eyes to his.

"Mother didn't like him, Mark. She hated him. You can't believe anything she tells you."

"Stop it, Leigh Ann; it's no good anymore. You've been able to manipulate me like a wind-up toy—but not anymore."

She reached out a hand to gently clasp his forearm. "Please, Mark."

He looked down at her hand and shook his head. "It won't work anymore, Leigh Ann."

She tightened her grasp and nodded her head. "Okay, he had hit me before. Mother knows. But he never meant to. He was sweet. You know that. There's never been anyone as sweet. It was the drugs." She nodded her head. "Like you told me you saw at the cabin. When he got on drugs it was like he became a different person. He hated himself afterward."

"But he went right back and beat you again, didn't he? He always felt guilty—Honey's rape, the drugs, seducing a teenager; but he went right back and did it again. And then when Julie said no, he killed her."

She shook her head violently. "No! He wouldn't have done something like that. He couldn't have. He didn't."

"He did, and you know he did."

She glanced at the telephone. "Have you told anybody else about the windowsill?"

He wet his dry lips with his tongue and shook his head. "No."

"Do you love me, Mark?"

He didn't answer.

"You do. And you know I love you, too. We can be together now. And I'll stick up for you—protect you. You would for me, wouldn't you?" She was nodding her head in short jerky nods. "I mean people that are married have to protect each other. What would you have done if you had come in and seen him sitting there sobbing, blood all over him? I had to protect him." She shook her head. "That whore! She led him on. It was her fault."

"Did he see her through her window, Leigh Ann? Saw her dressing, got turned on, went over there and she turned him down."

She shook her head. "I don't know why he went over there the first time. I had started looking for him—to apologize for our fight. He wasn't in his study. I went to the garage door. He was walking back from her house and I got mad again, tore into him. Said I had taken all I was going to take. It was my fault he got so mad. If I hadn't driven him into such a rage—" She shook her head again. "I left, went to Mother's. I was nearly out of my mind."

"When you left he went back over there again."

"When I was backing out of the drive, he saw her and the boy in the headlights. He watched them after I left. Then when the boy left, Jack went over to meet her. She insulted him—said terrible things about him. She taunted him, Mark; didn't have her T-shirt on and left it off as she talked to him—purposely flaunting herself and laughing. He started back. She kept laughing at him. He saw the knife—where he had been cleaning fish out by the edge of our yard. He got it and went back up to scare her. That's all. He told me, that's all. She slapped him, laughed again, and started to put her T-shirt on. He—he—it was just a reflex on his part. He struck out at her. It was an accident." She shook her head again.

Ramsey shook his head. "He stabbed her a dozen times, Leigh Ann—an accident?"

She raised her eyes to his, shook her head.

"Mark, I'll do anything you want—anything. Just don't tell them Jack did it. And not for him, for the twins. Don't tell for their sakes. You don't want everyone in town knowing their father was a murderer. You told Jack what that would do to them. They're little children. You wouldn't hurt them like that, would you? Please? For their sakes. What difference can it make? It's not going to hurt anybody if they think Johnny did it. He'll never be tried for it. You told me that yourself. Let everybody keep thinking he did it. I beg you." Her lip trembled.

As he continued to stare without answering her, her face began tightening. Her tone became cold. "I thought you loved me," she said. "I was just testing you. Jack didn't do it. I just told you that to see if you cared at all about me—if you would help me if I needed you to."

"Leigh Ann, quit; give it up."

"No! I'll say you're lying, making it up because you're jealous of Jack—because you couldn't have me." Suddenly her cheeks glowed red. She lunged up from the bed and came after him with her fingernails raking.

"You're not going to do my Jack that way!"

He tried to step back from her, grabbed at her wrists as she slammed into him; her momentum was so much he stumbled and they both fell backward to the floor. He forced her off him and rolled over on top of her, held her arms tight against the carpet. She struggled a moment, then lay silently, glaring up at him. Then, gradually, her face began to soften.

"Please, Mark," she said in a soft voice. "Please."

He released her arms and rose to his feet, looked down at her for a moment, then started for the door.

"No, Mark, please don't tell."

When he stepped out the front door of the house she was close behind him, pulled at his arm. "Please."

He stopped without turning to look back at her. "I'm not going to say anything."

"Oh, thank you, Mark. Thank you. Oh, thank you. Mark, we can—"

He moved on toward his car.

When he opened the door to climb inside, he glanced back at the house.

Leigh Ann had gotten down on her knees in front of the window Johnny had come through. Her hands were busy wiping the dust from the windowsill.

CHAPTER

42

Ramsey stared forward through his windshield as he neared his company's drill site. He had been thinking about Leigh Ann ever since he had driven out of Belle Colline Heights. She had started planning Jack's defense from the moment she came back from her mother's to find him sitting bloodied in the house.

First she wanted Jack to be able to refuse a polygraph without causing any suspicion. That's why she had told Ramsey about Honey, and let him know that Jack wouldn't be able to take a lie detector test because of his guilt over that incident. What Ramsey wondered was if she really knew Jack had raped Honey, or had she believed Jack when he said he didn't? Probably believed him.

But whether she did or not, she knew the story would eventually get back to the D.A., and she had no choice but to get Ramsey to go talk to the girl. The most important thing was to have a reason to refuse a polygraph without the refusal causing suspicion.

Ramsey also thought about Jack's fingerprint found in Julie's bedroom. Leigh Ann had spoken of the time she had arrived back at her own house to catch Jack and Julie. Jack had spoken of a time he had made love to Julie in his office. How many times had they made love in the girl's own bedroom?

Ramsey had told Leigh Ann he wasn't going to give away that Jack was the killer, and he wasn't. Who would be served by the telling? Johnny was thought to be the killer, but he would never be tried for the murder. The doctor would be set free. The twins were already absent a father. To have their mother taken from them and sent to prison for the coverup she attempted would gain nothing. As insanely in love with Jack as she was, and knowing he was the killer, she was already faced with punishment enough.

In love with Jack as she was, Ramsey thought again. He smiled sheepishly and shook his head as he remembered how he thought she had married on the rebound from a failed modeling career and from his not coming with her to New Orleans.

He shook his head once more. He felt like a fool. But there were other men he was sure who had acted a fool over their first love. And how would those men have acted if in the succeeding years they had not fallen for anyone else and then been given a second chance at that first love again? For that's what it had really been—in his mind anyway—a second chance.

He couldn't believe he didn't feel any worse than he did. Ever since he had walked from her house to his car he had kept waiting to grow despondent. But he hadn't, still didn't feel the least bit that way.

His mother had once told him that age and being grown up were not synonymous. She said the way you can really tell when you've grown up is when you finally become mature enough to put things behind you and go on with your life.

Welcome to the adult world, he thought. He hoped!